GROOVY GUMSHOES

Private Eyes in the Psychedelic Sixties

Michael Bracken, Editor

GROOVY GUMSHOES

Private Eyes in the Psychedelic Sixties

Down & Out Books
3959 Van Dyke Road, Suite 265
Lutz, FL 33558
DownAndOutBooks.com

Cover design by Zach McCain

ISBN: 1-64396-252-3
ISBN-13: 978-1-64396-252-8

For Temple
My Love, My Muse, My Everything

TABLE OF CONTENTS

A HARD NIGHT IN HAMBURG

Tom Milani

Hamburg, Germany, October 21, 1960

In the three weeks Tony Martin had been in Hamburg, he'd grown used to the damp nights, the slippery cobbled streets, the moldy brick ruins, even the despair that was part of the atmosphere. But not the cold. Hands in the pockets of a too-big leather jacket he'd traded his duffel coat for, Tony tried to ward off the chill. He was staying at the British Sailor's Society on Johannesbollwerk 20, hard by the Elbe. There, he could get good food, but no alcohol, and he couldn't bring a girl to his room, so at night, he ventured out.

He turned down Grosse Freiheit, the cobbled lane lined with strip clubs. In the distance, a neon elephant bridged the street, announcing the Indra, a club he'd yet to set foot in, and close by was the Bambi-Filmkunsttheater, a cinema. Tony was still learning his way around Hamburg, but reliably found himself in the St. Pauli district, drawn here by the sex and violence, reasons like most any other man's.

Sounds seemed to rise from the ground beneath him, and he stopped, cocking an ear like someone hard of hearing. It wasn't his imagination. He counted along to a four-four beat. On top of that, not quite in time, were bass notes. Noticing a small window at street level, Tony squatted. He couldn't see much through it—just tables full of drunken Germans—but the music was louder now, with real rhythm and voices in harmony.

The sailor he'd traded jackets with was into rock and roll. Elvis, of course, but also Duane Eddy, Carl Perkins, Eddie Cochran, acts lesser known to Tony. None of it was really his thing, but he saw that it could be dark and menacing, and at the same time filled with the promise of excitement, making it the perfect soundtrack for the Reeperbahn.

Halbstarke—"half-strong"—toughs stood smoking by the entrance to the Kaiserkeller, but Tony paid them no mind, pushing through the door as if he were a German regular, not an American who'd been in town for just a few weeks.

Inside, the music pulsed in his chest like a second heartbeat. Tony smelled spilled beer, and a fog bank of cigarette smoke hung low over the room. Incomprehensible shouts rose in disjointed counterpoint to the guitars. He wove his way around groups of standing men. At one table, a gangster with a face that looked chiseled by a farsighted sculptor yelled, "*Mach shau!*" and the music somehow became louder.

Tony looked around, careful not to make eye contact, stopping when he saw three people sitting at a table in the corner near the stage. Two men and a woman, all in their early twenties, the girl and one of the men fair, the other man with darker hair, the three of them with identical hairstyles, long and combed to the side, something he'd never seen before. He took a table behind them and found he couldn't take his eyes off the girl, whose skin and large eyes were luminous in the haze.

The three seemed transfixed by the band, and now that Tony was settled with a stein of beer, he turned to the stage just as the band was starting another song. He recognized the riff right away from hearing Barrett Strong on Radio Luxembourg. The five-piece band was young. They all had slick-backed hair, and the bass player wore dark glasses. They sounded like they were from the US when they sang, but when they spoke their accents were English.

The guy on rhythm guitar was singing lead on "Money," that most American of desires, putting everything he had into the vocals. Tony himself played jazz piano—something he had the ear and discipline for—but the band's music was everything jazz was not. The drumming was loud, yet rudimentary, and the bass playing was just passable, even though the guy in sunglasses looked cool doing it. The other three band members were something else entirely. Guitarists all, one left-handed, they traded lead vocals and had a presence that drew him in.

When they finished "Money," the three seated at the table in front of him applauded, and Tony looked more closely at the girl. Convincing himself she wasn't the girlfriend of either man sitting with her, he thought about asking if he could join them—one out-of-place visitor to another—but saw that the girl had caught the eye of the sunglasses-wearing bass player, saw that it was just one more thing that wasn't going to go his way.

Richter hated Europe. Hated the small rooms, hated the narrow streets, hated the post-war poverty of the place, the cities still with bomb damage fifteen years after the war. He thought Germany would be the worst, its people not having come to terms with the war they had started and so were guilt-ridden or in denial, but he recognized that Hamburg was open in ways the US never would be, could see a kind of freedom here he couldn't envision back home.

After Korea, he didn't believe in anything, other than the job. And he believed in the job for only as long as he was working it. When he finished, he didn't believe in anything until the next job came along. His client was Major Frank Waters, whose son died in Germany while he was on liberty from the USS *Fiske.* Details were hard to get. Waters's son was named Philip, and his record as a sailor was unremarkable. Not surprising in that it was difficult to distinguish yourself in post-war service. The men Richter had known who *had* distinguished themselves when he served were all dead.

Major Waters had pushed for answers but gotten nowhere. Richter knew the military bureaucracy was balky, that its gears often ground, but he also knew the gears never stopped and that Waters wasn't telling him everything.

The next time Richter saw Waters, he reported what he'd learned through his contacts in the Navy—that Philip had been a victim of a random assault in Hamburg. No suspects or witnesses had been found. Richter had talked to Carl Fischer, an official at the American Consulate in Hamburg, who'd been referred to him through his network. The call had been unsettling, but the pieces began to fit. Richter wasn't sure how much Major Waters wanted to know about his son. He reflected that the case could be over before it started, but such was the nature of the job.

"The Navy isn't interested in Philip's death," he told Waters.

The major steepled his fingers under his chin and for a long moment said nothing. He placed his hands flat on the desk blotter.

"My son was killed because of who he was."

Richter raised an eyebrow, waiting.

"He was homosexual. And because of that, the Navy wants to sweep his death under the rug."

Fischer had told Richter that Philip had been found with semen on his clothes. The Navy didn't want any scandal.

"And you want justice for your son," Richter said.

Waters nearly spat, surprising Richter. "Justice? There is no such thing as justice. Before I hired you, I looked into your Marine Corps record. You saw a lot of action in Korea. What did that do for your sense of justice?"

Richter examined the major more closely, as if seeing him for the first time. He liked most of what he saw, but he also understood that Waters wasn't willing to rattle the bureaucracy on behalf of his son because it could cost him his career.

"Combat was all about getting the other guys before they got you," Richter said. "And if they got your buddy, you did your best to kill as many of them as possible." The calculus was simple, the ensuing costs to his sleep and his soul less so.

"I want you to find the man or men who killed my son."

When Waters didn't go further, Richter said, "And?"

The major produced a thick envelope from inside his jacket and pushed it across the blotter to Richter. Richter thumbed through the hundred-dollar bills inside, doing the math. The amount was much more than his daily rate, much more than even that plus the round-trip airfare to Germany.

"I'll pay you the balance when the job is complete. And your expenses, of course."

Richter wondered how Waters had come up with the money and how he'd known Richter would take the job. The major may have been anonymously mired in a small office in the Pentagon, but Richter could see there were depths about the man.

The next day he landed in Hamburg.

The USS *Fiske* was back at sea, so he had no way of interviewing any sailors who had known Philip Waters. At the American Consulate, Fischer had invited Richter into his office.

"Coffee? Cigarette?" he'd asked.

Richter had been trying unsuccessfully to quit for several years but saw no reason to refuse Fischer's offer now. As he smoked, Richter studied Fischer. So much of his height was in his torso that he seemed to be sitting at a schoolboy's desk. His hair was greasy and thinning and needed combing. His fingernails were tobacco stained and his skin was sallow. In contrast, his office was a model of organization and efficiency. Inbox to the left, outbox to the right. Pelikan fountain pen and inkwell centered at the top of the blotter. Legal volumes in the barrister bookshelves behind him. German-English dictionary on an adjacent stand. No personal photographs on the desk or shelves, but three very good still lifes hung on the wall in showy contrast to the drab office in the drab building in the drab city.

"Thank you for seeing me on such short notice," Richter began.

Fischer waved a hand but said nothing.

"Philip's father doesn't believe his son's death was random. What do you think?"

Fischer rocked back in his chair. "The Navy doesn't want Philip's *proclivities* brought to light, it's true. His body was found on Schmuckstrasse, where the transvestite prostitutes like to peddle their wares. A woman scavenging in the early morning literally stumbled across his corpse in an abandoned building. Philip had been dead for hours."

Fischer opened a desk drawer and retrieved a manila folder. He rotated it and passed it to Richter. Inside were two large black-and-white photographs of Philip Waters. Even in death, lying on his side, he had a handsome face, the strong jawline lined with stubble, the cheekbones defined. His lips were thin, perhaps too thin for his dimpled chin. Broad shoulders stretched the T-shirt he'd worn, despite the cold, and his stained trousers were tight around his thick legs.

The second photo showed Philip after he'd been rolled onto his back. His T-shirt was darker on the left side, and it took Richter a moment to see the gash in the fabric.

"Stabbed in the heart," Fischer said. "He would have bled out very fast."

Richter tried to picture it. Two men standing close to each other, one not expecting what was about to happen. Had the other been planning it all along, or had it been spontaneous?

"Do you think Philip knew it was coming?" he asked.

Fischer tapped the desk. "Being there late at night would have been exciting and dangerous—which was the appeal, I'm sure. My guess? He went there willingly for a tryst and got killed by whomever he was with."

Richter thought the same thing. He could believe that no one witnessed the killing, but at some point Philip and his killer surely had been seen together. The problem was time. It had been eleven days since Philip's murder, and memories were short. He picked up the photo again. In black and white the young man was like a matinee idol—he doubted such a face would be forgotten.

"His service record was clean," Fischer said. "He did his work, was apparently well liked. He drank a lot while on liberty, but that hardly distinguished him from his shipmates."

"May I keep these?" Richter asked.

"They're copies." Fischer pushed another folder across his desk. "Photos of him in uniform."

Richter glanced at them. Formal portraits, they revealed less of Philip than the others had. And if he had ditched his uniform soon after he left the ship, which appeared to be the case, they would be less useful when he questioned people.

He thanked Fischer for his help. As they stood and shook hands again, Fischer said, "Philip loved rock and roll. Apparently had encyclopedic knowledge of it."

It was a start, Richter thought.

Tony wasn't listening to the band anymore. They were doing a Little Richard number, the left-handed guitar player sounding for all the world like a Negro, despite his pasty skin—but he'd grown tired of their act, the screaming on stage, the way the guitarists stomped their feet to help the drummer keep time.

He was about to leave when a man who looked to be in his early thirties approached the table with the three Germans, leaned toward the darker-haired man's ear, and spoke. The young German nodded, and the man pulled up a chair and sat. He was slightly built, but his body seemed defined by right angles: rigid shoulders, squat neck, long fingers, broad brow. He wore woolen trousers, black boots, black turtleneck, gray corduroy jacket. His hair was cut close to the scalp. Tony would have guessed him to be an art student, except for his eyes, which had no light, no emotion.

Tony caught snatches of the man's German, but when he heard him say something in English, realized he was an American. As soon as the band stopped playing, the dark-haired young German approached the leader, who pointed him in the direction of the bass player, who soon joined all of them at the table. The American showed the bass player a photograph Tony couldn't see. The bass player bent over the photo as if it were a holy book, then shook his head. The American pocketed the photo and clapped the bass player on the shoulder. The band's leader, still on stage, raised his eyebrows, and the American said, loudly enough for Tony to hear, "You're going to make it big in America." For an instant, time stopped, and the three guitarists froze as if peering into the future, as if they actually believed him.

Tony turned away, thinking he'd seen and heard enough. His jacket fell off his chair. He picked it up and was brushing off the back when the American spoke to him.

"Do you mind if I join you?"

Tony turned, the American now standing with one hand on an empty chair, head tilted to the left.

"Please sit," Tony said, slipping his jacket onto the back of the chair again, happy to have someone to talk to, and curious, too, about the man who seemed to have his feet in two cultures.

"My name's Richter," he said, holding out his hand.

"Tony Martin," he said, shaking Richter's hand.

"Quite the band, don't you think?" Richter said.

"I prefer jazz myself."

Richter leaned forward. "Bill Evans, Dave Brubeck?"

Tony raised his glass, and Richter tapped his stein against Tony's.

"Do you play?" Richter said.

"Why do you ask?"

Richter nodded. "You have a musician's hands."

Tony glanced at his long fingers, saw the misshapen knuckle on his right hand. He still couldn't fully straighten his ring finger.

"And, frankly, your disapproving look when the guitarist

played the piano," Richter went on. "Not that I can blame you."

Tony laughed. "I've played in some piano bars around DC. The kinds of places where elegant people like to hear music as they eat and drink."

"Like Maurice's?"

Tony brightened, then became immediately wary. "How do you know Maurice's?"

"I live just outside Washington and like to go to clubs. I work at the Pentagon, and they sent me here to do some translating at the American Consulate. Tedious work, but I get to see a bit of the world, hear some music."

"Where did you learn German?"

"From my grandmother. She grew up in Munich, liked the finer things in life. My parents brought her with them when they emigrated in 1931, and I was born a few months later."

Richter's feet ached. He'd been to clubs up and down the Reeperbahn, talking to people, showing them Philip's photograph, asking if anyone had seen him. Despite his fluency, people regarded him warily, not-answering-inconvenient-questions being a universal survival tactic.

He stood in a closed shop's doorway to get out of the wind. The sun had gone down hours ago, but the neon signs created a glow like fallout. In Korea he'd seen Chinese soldiers set ablaze with flamethrowers, and in his dreams he still heard the expiration of their seared lungs before he woke up gasping.

Richter shook his head, trying to push away the flicker of memory. He realized someone was speaking to him and looked down from the shop's threshold. A young woman was asking him for change. Her cheeks were rouged and her eye makeup had started to run. Richter looked more closely. She turned away, and he said, "*Waten.*"

"I speak English," she said, facing him.

Richter sighed, aware now of how obvious his foreignness

must be. "Can I ask you some questions? I'll pay you for your time."

"What is your name?"

"Richter."

"Richter," she said, pronouncing it with a voice that reminded him of his grandmother's, worn from years of smoking.

She bit her lip. "You can call me Petra."

"Will you talk with me?"

"Come on."

She turned without waiting to see whether Richter would follow. They walked for a few blocks, away from the seamier parts of Grosse Freiheit. Richter didn't think he was being set up, but he was aware of everyone around them. The cafe where they finally stopped was nothing more than a few plain wooden chairs and tables, Hemingway's clean, well-lighted place. Richter felt himself relax.

Inside, they sat by the window and ordered coffees. When the light above their table touched Petra's face, Richter saw the shadow under the rouge, saw the bob of an Adam's apple not quite hidden by a collar.

"What is it you want to ask me?" Petra said.

Richter showed her one of the photographs of Philip.

"Beautiful boy," Petra said, not turning from the photo.

"Yes, he was," Richter said, the truth undeniable.

Petra handed the photo back to Richter.

"Have you seen him?" Richter asked.

"He's the American sailor who was killed here."

"His name is Philip Waters. He served on the *Fiske,* which came into Hamburg a few weeks ago."

"Yes, yes. That I know."

"I'm trying to find who killed him."

"You are not with the police."

Richter wasn't sure whether it were a question or a statement, not that it mattered. "His father hired me to find his killer."

"Nothing you do will bring his son back."

Richter hadn't expected Petra to be a philosopher. "He knows that."

"And what will you do when you find his killer?"

"Bring him to justice." Richter lied automatically.

"Is that so?" Petra said.

Richter felt momentarily disarmed. Petra didn't regard him with suspicion, the way nearly everyone else he'd spoken with had, but instead appeared to see his search for what it was.

"You're not frightened that whoever killed Philip could kill you next, or someone you know?" he asked.

"Why would he do that?"

Richter folded his arms across his chest and waited.

"Because I look like this?" Petra finally said. "I think that you and I are not so different."

"Precisely."

Something had broken through Petra's facade, and her eyes softened. "I saw Philip."

Richter leaned forward to hear.

"I think it was him. He was wearing a leather jacket and was with another man."

"Can you describe him?"

Petra closed her eyes and tilted her head back, as if summoning a vision. "He was shorter than Philip, with olive skin, wavy hair. Cruel eyes." Petra faced Richter. "I'm sorry. It was at night, and they were just passing by the harbor."

"When was this?"

"Nine October."

The day before Philip was killed. "Can you think of anything else—anything that stood out?"

"Philip's jacket had a design on the inside pocket. He had it unzipped, and when he passed under a light and raised his arm, the man with him pointed to it. The stitching was in red, but I couldn't make out what it was."

Richter squeezed Petra's hand. "Thank you," he said, and squeezed again. "This is very helpful." He reached into his wallet.

"Not here," Petra said.

Richter shrugged.

"I have a room," Petra started. "We could go there. If you want to, I mean."

Richter looked Petra full in the face and allowed himself to think about pleasure, about the temporary oblivion it brought.

"All right," he said.

When Richter asked Tony if he wanted to go someplace "more private," the revulsion and excitement Tony felt were familiar, comforting even. Something in Tony drew men to him. One or two had told him it was his eyes, another, his Mediterranean skin. When Tony was twelve, his uncle had said it was his lips.

Tony grabbed his jacket from the back of the chair and followed Richter to the door. Outside the Kaiserkeller, the street was silent in comparison with the club, though his ears still rang, and the wind was cold and biting.

He zipped up his jacket. Richter seemed unaffected by the cold, but Tony could see hunger in his eyes, the same hunger Philip had, the same hunger the other men had.

He led Richter away from Schmuckstrasse and toward the Reeperbahn. He was looking for an empty alley. They would only be there for a few minutes—long enough for Richter to get on his knees, long enough for Tony to take care of him. Even the much larger Philip had gone quickly, though Tony had made the mistake of underestimating his strength. As Philip was bleeding, he'd tried to wrench the knife from Tony's hand, but succeeded only in breaking Tony's finger.

The cold had driven nearly everyone indoors. The few men Tony and Richter saw gave them a wide berth. Tony shoved his hands inside the pockets of his jacket and grasped the handle of his knife. He'd honed and stropped the blade so that the edge was sharp enough for a dry shave, worked the pivots so that it opened as silently and quickly as a switchblade.

"I haven't really done this kind of thing before," Richter said, his voice sibilant.

Tony knew it was a lie, the same lie Philip had told him, the purpose being to excite him. He gripped the knife more tightly, picturing himself slashing Richter's throat, reminding himself to step back from the spray of blood that was sure to follow.

"Don't be frightened," he said. Richter's posture didn't change. Maybe he *was* scared, Tony thought. All the better.

He slowed at the mouth of an alley and glanced around him, making sure they were alone. "After you." He motioned toward the opening, and Richter turned without hesitating. Tony remembered the easy way Richter had interacted with the Germans—even the girl—and with the band, how conversation came quickly to him, how he moved through the world in a way Tony never would. He no longer cared about seeing Richter on his knees. Snapping the knife open, he lunged for the back of Richter's neck.

Tony found himself on the ground, the wind knocked out of him, his elbow throbbing, his right hand numb and useless. Richter straddled him. Tony tried to raise his body, but Richter was immovable. A loop of piano wire flashed in front of his eyes. Tony reached for it, but he was too slow, and the wire pressed against his throat, the pain searing. He felt Richter's hot breath against his ear.

"This is for Philip and Petra," he said.

Tony didn't know who Petra was. He tried to ask Richter, but the world had turned red, and now it was darkening, now it was black.

Richter used Tony's knife to cut out the inside pocket of Philip's jacket. He tossed the knife into a sewer grate and the garrote into a rubbish bin. Looping one of Tony's arms over his shoulder as if he were a drunken companion, Richter walked his body deeper into the alley until he came to a narrow passage between two buildings. Holding Tony against the bricks, he leaned into the opening, his shadow causing rats to scurry. He managed to walk Tony twenty paces down the cobbles, where he let his body fall.

Back in his room, he placed the pocket from Philip's jacket on his nightstand, smoothing the fabric. A three-masted clipper ship was embroidered in red. Below it were the letters PJW USN—Philip Jon Waters, United States Navy. It would be all the proof Major Waters needed.

Before he sat with the young Germans in the Kaiserkeller, Richter had stood near the stage, listening to the guitarists singing in three-part harmony, their voices aching with promise and possibility. Even in a room full of drunks and gangsters, none of whom were really watching the band, they'd put on a show. To see them now, as they got better night after night, to be a part of it as they grew, would be a once-in-a-lifetime thing, he thought. He envied the young Germans who were witnessing this history unfold.

Last night he had experienced his first dreamless sleep in months. Even without the balance of what Major Waters owed him, Richter had enough money to live for a year or two here. He knew Fischer could get papers for him and take care of delivering the pocket to Waters. But who was he kidding? Soon, there would be another job, and he'd forget Hamburg, the way he'd forgotten Nice and Copenhagen before it. In another life, he'd take his chances with the Polizei and stay in Hamburg. But not in this one.

A mechanical voice announced that his plane was boarding. Businessmen stood, valises in hand. A single couple walked arm-in-arm away from him. Soon, the same mechanical voice announced final boarding.

Richter watched the last passengers depart. He turned and left the airport.

DEATH IN CAMELOT

Michael Bracken

Dallas, Texas. Friday, November 22, 1963. 12:30 p.m.

Stone DeSoto, operative for Evan Goodnight Security & Investigations, glanced at his watch. The president's motorcade was running late and would soon be passing through Dealey Plaza. The woman he was tailing had stopped next to a man standing on a concrete pedestal holding a Model 414 PD Bell & Howell Zoomatic Director Series Camera. She said something to him, but DeSoto was too far away to hear what she'd said. The man with the camera did not respond.

EGS&I—known behind the owner's back as Eggs and I—had been hired to tail Mary Margaret McCarthy twenty-four hours a day. A thirty-three-year-old dishwater blonde with an hourglass figure, courtesy of a particularly tight, waist-slimming girdle, she stood five foot seven—sans heels and bouffant—and had green eyes DeSoto had never gotten close enough to see. That Friday—his third day tailing her, the firm's seventh—she wore a knee-length teal polka-dot swing dress with matching teal purse, heels, and hairband.

A moment later John F. Kennedy's limousine made a sharp left-hand turn from Houston onto Elm Street. Within a matter of seconds, DeSoto heard three shots, watched the president raise his fists and turn toward his wife, watched Mrs. Kennedy climb out of the back seat onto the rear of the limousine, watched a Secret Service agent climb onto the back of the car, watched the agent shield both the president and the first lady, and saw the limousine race away as sirens began wailing.

What DeSoto did not see was the blonde disappear. When he returned his attention to the spot where she had been standing, she was gone.

"You lost her?"

Stone Desoto stood in Evan Goodnight's office, hat metaphorically in hand. "I only looked away for a second."

"You looked away?"

"But the president—"

"Were we hired to follow the president? No? Then why were you watching him?"

DeSoto said nothing.

"I already have operatives watching Miss McCarthy's apartment and her employer's office," Goodnight said, "but she hasn't returned to either one. You find her, and you find her before our client knows we've lost her, or I'll have your nuts in a vise."

DeSoto backed out of Goodnight's office, leaving the granite-haired company founder railing at him for his ineptitude. He returned to his desk and grabbed a file folder that contained copies of everything the firm knew about Mary Margaret and all the reports he and the other operatives had submitted during the seven days the firm had been tailing her. He carried it outside to his white Ford Fairlane, rolled down the front windows, and sat in the driver's seat with the folder open across the steering wheel. He had read everything at least twice before, so he skimmed the three-dozen pages and examined the half-dozen photos. He didn't learn anything new, and he also didn't learn who was paying the bill for the tail job. Goodnight had taken the case, and he had kept that information out of the case file, something he only did when the client was wealthy, well-connected, or both.

Mary Margaret worked in the secretarial pool of a large insurance company located a few blocks from Dealey Plaza. She was available to assist any executive not far enough up the corporate ladder to have a personal secretary. Unmarried and with no known romantic entanglements, Mary Margaret lived with a roommate named Betty Sheridan in a shoebox apartment a short bus ride away from her employer's office. During her lunch break each day, she walked unaccompanied to Dealey Plaza, took a wax-paper-wrapped sandwich from her purse, and ate it in the company of other people employed nearby who were also on their lunch break. She had exchanged pleasantries with a few of them, but never the same person twice. After work, she rode the bus home and she remained at home until the following morning.

EGS&I had not been tailing Mary Margaret long enough to know her weekend routine, but the previous Saturday morning she had visited her gynecologist and later browsed the magazine rack at her local pharmacy while she waited for a single prescription to be filled. The following morning, she attended Mass, went to lunch with Darlene and Delores Talbert from her parish, visited a grocery store near her apartment, and spent almost two hours in a laundromat. Operatives had been unable to determine the nature of her visit to the doctor or the exact medication purchased at the pharmacy, but they did provide a list of items purchased at the grocery store, noting that Mary Margaret seemed partial to *Life* and *Look* magazines.

Dallas traffic was a mess, worse than usual because of what had happened at Dealey Plaza, but DeSoto managed to park his Fairlane six blocks from the office building where Mary Margaret's employer occupied the top five floors. He found Kurt Myers sitting in the lobby, pretending to read the previous day's newspaper, and he settled into the nearest chair. "She come back?"

Myers folded the paper closed. "Not yet."

"You certain?"

"This ain't my first rodeo," Myers said, and, mixing his metaphors, added, "and I ain't the one who lost the sheep."

"But you're certain?"

"There's a hot little number upstairs who works as a receptionist for the insurance company. Everybody who goes in or out has to walk past her, and I slipped her ten bucks to call the guard desk over there if McCarthy walks in." He glanced at his watch. "The workday's almost over, and I don't think she's coming back."

DeSoto drove to Mary Margaret's apartment building and found Eddie Carville sitting in a Ford F-150 parked where he could watch the building's entrance and the windows of Mary Margaret's second-floor apartment. DeSoto moved from the driver's seat of his Fairlane to the passenger seat of Carville's pickup.

Before DeSoto could say anything, Carville said, "She hasn't come home. I slipped the lock when I first got here, and the place was empty. I'd be surprised if she could get past me—"

A light came on inside Mary Margaret's apartment.

"Damn," Carville said. "That must be her. Her roommate isn't due for an hour."

DeSoto opened the truck's door and slid out. "I'll find out."

He quick-stepped across the street, pushed through the apartment building's front door, and took the stairs two at a time. He was about to knock on Mary Margaret's door when sounds coming from inside made him think someone was tossing the place. He drew a snub-nosed .38 from the holster under his left arm, slowly twisted the knob, and eased the door open.

"Who the fuck are you?" was followed by a right cross that turned out his lights.

* * *

DeSoto woke a few minutes later to find the place ransacked and his wallet on his chest, open to his private investigator's license. He pushed himself to his feet, returned his wallet to his pocket, and then fumbled around until he found his .38 under the couch. When he stood, he found Carville standing in the open doorway.

"What'd you do to the place?"

"Wasn't me," DeSoto said. He took one last look around, didn't know what he expected to see and didn't see it, and added, "We should leave before the roommate gets home and finds this mess. We don't need to explain our presence to any cops."

DeSoto wiped off the doorknob—the only thing he'd touched—and then led Carville down the stairs. They returned to Carville's pickup truck and, once there, he explained what had happened. "I never saw the guy's face—I barely saw the brick he hit me with—but I think I'd recognize his voice if I heard it again. I think he was chewing gravel. You see anybody leave the building while I was in there?"

"Nobody came or went."

A city bus stopped at the corner. When it pulled away, it left behind a plump brunette wearing a navy-blue skirt and unbuttoned matching vest over a white blouse. Carville said, "That's Betty, the roommate."

DeSoto wanted to talk to Mary Margaret's roommate, but he didn't think the timing was right. He opened the truck door. "I'd better go. Keep an eye on things here and let me know what happens after she calls the cops."

"Where you going?"

DeSoto shrugged. He had two options and had yet to flip a coin to decide which would be his first stop.

"You might want to do something about your face. You're starting to bruise."

DeSoto returned to his Fairlane, drove several blocks and then circled back so he could approach the apartment building without Carville seeing him. A quick look let him know the building's rear door had been jimmied, probably with a crowbar, but he knew the police would find no fingerprints. The man who had ransacked Mary Margaret's apartment had been a pro.

He drove away, mentally flipped a coin, and it came up Jesus. His next stop was the Catholic church where Mary Margaret had attended mass the previous Sunday. Parishioners filled many of the pews, and he soon realized they were there because of the assassination earlier that day.

Father Mike Javorsky walked among them, offering solace.

DeSoto caught the elderly priest's attention and drew him away from his parishioners.

Father Mike glanced at the bruise purpling on DeSoto's chin and asked, "How may I help you?"

DeSoto displayed his private investigator's license and asked about Mary Margaret McCarthy. "Do you know her?"

"I do."

"I think she's in trouble."

"Oh?" Father Mike glanced over his shoulder at a new arrival sliding into the rear pew. DeSoto followed the priest's gaze, saw a thick-bodied man in a dark suit, but returned his attention to Father Mike when the priest asked, "And what kind of trouble might that be?"

"I was hoping you could tell me," DeSoto said. He couldn't tell the priest he had been following Mary Margaret, but he could spin a tale that was mostly true. "She left work at lunchtime today and didn't return. She hasn't been home, either, and I need to find her."

Father Mike said nothing.

"Maybe she told you something that would help me."

"Whatever she might have told me is protected by the sanctity of the confessional."

"So, she did tell you something."

Father Mike took a deep breath and let it out slowly. Then he said, "Follow me."

DeSoto followed him to the end of the seventh pew, where

a pair of dark-haired women in their late twenties sat. He recognized Darlene and Delores Talbert from one of the photos in Mary Margaret's file. The previous Sunday, they had gone to lunch with the missing woman.

Father Mike bent over to talk to the two women. "This man is a private detective, and he seems to think Mary Margaret is in trouble."

The two women stood. As Darlene used a white kerchief to wipe tears from the corner of her left eye, Delores asked, "What do you think's happened?"

DeSoto asked the priest, "Is there somewhere we can talk in private?"

"Use my office," Father Mike said. "Darlene and Delores will take you there."

DeSoto followed them out of the nave and down the hall to the priest's office, a room twice the size of his own living room, with a desk large enough for a game of table tennis. A small couch and a pair of overstuffed chairs made for a conversation pit at the far end of the room, and they settled into place. To make conversation, DeSoto asked the sisters how long they had known Mary Margaret.

"Since July sixteenth, 1960," Delores said. She looked at Darlene for confirmation, and her sister nodded.

"That's quite specific."

"That's the day after the Democratic National Convention ended," Darlene said.

"Mary Margaret volunteered to work for Kennedy's campaign," Delores said. "We all did. That's how we met. We stuffed envelopes and handed out flyers and made phone calls."

"But Mary Margaret did more. Her secretarial skills came in handy during the campaign," Darlene said. "She knows shorthand, and she types seventy-three words per minute—probably faster now on one of those Selectric typewriters."

"The three of us worked every evening and weekends—Sundays after Mass—from mid-July until the polls closed on

November eighth," Delores said. "Sometimes Mary Margaret stayed late to finish typing something or to take dictation from one of the men running the office."

"We've been friends ever since."

"But we don't know what we can tell you. Have you talked to Betty, Mary Margaret's roommate?"

DeSoto didn't want to admit that he had visited Mary Margaret's apartment only a short time earlier. "Not yet."

"Well, she should have some idea where Mary Margaret might have gone," Delores said as she stood and crossed the room to the priest's desk. She picked up the phone, dialed a number, and before she could do much more than identify herself was interrupted by the person on the other end of the line. After several minutes, during which she barely squeezed in half a dozen words, Delores ended the call, turned to DeSoto, and said, "Betty hasn't seen Mary Margaret since breakfast, she doesn't know where she is, and someone tore up their apartment and she didn't know why."

DeSoto wanted answers to the same questions but knew he would have to wait to get them. He used the phone on the priest's desk to call the EGS&I switchboard. Beatrice Johnson, recently back at the office after maternity leave, was working the phones that night. She told him that Mary Margaret had not returned to work before the office closed and that Kurt Myers, the operative assigned to watch for her, had clocked out for the day. Eddie Carville had also reported in after being replaced at his post surveilling Mary Margaret's apartment building. She had not returned home, and police had spent more than an hour with Betty at her apartment.

After ending the call, Stone handed his business card to Dolores and Darlene and left a third card on the priest's desk. They could not call him directly but if they left a message at the switchboard, DeSoto could get back to them. He thanked the two women and was about to leave when he turned back. "Do you have any idea why Mary Margaret visited a doctor earlier this week?"

"Her gynecologist?" Dolores asked. After Darlene gave her a sharp look and an elbow, she continued, "Female problems. That's all."

DeSoto couldn't get anything more from the sisters. So, he left them in the priest's office, walked back through the nave on his way out, and passed the man who earlier had slipped into the last pew while he was talking to the priest. He caught a glimpse of the man's right hand and saw his busted-up knuckles.

The EGS&I operative continued walking and pushed through the heavy doors to the outside. Instead of continuing down the wide stone steps, he stepped to the side and waited. A moment later the man followed.

"You know who the fuck I am," DeSoto said as he threw a haymaker at the man's jaw. "Who the fuck are you?"

The man absorbed the punch like Sonny Liston, shook his head and rubbed his jaw, and then offered his hand. "Carter Colson," he said. "Secret Service."

DeSoto didn't take the offered hand. Instead, he flexed his own, hoping he hadn't broken any bones. He asked, "What's your interest in Mary Margaret McCarthy?"

"I'm the one who should be asking the questions, Mr. DeSoto. What's *your* interest?"

"I was tailing her when—" DeSoto unexpectedly choked up. He'd been bottling up his feelings ever since seeing the president's assassination. "I took my eyes off Mary Margaret when the president was shot, and she disappeared."

"Why were you tailing her?"

"Why? That's above my pay grade. I was given the assignment, and I didn't question it."

"And now you're trying to find her."

Colson hadn't asked a question, so DeSoto didn't feel the need to respond directly. "I take it you didn't find anything of value in Mary Margaret's apartment or you wouldn't be here now."

***

A diner three blocks from the church served hot coffee and provided more privacy than the church steps. So, several minutes later, the two men sat in a rear booth, nursing coffee served by a pimple-faced brunette who couldn't have been old enough to vote.

DeSoto asked, "Why are you looking for Mary Margaret?"

"Our job is to protect the president."

"Looks like y'all screwed the pooch today."

"Not our finest hour," Colson admitted. "But it isn't just the president's body we protect. We also protect his reputation."

"Like quashing the rumors about him slipping it to Marilyn Monroe?" Colson didn't respond, so DeSoto followed up by asking, "So, how could a secretary from Dallas impact the president's reputation?"

Colson said, "I can't tell you that until you show me what you've got."

DeSoto showed Colson the file EGS&I had created, and the agent quickly thumbed through it. When Colson finished, he looked up, "You've been following Mary Margaret for a week and this is all you've got?"

The EGS&I operative shrugged. "The woman doesn't *do* anything or go *any*where."

Colson tapped the file folder. "Work, home, church, grocery store, pharmacy, doctor's office, and Dealey Plaza. Any of these strike you as unusual?"

"Not particularly," DeSoto said. "Except today. Going to Dealey Plaza wasn't unusual, but what happened was."

Colson pushed the folder back across the table and stood. "You have nothing," he said, "so I'll give you this: Bendectin."

Colson left DeSoto sitting at the table as he exited the diner, and a moment later the waitress brought the check for their coffees.

* * *

DeSoto didn't know much, but he knew more than he had before getting stiffed for Colson's coffee. He knew the Secret Service was interested in locating Mary Margaret and that, even with all their resources, they weren't having any better luck finding the missing woman than he was. He also knew they were looking for someone named Ben Deckton.

After he paid for their coffee, DeSoto located the diner's payphone between the restrooms in the back hall. He thumbed through the telephone directory chained to the wall and found no one and no business by that name. So, he called the EGS&I switchboard. Beatrice Johnson was still working the phones and, when she answered, he told her he needed to get a line on a guy named Ben Deckton.

She repeated the name and then asked, "Are you sure?"

"I think so. Why?"

"Bendectin is an anti-nausea drug. My obstetrician prescribed it for morning sickness when I was pregnant with Tommy."

More to himself than to Beatrice, DeSoto said, "She's pregnant."

"Excuse me?"

"What's an unmarried Catholic girl do when she's pregnant?"

"Damned if I know," Beatrice said. "I'm a Baptist."

"Thanks, Bea," he said. "I—"

"Stone," she interrupted. "Goodnight left a message for you if you phoned in. He wants you to pack it in and go home. He's already pulled the surveillance off Mary Margaret McCarthy's apartment and—"

"Someone's found her?"

"I don't think so," Beatrice said. "I think the client found out we'd lost her and is shutting us down."

DeSoto hung up the phone, returned to his Fairlane, and drove to Evan Goodnight's home. Even though it was a clear breach of etiquette for an operative to brace the company's founder at his residence, DeSoto felt he had no choice. Friday was rapidly slipping away, and he needed information that Goodnight had not shared with his operatives.

He parked in the long circular drive behind a dark blue Lincoln and a moment later stood on the porch, leaning into the bell. A slender woman in a black-and-white maid's outfit opened the door. She asked, "May I help you?"

"I'm here to see Goodnight."

"Mr. Goodnight is not receiving guests at this time."

She started to push the door closed, but DeSoto jammed a size-eleven Florsheim between the door and the jamb, preventing that from happening. She offered little resistance when he pushed the door open and said, "I wasn't asking."

Goodnight must have heard the commotion at his front door because he stepped into the foyer and closed a set of pocket doors behind him. He wore a blue pinstripe suit over a crisp white shirt and a bold red tie. "This is an inopportune time to meet with you, DeSoto," he said. "Whatever brings you to my home this evening can be discussed at the office on Monday."

"I don't think this can wait," DeSoto told him.

Goodnight said nothing.

"You were all over my ass this afternoon for losing the tail on Mary Margaret McCarthy," DeSoto said. "Now you want us to close the case. Why?"

"Our client has terminated the contract," Goodnight said. "It's as simple as that. Now—"

"Is it because the Secret Service has gotten involved?" DeSoto asked. "Or is it because—?"

"Lower your voice," Goodnight commanded. "I have important guests, and you are interrupting what had been a rather pleasant evening."

"But—"

"The vise is tightening on your nuts, DeSoto. Do you feel it?" Goodnight asked. "Leave now or tender your resignation. The choice is yours."

"This stinks every way from Sunday," DeSoto said. Then he turned and stalked out the door.

He didn't go far. He parked his Fairlane where he could watch Goodnight's house but could not be seen by anyone inside. Midnight came and went before the front door opened and Goodnight's two guests exited. When their Lincoln drove away, DeSoto fell in behind it. Nothing that happened during the next half-hour indicated that the driver knew he was being followed.

When the two men exited their car in front of a home that made Goodnight's look like a piker's, DeSoto was close enough to see their faces. He recognized Carter Colson as the driver and the passenger as one of the men who had helped orchestrate JFK's narrow victory in Texas. Colson waited until his passenger entered the house. Then he drove the car into the garage. DeSoto watched the house until the last window darkened. He presumed the two men had found their beds for the night, but he continued watching until he, too, fell asleep.

He woke shortly after dawn, knew he had missed anything that might have happened at the house, and had no idea what more he could learn by waiting. So, he drove across town to Mary Margaret's, and he pounded on the apartment door until her roommate jerked it open. He had clearly awakened her because she had bed hair, no makeup, and wore a floral robe held together with one hand. "Who are you and what do you want?"

He held up his private investigator's license as he introduced himself to Betty Sheridan. "I'm looking for Mary Margaret."

"She isn't here."

"I know that," DeSoto said. "Where is she?"

"Why are you looking for her?"

"I don't know," DeSoto admitted.

That caught Betty by surprise.

"Let me in and I'll explain."

When he finished telling Betty about EGS&I being hired to tail Mary Margaret and about everything he'd been through since losing her at Dealey Plaza—including his encounter with the man who had trashed their apartment and bruised his chin—he leaned back on the couch and waited for her reaction.

"Why didn't you come to me right away?"

"You weren't supposed to know we were following your roommate."

"But it's okay for me to know now?"

"I doubt it," DeSoto said, "but I don't care. I think she's in trouble. Did you know she was pregnant?"

"I—" Betty hesitated. "Mary Margaret never told me she was, but she couldn't hide it. How did you know?"

"Colson told me he found her anti-nausea medicine when he tossed your apartment."

"And you think that's why she's in trouble?"

"She's an unmarried Catholic girl," DeSoto said.

"An unmarried woman doesn't need to be Catholic to be in trouble," Betty said. "We have the same doctor, so maybe he can tell us something."

She phoned the gynecologist's office and told them she had an emergency. When Betty ended the call, she turned to DeSoto and said, "Eleven. The doctor will see me at eleven."

At five minutes till, they sat in the waiting room and, at precisely eleven, a nurse called Betty's name. DeSoto followed them into one of the examination rooms.

When the nurse realized he'd followed them, she said, "You should wait—"

"It's okay," Betty said. "He's with me."

"But—" The nurse looked from one to the other. "This is highly unusual, but you know what to do. There's a gown hanging on the back of the door."

The nurse stepped out and both Betty and DeSoto looked at each other.

She ignored the gown. "I've never done anything like this before."

The doctor pushed open the door, took one look at DeSoto, and said, "You really need to wait outside."

DeSoto flipped open his wallet and showed the doctor his private investigator's license. "One of your patients, Mary Margaret McCarthy, is missing. Betty is her roommate, and we both think you may know something about her disappearance."

"I'm sorry, I can't tell you anything," the doctor said. "Anything I know would be protected by doctor-patient confidentiality."

"Mary Margaret is pregnant," DeSoto said. "We know that. You prescribed Bendectin for her morning sickness. We know that as well. She isn't married and has no prospects, as best we can tell. Imagine what will happen if she carries the baby to term—"

Betty interrupted. "You don't have to tell us what happened to her, but what would you suggest if I were pregnant and didn't want the baby?"

"I—"

"Mary Margaret is missing, doctor," DeSoto said. "She hasn't been seen since twelve-thirty yesterday. She didn't return to work after her lunch break, she hasn't returned home, and none of her friends have seen or heard from her."

"That's unlike Mary Margaret," Betty added.

The doctor looked from one to the other and then spoke to Betty. "If you were pregnant and couldn't keep the child," he said as he wrote the name of a motel on the back of a scrap of paper. "I would suggest you check into room six, and I would suggest you forget ever discussing this with me."

***

A dark blue Lincoln was already parked outside room six when they drove up. DeSoto parked his Fairlane on the far side of it, told Betty to wait, and then slipped out of the car. He eased up to the door and listened. He could hear a male voice inside but nothing else.

He tried the knob and found it unlocked. When he pushed the door open, he saw Mary Margaret sitting on the side of the bed with Colson gripping her arm and trying to pull her to her feet. She was pale, didn't appear able to stand on her own, and wore the same clothes she'd worn Friday. Blood stained the lower half of her teal polka-dot swing dress.

"Let her go," DeSoto said.

Colson spun around to face him. "She's coming with me."

"I don't think so." DeSoto knew he wouldn't win a fistfight with Colson, so he drew the snub-nosed .38 from his shoulder holster.

Colson snorted derisively. "You wouldn't shoot a federal agent."

"Maybe not," DeSoto said as he squeezed the trigger, "but you're just a bodyguard."

Colson released his grip on Mary Margaret and staggered backward, but he didn't go down. He reached under his jacket and drew his own sidearm.

DeSoto shot him a second time.

This time Colson dropped to his knees. He swayed for a moment, and then he fell on his face.

DeSoto kicked Colson's semi-automatic pistol out of his hand.

He turned his attention to Mary Margaret, finally close enough to see her green eyes. They were dull and lifeless. "We need to get you to a hospital."

After he yelled out the door for Betty, DeSoto grabbed Mary Margaret's purse, shoes, and hairband. Then they helped her to his car. He drove directly to the Emergency Room at Parkland Memorial Hospital, the same hospital where the president had been pronounced dead the previous day.

Betty paced the waiting room while DeSoto phoned the Talbert sisters and Father Mike, letting them know that Mary Margaret had been hospitalized. Then he phoned the Dallas police and told them where they could find the body of a man who had been passing himself off as a Secret Service agent.

The police already knew about the shooting at the motel, and a pair of officers came to the hospital to collect DeSoto.

He spent the rest of the day and most of the night being interviewed by homicide detectives. He was finally released the next morning after the man who employed Carter Colson denied any knowledge of Colson's relationship with Mary Margaret. DeSoto suspected it wasn't Colson who'd had the relationship but his employer, the man who'd asked Mary Margaret to stay late those nights during the Kennedy campaign. He suspected the relationship hadn't ended with Kennedy's inauguration, but the man's wealth and political connections prevented the police from asking further questions.

As the homicide detectives walked DeSoto out of the station, he asked if they knew anything about Mary Margaret's status.

"The baby's gone," one of the detectives said, "but Miss McCarthy will survive. She faces two to five years imprisonment for her actions, but she might be able to get a plea deal if she rolls over on the abortionist and the person who introduced her to him."

The detectives left DeSoto on the front steps and disappeared inside. He caught a city bus and rode it back to the hospital. If he'd been a religious man, he might have sought out the hospital's chapel and offered a prayer for Mary Margaret, but he wasn't and he didn't. He considered seeking out Betty, the Talbert sisters, or Mary Margaret's priest for an update, but he decided not to intrude. He retrieved his Fairlane and drove home.

***

Sunday, November 24, 1963. 11:21 a.m.

Stone DeSoto opened a beer and tuned in to NBC to watch detectives lead Lee Harvey Oswald, the man arrested for the assassination of President John F. Kennedy, through the basement of Dallas Police headquarters, on their way to an armored car that was to take him to the county jail. DeSoto and millions of other viewers watched as Dallas nightclub owner Jack Ruby stepped from the crowd and shot Oswald once in the abdomen.

An hour and forty-six minutes later, Oswald died.

NICE GIRLS DON'T

N.M. Cedeño

If I wasn't a teetotaler, I'd probably have been a cliché, an alcoholic private investigator, drinking to numb the chronic pain from my blown-out left hip and squashed dreams. Because I didn't drink, and morphine made me want to scratch my eyes out, I settled for popping aspirin whenever my hip pain flared. Then, I threw myself into my work to shake off the dismals I got from no longer being a police officer. Consequently, I was down in the dumps, feeling broken, but financially stable and sober when I took on the Marquez case one Monday evening in September 1966.

Grief etched the stony face of the middle-aged man and clouded the red-rimmed eyes of the fragile woman who entered my private investigations office that night. At a glance, they were an upper-class Tejano couple who'd suffered a recent bereavement. The husband, wearing a black tailored suit, was soft in the middle, but I could've read his military history in his posture even if his missing left arm hadn't testified to it. The wife, slender and bird-like in a black sheath dress, clung to her husband's right arm as if she needed support to keep from sinking beneath one of life's tidal waves.

I straightened my tie against my white shirt and buttoned my suit jacket as I rose to greet them. "Welcome to Milam Investigations. I'm Jerry Milam. How can I help you?" The fog of grief surrounding them suggested they had come about a death. I hoped it wasn't another case where the evidence pointed to suicide, but the family refused to believe it. Those cases rarely ended well.

The man collected himself and said with a strong Texas twang, "My name is Esteban Marquez, and this is my wife Gloria." He evaluated me for a moment before he moved his stumpy left arm almost imperceptibly. "Army. In France. You?"

"Army. Pacific Theater."

He nodded, satisfied with my answer and ready to trust me. Introductory conversations with clients my age—upper-forties—frequently began with brief summaries of our service in the world war that had defined our youth.

"Have a seat." I gestured to the sturdy wooden chairs in front of my desk. As the couple sat, I sank into my chair before I started sweating from the strain of standing. Ironically, I'd survived the war unscathed, only to be injured at home. Excruciating pain, a remnant of the car accident that ended my career with the Austin Police Department, knifed through my left hip.

Once seated, Mr. Marquez said, "We want you to investigate our daughter's death. We believe she was murdered, but the police closed the case, saying she overdosed. Lizzie lived at home with us while attending college. She never used drugs. She couldn't have overdosed."

"I'm sorry for your loss. I worked as a police officer for ten years before moving into private investigations, and I can tell you the police don't usually overlook a homicide. Many parents are surprised to discover their child has used drugs. And even if your daughter never used drugs before, she still could have died the first time she tried them."

Mrs. Marquez bit back a sob and thrust an embroidered handkerchief over her pinched mouth and delicate nose.

"This is different," Mr. Marquez insisted. "They didn't question anyone or investigate anything. I asked a friend with connections to look at Lizzie's file, and it's mostly empty except for the doctor's report on the cause of death. The police ignored Lizzie's case because they were overwhelmed. She died Monday, August first, the day of the Tower Shooting."

My eyebrows rose. "I see."

August 1, 1966, had been a hellish day for law enforcement and for citizens in Austin, Texas. Charles Whitman, a mentally disturbed former Marine, used the observation deck of the University of Texas Tower as a sniper's perch and rained death on the city for ninety-six minutes, killing fourteen people and injuring thirty-two more. I'd itched to get my hunting rifle and join the civilians shooting at Whitman, knowing the sidearms carried by the police didn't have the range to reach him. That day my injury rankled as I wished that I was still on the force and capable of racing up a tower to stop him. I dragged my thoughts back to the present. "Can you think of any reason someone might murder your daughter? Did she have enemies?"

"Yes," said Mrs. Marquez in an icy voice, dropping her handkerchief to reveal a face contorted with rage. "That Lamp boy hated her because she was smarter than he was! Now that she's dead, he'll get her teaching assistant position."

Mr. Marquez patted his wife's knee. "August first was Lizzie's last day of summer class at UT. She took an organic chemistry lab this summer so she could graduate early and start her master's degree in chemistry this fall. She left our house at nine a.m. to go to campus and turn in a final lab report."

He reached into his suit coat pocket and removed two notebooks. "Here are Lizzie's calendar and her personal address book with names, phone numbers, and addresses for her friends and classmates. On her calendar for August first, she noted three names: her boyfriend Martin Madrigal, a fellow chemistry student named Albert Lamp, and someone named Carl Schmidt. We don't know Schmidt, and we don't know when she was supposed to meet Lamp, but Martin told us Lizzie was supposed to meet him at eleven-thirty for lunch." Mr. Marquez slid the books toward me. "The police think Lizzie died in the morning, before the shooting started. Will you investigate for us? Find out what really happened?"

I flipped the calendar open. The pages were filled with notes and names written in a tidy, sloping cursive. Directing a warning look toward Mrs. Marquez, I said, "I may discover things about your daughter that you don't want to know."

Mrs. Marquez leaned forward, still clutching her handkerchief. "We know, but we need the truth!"

After explaining my fees and collecting a retainer, I promised regular updates on my progress. Then, the grief-stricken couple shuffled out of my office.

I picked up the phone and dialed an old buddy in the Austin PD, Mutt Prichard. He could tell me about the police investigation, or lack thereof, into Lizzie Marquez's death. As a private investigator, I don't mind stepping on police toes when I work, though I try to tread lightly. I believe in the ideological concept of a police force, striving to attain justice for all. However, what we strive for is what we haven't yet achieved. Police officers are human, subject to stressors, personal prejudices, and poor decision-making. When I find mistakes, some officers' toes get mashed. "Hey, Mutt, it's Jerry. I need a favor."

"You're gonna owe me a beer. What can I do for you?" he asked in his East Texas drawl.

"I'm looking into a death classified as an overdose, Lizzie Marquez. She died the day of the Tower Shooting. Can you tell me what's in her file?"

"Give me a minute."

I heard him put the phone down with a thunk. A hum of background noise and snatches of conversations buzzed through the line as I tapped my pencil against the pad of yellow paper in front of me. After what felt like forever, Mutt returned.

"Got the file, but it's an open-and-shut case. Nothin' to it."

"What do you mean nothing?" I asked.

"The file says an anonymous caller reported a body in an alley behind a business off Guadalupe Street, north of the UT campus. The caller thought the body might be another Tower Shooting victim who'd fled the scene and died. The medical report says the girl died of an overdose of orally ingested tranquilizers sometime between nine in the morning and noon. The detective wrote that the victim had a paper due by eleven, but never turned in her assignment. An overdose. Case closed."

"That's it?"

"Hold on. Let me read the medical report." He paused, muttering to himself as he read the doctor's report. "She had sex shortly before her death. The doc thinks someone moved the body from somewhere else."

"That could be a sign of foul play."

"Or not. If she overdosed in a friend's place after a wild night, someone might have moved the body to avoid dealing with the fallout. We have plenty of university students who don't want blotches on their records that might mar bright futures. Moving a body is tampering with the scene of a death, or failure to report a death, but not murder." Mutt cleared his throat. "This is tragic, but not worth damaging someone's reputation or wasting man-hours."

"Her parents say she left their house at nine to go to class. That rules out the wild night theory."

I heard him thumbing through papers.

"Her parents don't want to face the fact that she wasn't the good girl they thought she was. Good girls don't sleep around and overdose. Besides, we had our hands full with real crime. A slut who overdosed didn't rate high on the priority list. We had Whitman's wife and mother dead, plus his shooting victims, and we didn't know if we'd find even more bodies in his wake." His voice, with its thick, syrupy drawl, dripped defensiveness.

He was already annoyed, so I bit back an argumentative response. If I suggested Lizzie could have been raped, Mutt would blame the victim based on the prevailing belief that nice girls don't get raped. My sister's personal experience, which spurred me into a career in law enforcement, had taught me the erroneousness of that belief. But lecturing Mutt would only aggravate him and limit my access to police files. Instead of burning bridges, I soothed him. "The death may be a simple overdose. I'm reviewing it for the parents' sake."

"Better you than me. It's a waste of time," Mutt said before someone interrupted him, and he ended the call.

Next, I called Martin Madrigal and arranged to meet him at a coffee shop at nine the next morning. Night had fallen and I was hungry, so I closed the office and headed home.

The Drag was the section of Guadalupe Street, mispronounced "Gwad-a-loop" by the locals, that ran along the edge of the University of Texas campus. Textbook stores, coffee shops, barbershops, and other businesses that catered to the university crowd were packed into that strip. As I strolled along the Drag toward the San José Café where I was meeting Martin Madrigal, students carrying books against their hips flooded across the street from the campus with scant regard for cars in the road.

Stepping from the bright sun and brilliant blue skies of a clear September morning into the dark, narrow coffee shop blinded me. I blinked rapidly to adjust my eyes to the darkness. Chattering students filled every table. Most of the young men were attired in short-sleeved, button-up shirts over dark trousers, but I spotted Madrigal quickly. He was a slender young man with narrow shoulders, short black hair, and a brown complexion. Alone, slumped at a table against the wall, he sat with a cup of coffee in his hand.

I walked up to him. "Martin Madrigal?"

He startled as I spoke. Apparently, he'd been lost in thought and didn't see me approaching. "Yes?"

I extended my hand. "Jerry Milam."

He shook my hand. "Pleased to meet you, sir. Join me." His voice was strongly accented, indicating recent immigrant roots.

I planted myself in a chrome chair that wobbled on uneven legs.

Martin said, "Señor Marquez told me that he would hire a detective. Do you think you can find who killed Lizzie?"

"You think she was killed? You don't believe she simply overdosed?"

"No. Lizzie studied chemistry. She'd never have taken drugs voluntarily because she knew what drugs would do to her body. Someone must have drugged her." His faced flushed with anger and his voice rose. "Someone murdered her!"

The hum of voices around us went silent as people turned to stare.

"Take a deep breath," I said as I patted his shoulder. "Who would have done that?"

"I've been trying to figure that out since she died." His eyes became glassy and damp, but he blinked back the tears, fighting to keep his composure.

"Do you think she was hiding something?" I asked, encouraging him to continue talking.

"I don't know," he said. "Her family is upper class. They arrived with a Spanish land grant before Texas Independence. The way Señor Marquez tells it, his ancestors were personal friends of Juan Seguin and Lorenzo de Zavala. Lizzie could talk to anyone with perfect poise and never show what she thought. My parents were uneducated Mexican migrant workers who came to Brownsville with nothing. It was like we came from different planets. Sometimes, I couldn't read her at all."

I recognized the class divide he was describing and the common story of the miscommunications that arise when a lower-class boy meets an upper-class girl. "Martin, I have Lizzie's calendar. On the day she died, she was supposed to meet you, right?"

He sipped his coffee and fingered the sturdy ceramic mug. "We were supposed to meet for lunch at the sandwich shop two stores down from here. She didn't arrive before the shooting started, and I was stuck inside until it ended around one thirty. I was afraid she might have been shot, but I was hoping she was safe inside a building somewhere."

"What did you do before going to the restaurant?"

"I had my final class for the summer semester at ten and spoke to the professor for a few minutes after class ended. I had to retake government over the summer because I failed last spring, so I wanted to make sure I passed the class with a B. Law and writing are difficult for me; I'm better at math. Then, I went to meet Lizzie. I knew she had to turn in a lab report. We agreed to meet at eleven-thirty, but she never showed up." His shoulders drooped.

"Lizzie left her house at around nine. Do you know if she intended to meet anyone before class? She had the names Carl Schmidt and Albert Lamp written on her calendar."

Martin's hand tightened on his coffee mug. "Schmidt? Why would she see him?"

"Do you know him?"

"He's a protester with mop-top Beatles hair. He wanted Lizzie to go with him to protests, like the ones held before every Saturday home game because the football team doesn't allow Black players. I'm on academic probation because I failed government. I couldn't risk getting into trouble at a campus protest. If I get kicked out of school, I'll be drafted into the military and never finish my degree. Without a degree, Lizzie's parents would never consider me worthy of marrying her." He shook his head. "I thought Lizzie decided to stay out of the protests, too."

Having gone to school after the war on the GI Bill, I knew college degrees could be earned after military service. I suppressed my inclination to lecture the boy on his long-term thinking errors and said, "Could Lizzie have been meeting Carl that morning?"

"I don't know!" Martin buried his face in his hands.

Part of me wanted to shake the boy and tell him to pull himself together, but I knew his grief was fresh. He needed time to heal. I softened my voice. "Could Lizzie have confided in a girlfriend?"

Martin's head came up. "Diane Brown. She and Lizzie were close. They were both planning to get a master's in chemistry."

I opened Lizzie's address book and flipped pages until I found Diane Brown. I would call on her next. "What do you know about Albert Lamp?"

Martin's mouth twisted into a disdainful sneer. "Lamp is a leech. He was Lizzie's lab partner, but she did all the work, and he copied from her. Lamp and Lizzie were both starting the master's program this semester. He's what we call in Spanish *labioso*. He wanted the same teaching assistant position that Lizzie did and would say anything to get it. He thought he'd get the job because he's a man and she was a Tejano girl. But the professor saw through him and gave the job to Lizzie."

I left Martin drowning his sorrows in his coffee and walked the few blocks to Diane Brown's home, my hip complaining with every step.

Diane lived in the Almetris Cooperative, which housed Black female students. Someone ran to tell her she had a visitor while I waited patiently in an oppressively warm entry hall. Five minutes later, a young woman with a dark chocolate complexion and a puzzled expression approached me. She wore a blue cotton dress with low-heeled shoes and had her tightly curled hair pulled into a fluffy ponytail on the back of her head.

I introduced myself as I extended my hand.

She hesitated, considering me, before shaking my hand. "A private investigator? Good! Maybe you'll find out what really happened to Lizzie. The police certainly don't care. They said she overdosed, but Lizzie would never take drugs."

"What can you tell me about Lizzie's plans for the morning she died?"

Diane motioned for me to follow her outside and into the shade of a century-old oak tree before answering my question.

"Lizzie told me she had to talk to Martin, a guy named Carl, and the brown-noser from her organic chemistry lab, Albert Lamp, but I don't know who she went to see first."

"Do you know why she wanted to talk to Carl?" I asked, noting how direct Diane was in her manner and speech.

"Carl is a cocky protester with an eye for pretty girls who sees the word 'no' from a woman as a challenge. Lizzie was pretty, so he repeatedly asked her to go to a protest with him, but she kept turning him down. Lizzie cared about people and wanted to help change the world. She wanted to go to a protest with Martin, but Martin wouldn't go because of his academic probation. Lizzie felt like she needed to get involved. She planned to tell Carl that she would go with him, but that she wasn't interested in him."

"Okay, and Albert Lamp? Why did she want to see him?" I shifted my feet as the stabbing pain in my hip flashed down my leg.

Again, Diane was forthright. "She had Albert's book, and she wanted to give it back to him. She was nice like that. They were lab partners, and she somehow wound up with Albert's organic chemistry textbook. The day she died, they both had to turn in their lab reports, but they didn't have a class, only a window of time to give the report to the professor. Lizzie planned to call Albert and ask him to meet her."

"And Martin? Did she have a reason she needed to see Martin, too?"

Diane hesitated, her hands fidgeting with the material of her dress. "I wouldn't tell anyone this if Lizzie weren't dead. She told me in confidence that she wanted to tell Martin that she wouldn't cheat on him and that he needed to stop being so jealous and insecure."

"So why was Martin jealous and insecure?"

"His family doesn't move in the same circles as hers. Lizzie could hold a conversation with anyone, smiling politely even if she was bored to death. Martin thought her smiles meant she liked wealthy bores. He was becoming clingy." Diane pulled a handkerchief from her pocket and dabbed the tears welling in her eyes. "I told her she could do better than Martin, but she said she loved him."

"Do you think Martin could have killed Lizzie?" I watched her face closely.

She contemplated the question before answering. "Shades of *Othello*, you mean? No. If she'd been strangled or killed in a fit of rage, maybe, but I can't see Martin feeding Lizzie drugs."

In the distance, the Tower clock began to chime. Diane glanced at her wristwatch. "I have to get to class."

Lizzie's address book listed only Albert Lamp's phone number. I called and let the phone ring fifteen times before hanging up and turning to the local telephone directory. I found multiple listings for the last name Lamp, but none for Albert Lamp, and none of the numbers matched the one Lizzie had recorded. My reverse directory didn't have the number either.

Turning my attention to Carl Schmidt, I found both an address and a phone number in Lizzie's book. I decided to approach him at home, as I had with Diane Brown.

Carl lived north of campus in a run-down apartment complex. I drove there, painfully climbed the stairs to his third-floor unit, and knocked.

A bleary-eyed, shirtless young man with a torso covered in dark hair answered the door. "If you're selling something, I'm not buying." He started to close the door.

"Excuse me." I blocked the door with my foot. "I'm looking for Carl Schmidt."

The man kept trying to close the door before noticing my foot. "Look, man, Carl's not here. He's in class."

"Who are you?"

"I'm Edgar, his roommate."

"Okay, Edgar. When will he be back?"

"I dunno," he said, rubbing his eyes. "Is it Tuesday or Wednesday?"

"Tuesday."

Edgar shook his head, as if trying to shake clouds of sleep from his brain. "If it's Tuesday, Carl won't be back until tomorrow. He has class, then work, then he's going to Marley's."

"Who's Marley?"

"Marley isn't a who. It's a place. Marley's Playhouse. You know, the music club in East Austin?" Edgar yawned and stretched.

"Where were you and Carl before and during the Tower Shooting? Were you together?"

"Carl left before I got up. He got stuck somewhere. I was asleep before the shooting started. Then I tried to drive to campus to watch, but the police blocked the roads. I parked and walked between buildings and arrived in time to see them bringing the bodies out of the Tower. It was bloody."

"Yeah. I know." I remembered the news reports from the day of the shooting. After the shooting ended, hundreds of students had crowded the South Mall at the base of the Tower to watch the removal of the injured and the dead. If Edgar was in the crowd, where was Carl? I'd have to ask when I found him.

Edgar yawned again. "I need more sleep."

"Then, I'll let you get to it." I left Edgar standing in the doorway.

Returning to my office, I ate the Dagwood sandwich I'd packed for myself and knocked the bottle cap off a Dr Pepper, all while trying without success to reach Albert Lamp by telephone.

Finally, I decided to try another route and called the Marquez house.

Mrs. Marquez answered.

I identified myself and asked, "Did the police return any of Lizzie's belongings to you? Anything she had with her when she died?"

"Yes—her books and purse."

"I'm sorry to bother you, but could I come see those items?"

"Of course. If you think it will help find who killed her."

After ending our conversation, I cleared up my lunch and drove to the Marquez home, a colonnaded, white limestone structure on a half-acre corner lot.

Mrs. Marquez met me at the door, looking like a delicate piece of china in danger of shattering. She walked me to her daughter's bedroom at the rear of the house.

"I haven't had the strength to touch Lizzie's things," she said, clutching her handkerchief with bird-like fingers. "Her purse and books are on her bed."

I followed her into the room, which featured a white canopy bed with matching dresser. The sunlight filtering through windows covered with green, eyelet sheers, warmed the pale green shag carpeting and gave the room a verdant, serene air.

I examined the books laying on the peaches-and-cream bedspread. The stack contained an organic chemistry textbook. Extracting it, I opened the cover, revealing the book was inscribed with the name Albert Lamp, followed by his phone number and, more importantly, his address.

Mrs. Marquez stared at the book. "Why did Lizzie have that?"

I explained how Lizzie had intended to return it. "Do you mind if I take this? I'm going to talk to Albert Lamp."

"I don't care what you do with it."

I hesitated, looking at the woman's brittle features. "I'm sorry, ma'am, but I need to search the room."

She bit her lip and closed her eyes, but said, "Yes. Go ahead."

I searched the well-kept belongings of a thoughtful and organized young woman. One dresser drawer contained a folder of leaflets advocating for social change hidden beneath neatly stacked clothing. Carl Schmidt was listed on the leaflets as the contact for information. The room hid no illicit drugs, and I found nothing to suggest that someone wanted Lizzie dead.

Walking back to the canopy bed, I picked up the chemistry textbook and tucked it under my arm, then asked Mrs. Marquez,

"Can you think of anywhere Lizzie might have gone before class? She left an hour early. Is there any place Lizzie liked to go regularly?"

Mrs. Marquez wiped the silently flowing rivers from her cheeks with her handkerchief. "I didn't want her to drink coffee because it stains teeth, but Lizzie liked a cup in the morning. She might have gone to the San José Café."

I borrowed a photo of Lizzie, took my leave, and set out for Albert Lamp's place.

I caught Lamp leaving his place in the West Campus neighborhood and introduced myself before returning his textbook. He was baby-faced, with round cheeks and brown, buzz-cut hair, and he wore the typical student outfit of dark gray slacks with a buttoned-up, short-sleeve blue shirt.

He said, "I didn't think I'd get this back. I can sell it to the University Co-op. Every penny counts when you're a poor graduate student." He glanced at his watch. "We can talk if you'll walk with me. I have class this afternoon, and I need to go to the Co-op to buy bluebooks before then."

"Fine by me," I said, stifling my frustration with my own physical limitations. My hip was throbbing after the walking I'd already done that morning. "If every penny counts, you must be glad you got that teaching-assistant position."

Albert stopped. "Look, mister, Lizzie's mother already accused me of killing Lizzie to get that job, but it's a lie! I didn't kill her."

"Did Lizzie contact you about returning your book? Her friend told me that she intended to return the book the day she died."

He started walking again. "Lizzie called me around eight the morning of the shootings. I was supposed to meet her outside our chemistry lab in Welch Hall at ten, but she never arrived. I waited for half an hour before I gave up and walked home. I was lucky not to be on campus when the shooting started."

Trying to minimize my limp and keep pace with the younger man was painful. "Did Lizzie say anything else to you about her plans for that morning?"

He side-eyed me. "We weren't friends. She didn't like me. The conversation covered returning my textbook, and that's it."

I thanked him for his help, and we parted ways on the Drag, a stretch of Guadalupe Street that borders the university campus on the west. I headed for the San José Café where I had met Martin.

It was well after lunchtime, so the coffee shop was considerably emptier than it had been that morning. Only two students sat at the tables. Behind the counter, a bored young woman with a bouffant lounged on a stool, leaning her chin on her palm, but she perked up when I approached her.

I placed Lizzie's picture on the counter and identified myself. "Have you ever seen this girl?"

The woman tapped the edge of the photograph with her index finger. "That's Lizzie. She came here for coffee in the morning because her mama wouldn't let her drink it at home. I heard she died the day of the Tower Shooting."

"That's right." I leaned against the counter to rest my leg. "Do you remember if she was here before the shooting started?"

"That day is seared in my memory. Lizzie was here talking to that rabble-rouser, Carl."

"Do you know what they talked about?"

"No. We were busy, so I didn't get a chance to talk to her."

"Did she leave with Carl?"

"No. Carl left, and then Lizzie waved to me as she left a few minutes later."

"So, Lizzie left alone? Not with Carl?"

"Yep. She was by herself. I remember she almost forgot her purse and had to come back for it. She was in such a hurry she almost tripped over a chair."

"What time did she leave?"

"Must have been close to ten because other students were

leaving to get to classes."

"You didn't see her again after that?"

"No." The woman shook her head. "That was a terrible day. One of my regular customers was shot and bled to death. All that gunfire sounded like a war zone. I'll never forget that as long as I live."

"I don't think any of us will." I nodded goodbye and returned to my office to review the timeline for Lizzie's morning. She called Albert Lamp at eight, left the house at nine, and met Carl at the San José Cafe. I only had Albert's word that she hadn't met him at ten as planned, but the fact that she hadn't returned his book suggested that she hadn't seen him. Also, she never dropped off her lab paper. If she had reached the chemistry building, she would have turned in her final assignment. Something had happened to Lizzie in the few minutes after she left the coffee shop, but before she was scheduled to meet Lamp at Welch Hall. Carl Schmidt was the last person to speak to her. Maybe he knew where she had gone. If he had no information, I'd have to take a harder look at Albert Lamp and question every shopkeeper on the Drag to see if anyone had seen Lizzie after she left the San José Café.

I had to kill several hours before I could find Carl at the nightclub, so I ate an aspirin for my aching hip and took a nap, thinking I might be in for a late night.

Marley's Playhouse was located in East Austin, across the new interstate highway from the University of Texas. East Austin was the Black side of town, but the club drew university students of all backgrounds. Outside Marley's, I ran into an old friend working his beat. He was sitting in his police unit with his partner, parked on the street watching the college kids stream into the club.

"Hey, Ray," I called.

Ray Andrews, in his Austin police uniform, turned in his seat and gave me a wide smile. He was tall, lanky, and Black, one of less than a dozen Black officers in the Austin Police Department. "Hey, Jerry, good to see you. What brings you here? Come for the music?" He gestured to the club.

"I'm working a case. They still got you working East Austin?"

Ray shrugged contentedly. "I chose this beat. I know the folks, and the folks know me. But I'm not stuck here anymore. Earlier this year, the chief decided to allow us to work any beat in town, and we are eligible for promotions now. With the college kids coming here and getting drunk, we've already had to arrest a few white boys. They were surprised that we could do that."

"I read about the changes in the newspaper. Congratulations." I glanced at the stream of young people flowing toward Marley's. "Do you know a white boy named Carl Schmidt?"

"Shaggy-haired protester and ladies' man? Yeah. Thinks he knows everything. He asked me why I would work for my oppressors and told me I should be out protesting." Ray shook his head. "Look. There's your boy. He's dressed liked the Beatles again, probably thinks he's more important than Jesus, too."

My eyes followed where he pointed and found Carl Schmidt, looking like a carbon copy of John Lennon, helping a vivacious girl wearing a short purple dress exit a blue Chevy sedan. "Thanks, Ray. Catch you later." I trotted painfully across the street to catch Schmidt and the girl, but they entered the club before I could reach them.

Inside, the club was crowded, loud, and smoky. Scanning the dimly lit room through a haze of cigarette smoke, I located Carl and the girl. They took a table near the band as the lead guitarist struck his first chords. If I tried to question Carl now, he'd never hear me over the music, and the band wouldn't appreciate the disturbance. I settled against a wall, cursing my lack of agility, and watched Carl.

After forty-five minutes of covering Motown hits, the band took a break, and I headed toward Carl's table. As I threaded my way across the club, the girl in purple stood and walked away. Guessing she was going to the ladies' room, I figured I'd be able to speak to Carl alone.

I was six feet away when I spotted Albert Lamp in the crowd also walking toward Carl. I changed direction and covered my face with my hand, pretending to cough. Albert dropped a tiny bag of powder on the table in front of Carl. A look passed between them, but no words. Carl dropped his hand over the bag. I thought I saw his hand flash over his date's drink. A moment later Albert settled at the bar, and Carl's date returned from the ladies' room.

Lounging against a wall with a vantage point to observe both Albert and Carl, I assessed what I'd seen. Albert delivered drugs to Carl. Albert was a chemist with lab access. Perhaps he was manufacturing drugs. Could Lizzie have discovered that? And had Carl put something in his date's drink?

As I turned my attention to her, the girl with Carl stood on unsteady legs. Carl caught her as she went limp. Instantly, Albert appeared to help.

Albert cleared a path. "Give her air. Move. We need to take her outside."

Seeing that they were leaving, I loped outside ahead of them, and whistled through my fingers for Ray and his partner, who were standing by their police car, to join me.

Now, everything made sense. Carl must have slipped drugs into Lizzie's coffee. She was disoriented, forgot her handbag, and tripped over a chair. He and Albert probably intercepted her outside the San José Café, taking her to a car. They were in it together.

As Albert and Carl supported the girl between them, I blocked their path on the sidewalk. "Hey! What did you do to that girl?"

"She had too much to drink, so we're helping her home," Carl said in a smooth, confident voice.

Albert stopped as he recognized me. His gaze darted around as if he were seeking an escape route.

The girl groaned and her eyes fluttered.

"So her condition has nothing to do with the drugs you put in her drink?"

Carl's eyes widened. He released the semi-conscious girl and tried to sidestep me.

I swung my fist and caught his jaw, rocking him back on his heels and stunning him. Grabbing his arm, I twisted it behind his back.

Albert abandoned the drugged girl and sprinted into the street. A car horn blared. I heard a sickening thud. Then, Albert Lamp was sprawled in front of a car with a pool of blood spreading around his head.

Ray ran to Albert's side while his partner ran toward me. Ray yelled, "What happened?"

"This guy and that guy in front of you drugged this girl. They were trying to drag her out of here," I said. "When I blocked them, Lamp bolted and got hit by that car."

Ray examined Lamp. "This one's dead. His skull cracked like an egg."

Ray's partner knelt by the girl in purple, who had collapsed onto the sidewalk. "This one's alive."

A crowd gathered around us. While his partner called for an ambulance, Ray handcuffed Carl. I ran into Marley's and caught a waitress carrying a tray of used glasses back to the kitchen. I made sure no one washed any of the glasses before they could be collected as evidence. The rest of the night vanished into a blur of questioning and formal statements.

I met with Mr. and Mrs. Marquez in my office the next afternoon. After summarizing the night's events, I explained what had happened to their daughter. "Police searched Albert Lamp's lab space this morning and found evidence that he was manufacturing a type of benzodiazepine. Albert gave the drugs to Carl Schmidt, who sold them and used them to incapacitate unsuspecting girls.

Upon questioning, Carl blamed Albert for Lizzie's death. He said Albert was afraid that if Lizzie got the teaching assistant job, she would discover his drug business. When Lizzie was awarded the job, Albert decided to eliminate her as a threat to his illegal operation."

A fire lit behind Mr. Marquez's eyes. He said, "Carl's trying to place all the blame on Albert? You don't believe that, do you?"

I leaned forward on my desk. "They were partners. Both Carl and Albert tried to get Lizzie alone. Carl asked her to attend protests, and Albert switched textbooks so that she would have to return his. Lizzie took the bait and met Carl, who drugged her coffee. I suspect both men intercepted Lizzie outside the San José Café." I left out the rape. No parent needed to discuss that.

"What happens now?" Mrs. Marquez asked.

"The police reopened Lizzie's case. With Albert dead, Carl is the main suspect, and he's already in police custody."

Mr. Marquez was red-faced with anger. "That rotten bastard is going to jail, right?"

"He's being charged with drug possession, attempted kidnapping, and assault of the girl he drugged last night. So, yes, he's going to jail."

"Thank you, Mr. Milam," Mrs. Marquez said.

"Thank you, ma'am. If you hadn't asked me to investigate, another girl would have been assaulted and left for dead."

As they left my office, my left hip twinged painfully, reminding me that if I had been faster, I might have talked to Carl before he entered the club. Then, I wouldn't have seen Albert give him the drugs. For once, being frustratingly slow and gimpy saved the day.

FOUR ON THE FLOOR

Grant Tracey

—1—

As the Plymouth rushed toward me, its grill work resembled the face of a snarling shark. I leaped clear, but Eddie's hot dog cart crumpled and hammered into pieces. The car then crunched a mailbox before stopping abruptly in front of Union Station. A hollow pole of a streetlight now covered the car like a bent Q-tip.

The driver staggered in my direction, bloody bellied. He wore briefs. Nothing else.

Snow fell.

There was no color in his face, and within seconds he wasn't breathing, either.

The cops figured the decedent was stabbed with a stiletto. There was no ID in his wallet, and not much in the car, just a cashmere sweater and a zippered key case with a single key in it. "Homosexual spat, sex crime," one of the blue said.

Before they arrived, I had found a yellowing business card in the fella's wallet: Hilary "Chip" Hampton, Assistant Professor of English, U of T. He had been my wife's favorite prof. Back in the day.

***

Hilary Hampton was now a professor emeritus. Yuletide was two weeks away, and his wife was busy baking sugar cookies. The smell was a heavy blanket. Through the bay window shone the black fencing of Sibelius Park glazed with evening frost. A group of kids were playing road hockey.

The dead fella had been identified, Douglas Gomery. Forty-two, a clerk for an insurance company. He was also a former student of Professor Hampton's, 1947–1948, and a member of his creative writing workshop, known as the Freedom Writers.

He had now been dead for nearly twenty-four hours.

"I heard you almost—were hit by—"

"The car was coming—that's for sure—four on the floor—"

The professor nodded. "Doug was a talented student," he said, "had real promise, but took freedom too far. Then it was *tea*, now he's into LSD." He made a face. His eyes were close-set and his nose too small for his face.

His wife nodded from the kitchen. "His writing was so sloppy," she said. "The drugs—no discipline—"

"She often reads my students' stories," Professor Hampton said by way of apology.

I played with the brim of my porkpie. "Why was your business card in his wallet?"

"Strange—they had a falling out—" His wife dabbed away sweat from her chin.

I handed him the faded card.

He looked it over. "This is old. I was only an Assistant Professor then. Old office address, old number." That office was the small, cramped quarters he'd worked in before the Serchuk series and tenure. "Didn't even have a window." He shrugged at the University's antiquated system of privilege.

"Serchuk—that's the—?"

"The hockey book, the beginning of the series I wrote. Yes." *A Boy on the Leafs Blueline,* the first in a six-novel run that had gotten him tenure in 1949. The professor grimaced, shifted in his oversized chaise lounge. "The fella had a grudge against me. That's for sure. But I thought that was over years ago—"

"Many of the Freedom Writers have gone on to place stories in national magazines, but Doug was compromised by his addiction," he said.

"He was delusional," Mrs. Hampton said. "He accused my husband of stealing his characters." She slathered white frosting and red bursts of sugar dust on the tray of cookies that had been cooling. She brought them to us. She wore a plain fifties-era dress, and her dusky hair was done up in a bun. She placed a plate by my side. Her skin was smooth like underwater stones, and her accent full of money.

"Go ahead—" The professor encouraged me to eat while he spoke.

I smiled my lopsided grin and dug in.

"The problem was that Doug suggested that my intellectual property wasn't my own, and in my field that's, well, treason," Hampton reasoned. "Anyway, I guess I had talked a lot about the series with Douglas over post-workshop beers at George's, and his drug-addled mind got to thinking that he had a hand in the plot trajectory of the first book." The professor shrugged and shifted uncomfortably in his chair. He unfastened the lower button of his tweed jacket. "Doug demanded financial compensation, co-author credit. Well, my reputation, and tenure, were at stake. The book was *all* mine—"

"He hire a lawyer or anything?"

"No. *I* almost did. I should have—" Professor Hampton's gaze wandered to shadowy figures chasing a hockey game through streaks of snow. Someone scored. Arms and sticks raised. "Just to get him out of my hair, I signed over my first royalty check, *to him*. Twenty-five thousand dollars."

"That's a hefty, signing bonus," I said. My first year with the Leafs, 1957, I made only seven thousand.

"I know—especially now that Evergreen Books, seventeen

years later, wants to re-launch the series—" All six books and they were going to let him write two new ones.

With Expo '67 coming up in Montreal, the whole world was Canada-conscious, Confederation, one hundred years young, and outfits like Evergreen were looking to promote Canadian writers, placing them in our public schools. The Evergreen board also wanted to push back against the era's high octane go-go style with Chip's retro hero, Chance Serchuk, a fifties fella with a buzzcut, not all that dissimilar from my own.

"Technically ten, not seventeen years later," his wife corrected. The sixth book in the series came out in 1956. "I think it's the best." A wry smile turned at the corners of her lips.

"Right." The professor nodded at some kind of private joke between them.

"A team of their writers is updating the six books, modernizing the fashions and hockey references, and—" He paused, slightly embarrassed. "And tossing in more kisses between Chance and Kitsey." Kitsey was Chance's girlfriend and co-star of the sixth book.

"So the new books are ghostwritten?"

"Well—" He seemed embarrassed and a little annoyed at my question.

I finished my cookie. "Did Gomery want another *royalty* check?"

"Tell him—" His wife removed a second tray from the oven, the mittens on her hands resembling small pillows.

The professor shrugged his coat-hanger shoulders. "All right, all right—" A month ago, Gomery had contacted the professor, wanting co-author credit.

Fresh bulky shadows and heavy rocks filled the glass of the bay window. A hard triple knock on the front door. The kind that spelled cop.

The cops, in their Sloan Wilson grays, had found a match for the key in the zippered case, a swinging Bay Street pad with lava lamps, pop-art posters, and Man Ray photographs. In a corner, near a window, they had also found dried blood that matched Doug's. The name on the lease for the pad: one Hilary "Chip" Hampton.

—2—

Stana Younger couldn't believe that her old professor was being held on suspicion of murder.

We were in her new office at *The Toronto Star*. Susan Gomery was about to visit and Stana wanted backup. "Susan's claiming that the first Chance Serchuk novel was written solely by her husband. She wants justice on Doug's behalf, wants me to write a story exposing my former professor as a fraud, and possibly a killer." Her lower lip pressed against the pencil resting against her chin. "Honestly, in terms of Professor Hampton's legacy, I don't know what's worse, being a killer or a plagiarist." She laughed at her own joke, the pencil shaking slightly in her fingers. Stana can have a bit of a dark sense of humor.

She shook her head, eyes flashing, the freckles on her upper cheeks dancing. According to her, the former-lover angle that the police were spinning was nonsense. "He's no homosexual," she said. "About every other year, Chip had an affair with a young grad student. His wife knew about it, too. Open relationship. Gomery—wouldn't interest him. At all."

I pointed out that Doug was killed in Professor's Hampton's apartment. "The blood matches," I said.

"No one's denying the matching blood," she said, "or that Gomery was killed there. But the place was a regular Union Station. Creative writing students were always dropping by to talk, chat, share their newest work with one another, catch a nap, have a romantic interlude with someone. The professor had an open-door policy. His Freedom Writers were free to write whatever they felt, free to be whatever they were; free of bourgeois entanglements, they lived lives to the fullest—"

"Uh-huh—" I dropped my porkpie next to the two Parker pens parked in their brass quivers. "So, you're saying every creative writer in this so-called Canadian Left Bank had a key to this pad?"

"More or less—" She dropped her pencil on a desk blotter the size of a living-room rug. A smile creased the corners of her eyes. "Now do you see why I don't think the police will hold Hilary for long? Doug had a key, from years gone by—I'd bet on it."

I rubbed at the edges of my mouth.

"Hampton's a libertine, but he's also a brilliant man—made you believe that you were brilliant. I don't think I would have become a reporter if I hadn't taken his classes." She reached for my hand.

If not the professor, then who killed, Doug and why? The bare feet and briefs had sex crime tattooed all over the joint.

The sky outside her window was red and Lake Ontario glowed as if little fires were dancing on the ice-capped blocks floating in broken waves.

There was an insistent knock on the doorframe that I felt in my shoulders. There stood Susan, a slight woman with dim hair the color of freshly fallen snow. On her right wrist was a hexagonal chain attached to a briefcase.

She was expecting her first child around Christmas. It took great effort for her to sit in the padded chair to which Stana directed her.

"You're Hayden Fuller— Scored the winning goal in the '62 Finals."

I smiled my lupine grin. I had played in the NHL for seven-and-a-half years.

Her tongue quickly darted across thin lips. "I'll keep this short." She pulled out a key, undid the lock around her wrist, and gently placed the briefcase on the desk as if it contained a nuclear isotope. From inside, she pulled out a sheaf of paper, inky blotches spilled across yellowed pages. The title, *A Boy on the Leafs Blueline,* by Douglas Gomery, 8/17/47. "Forensics has already looked at this. The wood fiber in the paper, the ink from the typewriter ribbon. This was written in 1947. Two years before Hampton's version. The words are different, but the plot is the same. Scene for scene."

"You show this to Hampton?" My lips pressed firmly against my lower teeth.

"I've shown it to him and Kittle the publisher—nothing—total denial—Evergreen says Hampton's a great Canadian artist and with Expo approaching, this is a time to uplift our artists, not denigrate them," she said. "Bunk I say—" She reached into a pocket of her bulky parka and removed a wax package of beige tea biscuits. "Sorry—I'm hungry all the time." She took tight, tiny bites.

In the distance blocks of ice bounced on the flame-colored water. Susan pushed forward in her chair, the rigid cuffs of her parka covering the fleshy parts of her hands. "Doug never wanted money, he just wanted to get his reputation back. Everyone called him a druggie. He hasn't done drugs in years—and he's no homosexual. I don't know how that rumor started—"

She said that she, too, was a member of the Freedom Writers Society, but admitted that her writing wasn't worth much beyond mediocrity. "Still, I learned a lot. Hampton had this exercise where you had a list of a hundred and twenty adjectives and were instructed to pick three to inhabit your lead character. Three. "And there were some weird words on that list, let me tell you. *Churlish. Parsimonious*—" She laughed, her blue eyes brightening. "*Peevish.*" She returned her gaze to the ice disappearing under red waves.

"What about the sweater found in the car? Your husband was like what, a hundred and forty pounds? The sweater was a double XL."

"A false narrative?" She finished what was left of her biscuit.

Stana jotted down notes.

"My husband may have been sterile, but that didn't mean he

didn't like the ladies—"

Stana and I shot each other a look.

"Doug caught the mumps when he was twelve." She patted her stomach. "The child isn't his—and he's, *was*, okay with that. He knows how much I want a kid—"

Stana flipped through the manuscript's pages, quickly catching some of the rhythms to the prose. "It reads like Chip," she said.

"Or Hilary Hampton reads like Douglas Gomery—"

"But there were five other novels after this one," I said.

"I want my husband to get credit for *this* one—"

"I'm surprised by the attitude of Evergreen, a so-called Christian Press—" Stana said.

"Stewart Kittle? A total company man, brown-noser. Kittle, too, was taking Hampton's creative writing class this very fall and refused to listen, to believe my story," Susan said. "I even gave him a copy of the manuscript to look at. Christ—"

We paused, waiting for her to continue.

She shook her head dismissively, the pink part of her hairline shining under clear white snow. "Thinks he's a love god. I mean, the fella runs a religious press and then has sex with me to give me what I want, a child, but it's all about what he wanted, to sleep with every woman in the class and then brag about it—"

"I'll look this over—" Stana promised, thumbing more pages of the "Gomery" manuscript.

"You'll learn a lot about the beloved professor by looking at that—"

"Some things, I wish I didn't have to learn," Stana said.

—3—

Framed posters of Evergreen books, including a new updated cover for *A Boy on the Leafs Blueline,* dwarfed the room, along with sentimental posters of aphorisms on success, optimism, and Christian love. Stewart Kittle offered me a Perrier. "Best thing for you," he said. "Lay off the coffee and the soda. Drink water."

"I'll take my water from the tap, thanks," I said.

"Old school, huh?" He had a high forehead that shone like a thin coat of car wax. His eyes were shaded smears of charcoal in a bright, robust face. Heavy trough lines ran around the sides of his mouth.

"I drink water this time of year," he said, "because look—" He gestured with two outstretched arms. On the granite tabletop and shelving behind me were platters of desserts: coconut-clustered dates, three kinds of fudge, and lemon and butter tarts. "Everybody brings treats to the office. Instead of a smoke break, you get a fat break." He patted his stomach. "I swear I've put on ten pounds since late November. But Mrs. Hampton has yet to give me any cookies." Kittle sighed. "Every year she makes cookies for all us Freedom Writers, wraps them up on colored plates with big bows. I don't know if you heard, but I'm a student of her husband's."

"Yeah, I heard." *I also heard that you're the father of Susan's child.*

And Kittle had heard the charges leveled against his client, the re-discovered boys' writer, and his personal mentor. Evergreen was rushing the first three books of the series to press, just to show the media and all involved in the case against the professor of Evergreen's undying support. "The book is his. The series is his. He's a great writer."

The top of the desk he sat behind was marble. The lamps were made of jade. The carpet was midnight blue wool. The whole room oozed an acquisitive lust for more.

I almost wished I smoked so I could flick cigarette ashes everywhere.

"And the second book, *Overtime*. Wow," he said. The North York Board of Education was assigning it to all their seventh-grade classes in the district. "Do you know what that means for our sales?" He squeezed his hands together. "The first re-printing of that book alone can pay for, well, just imagine what it can pay for, for a small press like ours. Moreover, we'll be bringing Canadian content into our schools. "Expo is forcing us to see who and what we are. It's nation building." He smiled.

"What if Douglas did write the first book and Hampton aped his style—what if you're wrong?"

"Then I'm wrong. But I'm not." Kittle leaned back in his chair, peeling cellophane off a cigar. He cut the end with a small guillotine gizmo. He struggled to light it. "Sure, sure, sure. Look, Chip told me something in confidence and I'm telling you in confidence—" He sat forward.

I'm never very confident with folks who share confidences.

"Hampton wasn't queer or anything, Fuller, but he wanted to know, like a writer, a scientist, what being a homosexual was all about. And he and Dougie boy, who was queer, carried on. Lovers. Well, Douglas was serious; Chip was just experimenting. And he felt guilty. Afterward. He felt he had been trifling with Doug's emotions. That's why he gave him the twenty-five thousand. It was severance pay."

"Hmm. Susan Gomery says her husband was straight."

"Susan Gomery says a lot of things."

"Like you're the father of her child?"

"She said that." He chuckled lowly. "Utter nonsense." He puffed on his cigar. "Anyway, back to my story. Apologies, promises of severance pay, a royalty check, wasn't enough. A peevish Douglas Gomery stole the original manuscript from the professor. *Stole it.* It was the only one Hilary had." He shifted in his chair. "You ever hear the story of Edna St. Vincent Millay, *Conversation at Midnight?* A collection of poems. Well, maybe a drama poem? Anyway—" He waved a hand, which was covered with five or six rings. "Nineteen thirty-six. Sanibel Island, Florida. Hotel fire, manuscript lost. She goes home and rewrites the whole thing from memory, and it was published the very next year. That's what happened with the professor. Dig? He rewrote the whole book, so of course the plot matches. That's what he told me." He sighed heavily, pushed some papers to a far corner on his marble-top desk. "And in order to defend himself, Professor Hampton has to admit to this—how shall we say—homosexual interlude. Can you imagine how that might affect sales of the Serchuk series?"

I looked over at the Christian Love poster and felt a block of ice melting in my stomach. "Severance pay, huh? Who wanted to sever Douglas permanently?"

"Probably the guy in blue cashmere—gay love gone wrong. Look, I believe in the professor, and I'm backing his story," he said.

"Right—" I rubbed at the edges of my mouth.

But so much about this wasn't right.

On my way out I grabbed a chunk of fudge and two butter tarts.

"Hey, hey, easy on the butter tarts, pal. I haven't tried them yet," he said. "Save me some."

—4—

"I don't believe the cashmere-sweater angle," Susan Gomery said over the phone later that night. Stana and I were watching *Combat!* "It's part of a smear campaign," she said. "And I have the key."

At first, I thought she was talking figuratively, but she meant a key to the apartment with the swinging Man Ray nudes and lava lamps. "I found something there—today—when I was nosing around the cabinets, drawers, and whatnot. It was crumpled up in the back of an office desk. Meet me there. Bring Stana. Workshop notes, and it's dynamite."

"You know, we just got the autopsy report on your husband?" As a reporter Stana had contacts in the police department. "Before he died, he was jacked up on secobarbital sodium. How he ever drove a car was—"

"Seconal? The stuff that helps you sleep?" Susan asked.

"Yeah—"

"Meet me. It's a twenty-minute drive from your house—"

The sky outside was black charred logs.

It took twenty minutes exactly to get to Bay and Bloor. Lava lamps glowed eerily in the dim dark, and the joint smelled of heavy disinfectant. The vinyl countertop and linoleum floors reflected the orange and red rusty-coin glow of the lava lamps. Susan turned on a set of lights. The Man Ray violin lady appeared to be staring over her shoulder at me, making me feel ashamed for gawking.

Fifteen minutes prior to our arrival, Susan said, Hilary "Chip" Hampton had been released on his own recognizance.

"This is where they killed Doug—?" Susan pointed to the couch, next to a radiator with a black, lacquered covering.

Stana nodded. "They?" She tapped her lower lip three times. "They?"

"The workshop," Susan said, tugging at the sleeves of her men's flannel shirt, and then handing us a piece of torn notebook paper with eight little words scrawled along its lines: *cashmere sweater; jealous; peevish; forbidden love; sex murder*. "I think they, members of the workshop, plotted a story, a narrative arc, only the character was real, not fictional—the character was my husband."

The word peevish jumped off the page, and I got to thinking about that list of one-hundred-and-twenty adjectives Susan had mentioned earlier, as well as something Kittle had said when describing Doug—"peevish" lover.

"Kittle, the professor, and probably others were in on it—" Susan glanced around the kitchen. "There were usually snacks here when we met to write or fuck. Mrs. Hampton's cookies, catered plates with those little cucumber and cream cheese sandwiches, and Red Chinese beer, with the communist star on the label. We all got a kick out of that."

"Anything else look different?" Stana asked.

Susan padded across the living room carpet into the bathroom. "The shower curtain."

The whole room smelled of fresh vinyl. "The old one has been replaced," I said. "It was probably used to roll Doug up in. They drugged him, stripped him—remember there were no fibers in the wounds—used the shower curtain to catch his blood, rolled him up and carried him out."

"Only he wasn't dead," Stana said.

"He wasn't dead." I exhaled sharply. "Then in the backseat of the Plymouth, Doug becomes a regular Lazarus, rising from the dead, delusional, and confused. Our killers are even more confused by Doug's sudden resurrection, so they leave him in an idling car."

"And I bet it was women in the car—men would have finished him off," Stana said. "Two women. At least."

—5—

In the morning Stana was slouched in the comfy chair of our living room, feet up on an Ottoman, a plaid blanket covering her hips and legs.

"How long have you been up?"

"I didn't sleep—" Her face was weighted with worry. On the coffee table to her left were the six books in the Chance Serchuk series. "I don't think he wrote it," she said. "Professor Hampton." She gently tossed a ream of the Gomery manuscript onto the adjacent wooden chair to her right. "The style *is* different—but not different enough."

"Coffee?" I scratched behind an ear, my eyes and mouth dry.

"Please."

In the kitchen I turned on the kettle and dropped a mound of grounds into the French press. Outside the sky was a bright blue, faded denim jeans. Little chevrons of snow graced the window. I rubbed at tired eyes.

"Chip stole that boy's work."

"How can you tell?"

"Three ways, all of them global revisions," she said. One, flashbacks. Gomery's are clumsy, roundabout: "'Sitting in the living room made him think back to a time when—' versus, 'Two years ago, Chance figured—' You feel the difference, hon? Professor Hampton's flashbacks are more direct, less filtered."

I nodded.

"Two. Dialogue." She smiled awkwardly.

The kettle whistled. I poured hot water into the press and set the timer for five minutes.

Tears crowded the edges of her eyes. "In the professor's dialogue he doesn't use tags much." Her fingers skittered through pages from the published book. "Here we go: 'I don't care what you think.' David leaned forward, his eyes narrowed. 'You'll do as we say.' You get that? The dramatic beats?"

"Yeah." I nodded.

She held up a hand. "Okay, okay. Here's the same passage in Gomery: 'I don't care what you think,' David said, leaning forward, eyes narrowing, 'You'll do as we say.' Chip likes removing said constructions. Gomery has them all over the place—"

"Hmm."

She sighed heavily. "God, I feel sick."

The timer beeped and I poured a cup of coffee and took it to her. "I'm sorry, honey, I know how much you admired him."

"We all did," she said, sipping slowly. "And I don't think he wrote the fifth and sixth books. Or, at least, I think they were largely co-written. The voice is much more interior—narrative telling as opposed to showing and scene work, and Kitsey has a much more dramatic role in both plots—"

I sat next to her, reached for her hand.

She pulled away, got up, and crossed slowly toward the TV and the runner's lip that led to the hallway. "I so wanted to find him innocent, to find my preconceptions to be true: The professor is noble; Douglas Gomery is an imposter. But damn, damn, damn—"

"All for an office with some windows," I said.

The professor, Kittle, and maybe Mrs. Hampton. They all had something to gain by Doug's death. Kittle runs a press with a financial connection to the professor. Mrs. Hampton wants to protect her husband's legacy. Hilary "Chip" Hampton wants to protect himself from being outed as gay and a plagiarist.

Just then the phone rang.

It was Susan. She was rushing her words, something to do with going out for smokes and coming back and finding a blue cashmere sweater under her Christmas tree.

"Lock the doors, call the police, I'm on my way—"

Her apartment was in Don Mills, ten minutes from our suburban home.

Faulkner once said something on revising sentences: "Kill your darlings." I was afraid that some members of the Freedom Writers had taken that edict to a new level—

Susan Gomery didn't answer when we knocked. I pulled out my side-holstered .38 snub-nose while Stana opened the door with an Esso card.

The click was a fallen icicle.

All the lights were off, except for the blinking of a Christmas tree and the hulking lines of lumpy shadows on the yellowy-gray linoleum floor. Next to the lumpiness were the remains of a cup with a broken-off handle, and two halves of a cracked china saucer. The lumpy shadows resembled a pile of uneven blankets.

Stana turned on the hall light.

The cashmere sweater was draped over the back of a kitchen chair.

The lumpy blankets turned out to be Susan Gomery, blood at both corners of her mouth. A stiletto was stuck between her breasts.

On the table: a teapot, a cast-aside cozy, three lonely sugar cubes, and sparkles of sugar dust that glinted like glass. A spoon rested in a ceramic mug.

Stana crouched near the body, staring into faraway eyes. "Someone wanted to keep the myth of the blue cashmere killer alive—" She pointed at the sweater, the stiletto.

Writers can be a stubborn bunch. Some hate to revise their damn plot lines.

"I bet she was given Seconal. Like our first victim, and then stabbed," Stana said.

I glanced at the two halves of the saucer on the floor, the C-shape handle, broken away from its cup. The clean Formica tabletop. "Susan was reaching for something," I said, "and that something has been removed from the crime scene. Look at the positioning of the body." I kneeled next to Susan. "What were you reaching for?" I opened her hands. In the left palm was a muddy smudge, like traces of wet beach sand.

"What's that?"

"What she was reaching for, Stana—" Beige. I recognized it. The wet remains of a tea biscuit.

—6—

Mrs. Hampton offered us cookies as soon as we came through her door, but I wasn't hungry and Stana was too mad to eat. Negative energy radiated from my wife's whole body, the freckles on her face vibrating like angry, excited atoms. I took off my porkpie hat and loosened my tie. Like a lot of old folks, the Hamptons had set their thermostat much too high. I undid the top two buttons of my chambray shirt.

The place smelled of porridge and moth balls.

Professor Hampton sat by the window, looking out at the snow-slicked street. Frost glazed the inside corners of the glass. He was far away and his shoulders were stiff with anticipation.

"Susan Gomery is dead," I said. "Murdered. Don Mills. The police are there now." I wiped at the edges of my mouth. "They'll be coming here—next—"

"Huh?" Professor Hampton turned from the window, his eyes looking through my shoulder, his face full of abstract lines, obscured meanings. "Here—?"

"And I don't think it's to have you autograph a few books."

"I—I—" His hands fell to his sides.

"The writing isn't yours, professor," Stana said. "I've read the original copy. The prose of the original is too near, too precise, when placed next to your revised prose. Sure, your revisions are much better, cleaner, more efficient, direct, lyrical. But line for line, the words are too alike. You couldn't have lost the original manuscript and then recreated it so perfectly."

"Simply put, Daddy-O, we don't believe the *peevish* lover angle—" I stood at the edge of the living room, the porkpie tapping my thighs.

"They *were never* lovers," Mrs. Hampton said. "That was Kittle's idea."

"*Peevish?* Really? That word popped up too many times on this caper and it was your undoing. Peevish," I said. "Don't you teach in your workshops how to make characters three dimensional and rounded? Complexities? When all the arrows point in one direction, I get suspicious, professor. Peevish? It was on your list of one hundred twenty adjectives. Susan mentioned it. So did Kittle. And the blue-cashmere angle. Another overdetermined detail. Bad plotting. Bad writing."

"Peevish was *my* idea—" Mrs. Hampton said. She sat in the chair across from us and tucked her legs closer, a red plastic plate balancing on her thighs. It was piled with four or five sugar cookies under cellophane with a red bow precariously tipped on top like a fedora's edge. "And it got overplayed— You're very smart, Mr. Fuller."

And the sweater?

"An unwanted gift," she said. "Buried in our cedar chest for years."

I wasn't sure which sweater she was talking about: the one in the Plymouth or the one in Susan's apartment.

"The police are coming to arrest me—for Doug's death and Susan's?" A thick strand of Chip's slicked-back hair had broken free and fallen across his face.

"Why did you do it, professor?" Stana leaned in with her shoulders. She wore a black beret, a pleated skirt, and an orange-and-black cardigan sweater, the pattern of which resembled a bunch of flying swallows.

"I didn't kill anyone—I— Tenure. I needed to get tenure." Back then he'd had a cramped office, but soon he'd have no office and no job. "In the summer of '47 Doug shared his book with me. The writing was very rough. But what a plot. The kid could write a gripping narrative." He invited us to sit down. "It's ironic, isn't it? The first story was his, but the next three were mine, all mine. It's like I needed that first plot to jumpstart my imagination." His hands fluttered. "I justified it to myself, you know, saying I was Shakespeare, taking someone else's plot and making it more beautiful, which I did. You can't deny that." The irony? "He saved *me*. Writing that book gave me the courage to write the next three on my own. It was like a catalyst. *Overtime* and *Five Minutes for Fighting* are all mine. So's *Shot on Goal*. It was like drinking a magic elixir. Right out of a fairytale: the student was the teacher, and the teacher was the writer-student. That's called situational irony," he said.

I was thinking of Poe's "The Oval Portrait," and how in order for the artist to live, his muse had to die.

"The fifth and sixth books, *I wrote*," his wife said, finishing a cookie.

"That accounts for Kitsey having more of a role and the greater interiority overall," Stana muttered.

"Thanks for noticing." She started a second cookie. "Chip, of course, worked with my work. He revised it, smoothed it out—he's so wonderfully lyrical—"

"Yeah, a regular William Wordsworth," I said.

"You sure you don't want a cookie?" She gently set the cling wrap and bow aside. "I made them yesterday. They're still fresh—"

"No thanks—" Stana said. "You're a plagiarist, Professor."

He winced at the words. "Don't say that—"

"He's an artist—" His wife corrected.

"Your husband's a Hallmark hack, putting greeting-card words to other people's narrative pictures," I said.

"That's not fair—" The professor's voice cracked.

"And you're also a murderer. That's why"—I glanced at my Timex—"the police should be here any minute."

"I didn't—" He bit heavily on his pipe. "I told you, I didn't, I didn't—"

"The Freedom Writers Society?" Stana asked.

A radiator clanked like a coin was loose inside, and the heat in the room rose ten degrees. The floor felt as if it were bending toward the sun.

"Evergreen was going to use my husband's work, our work, to celebrate Canada," Mrs. Hampton said. "Cultural identity. Susan Gomery threatened to ruin that and she had to pay." Suddenly, Mrs. Hampton's accent had slipped from its refined origins of privilege into the ergot of Cabbagetown and Regent Park, where I had grown up. "She was a real bitch!" she said, holding the red plastic plate tightly, one of the cookies teetering near the edge.

She took another bite of cookie. "Yes, my husband stole that boy's blueprint, but he transformed it into something beautiful. That should count for something—"

"And to keep quiet about Doug's legacy, Susan had to die—" I pointed a stubby finger.

"It wasn't about Doug's legacy, it was about her legacy and the baby—" Mrs. Hampton said, her voice a scabrous grind.

Her husband couldn't look at her; the pipe trembled in his hands. "The child—"

"Exactly, the child. Your child-bride was taking far too much for granted—" Mrs. Hampton finished the last of the cookies. "To keep her quiet about the baby's father, Kittle had promised her the right to write the eighth book in the series, a book he had initially promised to me—"

"So, you had no idea about these killings—" Stana's words rained hard on the professor.

"He didn't until yesterday. Kittle and I returned here, after killing Susan, and I felt my dear hubby should know. I was the one who put the Seconal in the cookies Doug ate."

"Cookies—that's what I figured—" I looked at the diminished plate in her lap. *She was always making cookies for people—it was her trademark, and that's why a dying Susan reached for the wet tea biscuit, a kind of cookie—*

Suddenly, Mrs. Hampton squeezed into a tight knot, the plastic plate dropping blithely to the floor. Her mouth moved but there was no sound. Slowly her face glazed into a ceramic mask.

"She's having a heart attack—" The professor reached for the phone and dialed the operator. He talked fast, a voice spackled with helium.

"It's not a heart attack— Those cookies were laced with cyanide."

And only a few minutes earlier, she had tried serving some to Stana and me. Red bow and all.

Mrs. Hampton, now from the floor, focused sharply on us, her heart and lungs failing, a series of theatre lights dim-dimming.

Cyanide is a long goodbye.

It took her two to five minutes, and she was aware of the pain.

When she finally died, she did so before the medics and the police arrived.

And with her death went her story, the accusations leveled at Kittle, the last standing workshop killer.

But I knew the story. Stana knew the story. And Kittle was about to know it.

—7—

He congratulated us on figuring it all out, as he licked bits of apple tart shortbread frangipani off his fingers. "As you can see, they're still bringing treats to the office. Hate this time of year—" He laughed at his joke, patted his belly. "Come on you two, lighten up." He grinned, a political candidate seeking re-election. "Get a little fun out of life."

Fun? Doug, Susan, Mrs. H. Three on the floor. And now, maybe, Kittle.

A Christmas tree stood in the corner, the tip of which kissed the ceiling. He was sitting on a leather couch with pillows the size of a Buick's bumper. On his left was a cabriolet with a bottle of J&B Scotch. In front of him, a low-slung coffee table decked out with fudge, tarts, and a red plate piled with sugar cookies. "Sit down. Sit down. Suicide, huh? Pills?"

"Yeah, you could say that—"

"That's tough. Real tough. But, hey, you figured it all out. You should be proud of that. But there's nothing you can do. You win—I win." He placed a hand to his heart. Winners everywhere, baby.

We didn't sit.

"My lawyers are with Chip right now. He's distraught, and he'll answer all questions, tomorrow. In the meantime, the doctors have given him a sedative. He'll collect himself, and in the morning, he'll realize that all of this can just go away." He waved a hand, fluttered some fingers. "Magic dust. It all can be pinned on a jealous wife. *She* killed Doug. With the help of Susan. And then, because I agreed to let Susan write one of the new forthcoming Serchuk books, *she* killed her, too," he said. "The fact that Susan was pregnant with Professor Hampton's child didn't help any." He shrugged and smiled sheepishly. "But we can keep that part out of the papers, can't we?" He winked.

"*You* killed Douglas. *You* were there when Lady Macbeth killed Susan. She told us," Stana said.

"Right, right. Hypothetically possible. But where's your witness, witnesses?" He smiled. It wasn't pretty. "This frangipani is delicious. You should try it. Delicious." He scraped shortbread crumbs from his fingers with a quick brush of his hands. "I have people who will vouch for where I was at the time of both deaths—" He shrugged.

"We have the manuscript," Stana said. "It proves—"

"What does it prove?" He cut her off. "What?"

"That Doug wrote the first draft—"

"Professor Hampton admitted as much," I said.

"He won't after tonight," Kittle said. "My lawyers will have a prepared statement. Like I said, a good night's sleep will get his mind right—" He laughed. "Your victory is a private one. Everything you surmised is highly probable, but that's all I'm willing to say—And the death of Mrs. Hampton will create sympathy around the professor and boost the sales of his books. Win, win, Baby."

"Susan was no killer—she was a victim."

"And the victors tell the stories, and in our workshop story Susan is the antagonist—You want to take some of this with you? I can't, or I should say, I shouldn't, eat all this."

"The police will be here soon," Stana said.

"I'm always willing to welcome the blue. Always." He held up both hands. "You have no witnesses. Bupkis, Baby. The coveted manuscript you do have in your possession? That's a first draft. Written by the professor. And Canada, overall, is better off," he said. A hockey series to celebrate Expo '67 and our illustrious hundredth birthday. "Hockey is Canada's game. The time is right for a return to traditional values. The Serchuk stories are morality plays." He laughed at the situational irony.

"You killed two people," Stana said.

"Right. Where're your facts—? Mrs. Hampton is dead. Susan is dead. Doug is dead. The professor will have a new story tomorrow for the press. The jealous wife angle works for me, and the press will eat *that* up." He winked again. "I'm glad I live alone—jealousy's a bitch."

I reached across the table and grabbed some fudge, a butter tart, pushed aside a green bow and nabbed three cookies off a red plate.

"Hey, easy on the cookies—I haven't had any yet—"

"You're a real fucking prick—"

"Happy holidays," he said.

We headed out. He didn't show us the way.

It was cold, the wind kicking up, and dusty snow sprayed around us. Across the way was the back of a scraggly strip of stores in dirty white brick: a donut shop, a One-Hour Martinizing, a Chinese food joint. An open dumpster sat crookedly by a gray bump of plowed snow.

"God," Stana sighed. "What a douche—" She kicked at the ground, bits of salt and ice pebbles splashed at the edge of the street. "Maybe we can work on the professor—"

"If we can get close to him—"

We headed toward our car.

"What was with the cookies?"

I stared down at the three in my hand. "He's a covetous son of a bitch." I rubbed at the edges of my mouth and wished I had worn my winter coat instead of a leather jacket. I side-armed the cookies toward the empty dumpster across the way. I watched them arc like wobbly clay pigeons and double thud into the metal box. "You saw the red plate?" I said.

"Yeah," she said. "Green bow."

"You didn't say a thing about it—"

"No—"

I nodded. "Can I buy you a drink?'

"Yeah," she said.

In the morning, before ten o'clock, when the police arrived for questioning, Stewart Kittle would disappoint them, because he was dead.

A cyanide goodbye.

He should have let Mrs. Hampton write the eighth book.

CREAKY JONAH

Jack Bates

"He ain't ever had but one name that I know of," the old man said. He leaned back in his folding lawn chair and filled his lungs with roach smoke. When Edmonds spoke again, the smoke came out in puffs like vapory little dragons. "People around here call him Creaky Jonah on account of the way his legs bend and unbend the way a marionette bobs on its strings."

Edmonds leaned forward and held the roach clip out to me. I shook my head. The apple crate I sat on creaked.

"Any idea why he'd come here?"

"Let's see." Edmonds rubbed a finger over his whisker-laden chin. "There's that music festival they're having down in Monty-Ray."

"Think he was hitching a ride to Monterey?"

"Could be. Couple of the surfer kids I buy my grass from told me King Carver told them he saw Creaky Jonah in a white coupe that pulled over."

"Is King Carver another surfer?"

"Yeah, man. Ain't you listening to me?" He coughed a bit, smoked more, carried on. "Carver said a woman with a scarf and sunglasses got out. Looked around like she didn't want to be recognized. She went around and opened the passenger door. King Carver said she pulled Creaky Jonah from the passenger seat."

"He didn't want to go?"

"That's what King Carver said. Told me the woman hugged the guy. Said she tucked some cash into the pocket of his Army shirt, then she got back in the sports car. Jonah watched the rooster tail of dust drop back to the road. Then he dropped the money in the dirt."

The old guy could be poetic. Might have been the grass he smoked. Maybe I had a contact buzz. Didn't matter. He had a folksy way of weaving the story surrounding my client's MIA son. The woman he spoke of had hired me to find Creaky Jonah, aka Martin Drexler, son and heir to Hollywood honcho Heinrich Drexler.

I grabbed two cans of Hamm's beer from his fridge and gave one to Edmonds.

Down the dune from us the Pacific broke over the beach. Slow-rolling waves carried surfers like little floating toys. The same waves pushed sea foam around the carcass of a dead sperm whale, fifty feet long and well over eight tons. A late afternoon sun stretched the shadow of the lost leviathan. The old guy didn't seem bothered by the dead beast. He was all aglow on mellow-grass and tiki memories.

"Hypnotic, ain't it? Yes, sir. After the war I knew I could never go back to Ohio. I was in the South Pacific aboard a Kilauea-class munitions ship and just didn't want to leave that beautiful sea."

"You were already in the service when Pearl got bombed."

"Joined the fleet when I turned twenty-one. Had ten years in when I got stationed in Hawaii. Boiler-buster. Kept that ship running fine until the day we got attacked. Back got broken. Ten weeks' survivor's leave in a hospital full of eager, pretty nurses full of honeysuckle and wine and me wrapped tight in gauze and plaster. Didn't stop me from getting to know a few, if you get what I mean." He winked. At the end of a raspy laugh he asked, "What about you?"

"Me? I was a fighter pilot."

"Young one."

"I may have lied a little about my age."

"And now you're a private detective? Why ain't ya flying?"

"Lost an eye at Midway."

No laws prevented me from flying with only one eye. I had other demons chasing me that kept me grounded.

"You're lucky that's all you lost."

"Very true, my friend." We tapped beer cans. "Very true."

We drank a bit in silence before I asked about the whale.

Edmonds looked down at the beach. "That beast washed ashore about the time Creaky Jonah showed up."

"That's why they call him Jonah." I drank a little beer. Belched. "Because of the whale."

"I thought it was his given name."

"No. His real name is Martin Drexler. The woman your buddy saw abandon him was his mother."

"That's cold, brother."

"Yeah, well she regrets leaving him behind. She asked me to bring him back to LA."

"Why'd she drop him here in the first place?"

"Maybe she liked the scenery."

"She wanted miles between the two of them, that's why. Los Angeles is six hours south of here."

"Annie Clancy never does something on a whim."

"Clancy? Thought you said his name is Drexler."

"It is. Clancy was her name when I knew her in college. Hey, where can I find King Carver?"

"He works the bar at the Sand Dooner up the road a bit."

"Well, sir, I thank you for your time." I stood up, took out my wallet. I held out a five. "For the beers, Mr. Edmonds."

He turned his head to the sea as he reached for the money. "You can call me Pete."

The Sand Dooner was a box on stilts overlooking the dunes

along the Pacific Coast Highway. A small patio deck behind it held three whitewashed picnic tables. The inside was cramped and smoky, the kind of place where the men all wore the same after-shave of sweat and soured beer.

King Carver was easy to pick out. Muscles rippling out of his tank top. Hair like a lion's mane. A pride of young women hanging out at a dive bar for no other reason than to have him strike a match and hold it under the end of the long white cigarettes tucked between their puckered lips. They laughed at everything he said. He was truly the king for the three princesses purring and pawing to be his queen. In his world, he didn't have to choose just one. I hated to interrupt his party, but I had a job to do.

He broke away from two brunettes and a blonde to take my order.

"What're you drinking, pal?"

"Give me a shell of Hamm's."

He held a glass under the tap. "Eighty cents."

I dropped a dollar on the bar. "Keep the dimes."

"Thanks. Anything else?" He scooped up the dollar, eager to get back to his inner circle.

"Yeah. I'm looking for this guy." I showed him a picture of Martin Drexler in his uniform, taken before he shipped out to Vietnam. "I think you know him as Creaky Jonah."

"Been a while since I saw him." King Carver held the photograph out for me to take. The blonde took it.

"We saw him the other day on the beach," she said. She handed me the picture, making sure our hands touched.

"He was talking to that dead whale," one of the brunettes said.

"Could you hear what he was saying?"

The brunette shook her head. "He was too far away. I wasn't going near him or the whale."

"Yeah," the other brunette said. "It looked like he was trippin'. He raised his hand like he was praying over it. Stared at the horizon, then he walked down to the surf with those broken, crooked steps. Walked right out into the waves. He would have kept going if those Army guys hadn't stopped him."

"What Army guys?" I asked.

"I don't know. Some Army guys. Kept walking around the whale."

"I heard he cut one with that knife of his," the first brunette said before turning a little pale. "What's the matter with your eye, mister? It's all white."

"It's glass. Sometimes it rolls. Any of you have a compact?"

"I do," said the blonde.

"Hold it open for me, would you, please, so I can adjust my eye?"

The blonde brought out a pink plastic compact from a crocheted shoulder bag. "How did you lose it?"

"Shot down over Midway two wars ago." I slid the eye back into place. With my good eye I caught the reflection of King Carver talking to the local sheriff.

The first brunette jetted smoke. "My dad always said no one comes out of a war without some kind of wound."

"God's honest truth," the sheriff said. The side of his overhanging belly slid along the edge of the bar as he moved closer. He held out his hand. "Stanley Cook. Second Marines. Guadalcanal to Tinian."

I shook his hand. "Jimmy Darling. Seventh AAF." I tapped my glass eye with my finger. It produced a tiny little ting like the tintinnabulation of a delicate little bell. "After Midway, I flew a desk in Hawaii. Now, I'm a PI."

"Not so bad. Hey, Bruce says you were asking about our uninvited guest."

"Bruce?"

Cook hooked one of his plump thumbs over his shoulder at King Carver. "The guy with the gals. So this guy you're looking for. What do you want with a beach bum?"

"His family hired me to bring him home." I said with a sip

and a shrug. "You didn't arrest him, did you? It would be great if you had him in a cell."

"If I arrested everyone who drifted through Duneville for vagrancy, the jail would burst at its seams. Too many free spirits coming and going all the time. That music festival down in Monterey isn't helping. County is crawling with the anti-establishment crowd, which apparently has no problem attending an organized event."

His voice rose on the last part of his griping, then lowered.

"Not a fan of the flower children?"

Cook screwed up his face. "I figured your guy would move on in a day or so. Nope. Not this guy. I've got people calling the station all hours about him talking to the dead whale."

"Where's he staying?"

"In the brush, I'm guessing."

"He's in the old school bus," the blonde said. She had separated herself from her friends. The pair had gone back to flirting with King Carver.

"The one up there on Beach Trail Road?" Sheriff Cook asked.

The blonde gave the sheriff the kind of incredulous look that asked, *Is there another one?*

"How do you know he's staying there?" I asked.

"It's always been a party spot. A few of us hiked up to it a few days ago to, you know."

"Get high?" The sheriff rolled his eyes. "Ball? Crochet? All of the above?"

The blonde spoke with a newfound terseness. "Discuss the ever-changing political climate. Anyhow, it started to rain. We were going to wait out the storm when we saw CJ."

The sheriff scoffed. "Don't you mean JC?"

"She means Creaky Jonah. Did you talk to him?"

"No. He made it pretty clear he didn't want us hanging around."

"He tell you that?"

"It's not what he said but what he did that scared us away."

"What was that?"

"Flashed this really big knife." She held her hands about ten inches apart.

"The one he used to cut the soldier?"

The blonde offered a slight lift of her right shoulder. Her long hair brushed over it. "I guess."

"You want I can run you out to the bus?" Sheriff Cook said. "Your friend just became a liability."

"Wouldn't hurt to have two of us out there."

The blonde protested. "Look, man, he didn't do anything. Just tried to frighten us away. He's marked his territory. Woe unto ye who crosses his path and the rest of that biblical horse-shit he espouses all the time. Maybe he wouldn't be so screwed up if he wasn't off fighting a war between capitalist mongers and communist overlords who just want power and control for themselves."

"Wait a minute," Sheriff Cook said. "Who's espousing horse-shit?"

The old bus in the dune was fifteen minutes north of the Sand Dooner. Sheriff Cook drove and spoke the entire trip.

"Sometimes I wonder why we fought so hard to save the world."

"Still steamed about what the blonde said back there?"

"Have you ever seen someone as ungrateful as her?"

"Ungrateful or opinionated?"

"What's the difference?"

"Not much."

Sheriff Cook laughed. "No. I guess not."

"She wasn't there. She's grown up with stories and history books. It's all a black-and-white movie to her."

Sheriff Cook turned left on a sandy, two-rut road. Ahead of us a red sun slowly sank over the edge of the Pacific Ocean. In the waning daylight I could see the metal hull of a mechanical beast dead in the sand. Like its aquatic counterpart, there was no easy way to remove the bus from its final resting place. Sheriff Cook didn't even try to drive up to it. He grabbed two flashlights and handed me one.

"No one knows how it got this far. Never had plates. No registration. Over the years it's been painted and repainted a bunch of times. It just kind of sits here like a—"

"Beached whale."

"Exactly."

We didn't try to sneak up on the bus. Didn't try to hide our lights. We spoke without whispering.

We didn't find Martin Drexler at the abandoned bus. We did find his Army duffel and one of his extra prosthetic legs. We found piles of small game bones and fish bones and possibly chicken bones scattered around a fire pit.

"Looks like he's doing what the Army taught him," Sheriff Cook said. He tossed small bones into the brush. "Guess the war ended early for him, huh?"

"I think his war is just beginning."

"I meant the wooden leg." Cook looked out at the surf. "Well, Mr. Darling, I'm afraid I can't wait around for him to return."

"I'm pretty sure he's nearby watching us."

"Yeah. I am, too. Kind of giving me the creeps. Kind of why I want to leave. You coming?"

"Yeah. I know where I can find him."

"All right. Let's roll. Between Drexler lurking out there and the smell from that damn dead whale, I am tripping out right now."

Cook walked a little quicker than I did. He seemed slightly irritated with what he referred to as my sauntering.

"What interest does the Army have in that dead whale?"

"Oh. They're trying to figure out how to get rid of it. They thought about pushing it or pulling with bulldozers, but the sand is too soft, and they're worried the dozers will get stuck. It's too heavy to airlift. Too big to bury."

"Not many options left."

"There is one. Dynamite."

"They want to blow it up?"

"The idea is the gulls will eat the smaller chunks and the rest will be easier to dispose of in the ocean."

"They're going to need a lot of dynamite."

Cook mocked a salute. "Sir! Yes, sir! That's the Army for ya."

He took me back to my car at the Sand Dooner. The blonde from earlier sat at an outdoor picnic table watching late-in-the-day surfers. Cook saw her and groaned.

"It's like she's been waiting for our return. Forgive me if I don't walk you to your car."

"Go home, sheriff. And thanks for the ride."

Cook drove away.

I went to my car. A '66 Plymouth Satellite. Ragtop, 383 V8 4-speed.

"Hey," the blonde said. "That your ride?"

"Free and clear."

"Nice wheels."

"Too much for a guy my age?"

"Age is all in our heads."

"Tell me that when you're forty-seven."

She smirked. "Did you find Creaky Jonah?"

"He wasn't there. And his name is Martin."

"I know where he is. At least where he'll be."

"Yeah? Where is that?"

"Where the whale is. It's like he's guarding it. If someone builds a bonfire, he goes all Holy Roller on them. I can take you there."

"Aren't you here with your friends?"

"That scene is a drag, man." She looked at my ride. "Put the top down. Get the wind in our hair."

I opened the door. "It's a top-down kind of night, isn't it?"

"It definitely could be."

I laughed. "Well, I appreciate the offer."

"I hear a 'but' coming."

"Yeah. Sorry."

"No, it's cool. You still love whoever it is you lost."

"No one comes out of a war without some kind of wound."

"It's not just wars, you dig?"

"You have a way home?"

"I'll hitch."

"This time of night?"

"I've done it before."

"Stick out your thumb."

She smirked again as she stood up from the picnic table. Her thumb popped up and her hip popped out.

"Where you headed, miss?"

"Into town. And my name is Carol."

"Hello, Carol. I'm Jimmy. Get in. It'll take a second to put the top down."

Ten miles seemed like a long way to go for a beer. Then I remembered she was twenty-two or something and had gone to the Sand Dooner for more than just beer.

I learned her life story. She was in her final semester at Monterey Peninsula College, studying acting. Her immediate plans centered on moving down to LA and finding an agent. She had a room in a house she rented with the two brunettes, Shella and Nikki. Shella was thinking about going with her to LA, but then again, she might become a stewardess with Nikki and see the world.

During the entire ride to her place Carol touched my arm, my hand, or my leg. Even after I pulled up in front of her building, she made a push to get me to come in with her. I gave her my card and told her if she was ever in San Francisco to call me.

Then she kissed me, and I let her.

"Who was she, Jimmy?"

I sighed. "Antoinette Clancy. We met our last year in college. We were going to get married. Before we could, Pearl Harbor was bombed, and we put our plans on hold. She was a nurse on the Big Island for a while and then volunteered for Corregidor. When that fell, she was taken prisoner. I didn't know this until after the war."

"You thought she was dead."

"I checked the missing-in-action lists every day. Some days I hoped I'd find her on the casualty list, just so I'd know and be able to find some peace. Selfish of me, I know."

"You were grieving and needed closure."

"I never thought I'd see her again. Then one day after the war I'm at a newsstand buying a paper and there she is staring at me from the cover of *Hollywood Bride Magazine.* 'Studio Master Weds Courageous Nurse.' Annie had sold her story to Roundhouse Studios. That's how she met her husband. She was home and safe and alive and I was alone and bitter and broken."

"There must have been other women."

"A few. But none like Annie. When I fell on hard times, Annie convinced Heinrich to give me a job at the studio."

"Look at me. Out with a movie man."

"I handled matters off screen. Did that for fifteen years."

"Kept you close to her, didn't it?"

"Maybe a little too close. Heinrich must have finally grown tired of me being around. He replaced me with this smarmy SOB with a soul full of sulfur. Lamont Sanders."

"Sounds like a great guy."

"He goes by Sandy."

"And you're certain you won't come up?"

"As tempting as this is, I have a job to do. I need to find Martin Drexler."

"You'll find him. And maybe after you do, we'll have another top-down night." She pressed into me, gave me her best eyes, squeezed my leg. Her kiss was gentle on my mouth.

I wolf-whistled as she headed up the outdoor steps to her second-floor apartment. She put a little extra swivel in her hips.

I drove off. Found a drive-in diner called the Patio. Home of the Slab Burger. I pulled into a spot and pushed the Order button. A young voice came over the speaker.

"Welcome to the Patio, Daddy-O. What can I get you?"

"Slab burger. Crinkle fries. RC Cola."

"On its way."

My mind wandered while I waited. I thought of the Annie I'd known before the war and the Annie I came to know after the war ended. I was the one who had contacted her after seeing her on the magazine cover. It was like talking to a cousin you only saw at weddings and funerals. Our post-war relationship headed in that direction, and I accepted it. Reluctantly.

I watched Marty Drexler grow up. He was a great kid. Loved baseball. He always wanted to play catch with me whenever I stopped by the mansion. I asked him once why he didn't play with his dad. Marty had shrugged, told me he didn't think Heinrich liked him. After that, I watched an ever-widening rift open between them, with Annie caught in the middle. By the time Marty was drafted, the father-son relationship had evaporated altogether.

Marty deployed and the rift closed. Annie and Heinrich fell in love again. Marty came home emotionally and physically crippled and the gap re-opened. Only way to close it was to send Marty away again.

I heard the regret in her voice over the four hundred miles between us when she called.

"Jimmy, I've done something awful and I need your help."

"Anything for you, Annie."

"I feel rotten for dumping my troubles on someone else."

"It's no trouble."

At the time I thought she meant me. Sitting in my car, watching a parade of happy families coming and going, something else pushed its way into my head. Marty Drexler telling me he thought Heinrich didn't like him. I couldn't understand why a dad wouldn't like a kid like Marty. He wasn't my kid, but I liked him.

He wasn't my kid.

Maybe he wasn't Heinrich's either.

I had seen Annie on an February magazine cover. Marty had a November birthday. Somewhere in those nine months was the connection to Duneville.

A carhop brought my food to me in a box.

"Here you go, Daddy-O."

The bill was a buck eighty. I gave her a five. "Keep the change."

"Hey, thanks, man. This will pay for my next semester of nursing school."

I dropped the box on the bench seat.

"...a hospital full of eager, pretty, nurses full of honeysuckle and wine...me up to my chin in gauze and plaster...didn't stop me from getting to know a few..."

Suddenly I knew why Annie had dropped off Marty in Duneville.

Pete Edmonds stepped out of his trailer and walked over to my car.

"I thought you might be back."

"Did you know?"

"That Drexler is my son? No."

"Annie never told you?"

"Why would she? It was only the one time in San Diego just after the war ended. She remembered me from the hospital. I told her I never forgot her. Small talk opens doors, don't it?"

"Apparently."

Edmonds's wrinkled brow flattened. "We both had wounds. We'd always have scars but right then, that night, we bared them to each other, happy it was all behind us. Hell, you remember those days, don't you?"

I didn't.

"I never saw her after that."

"How did she know you were here?"

"Figured she put you on my trail."

"I didn't know anything about you, Pete, until I got here this afternoon."

"Someone found me for her."

"I'm not the only PI in California."

"No, you're not."

"You talked to someone."

Edmonds shook his head like he was upset with himself. "Sheriff Cook showed up with this fella one day a while back. Started asking questions about the war and what all I did. Said he was looking for stories for some television program."

"This fella tell you his name?"

"Sandy something. I got his card...."

I shook my head. Lamont Sanders had been there doing what I used to do. Fixing a problem.

The low wail of sirens caught our attention. Flashing lights headed to the shoreline.

"Get in," I said.

Edmonds picked up the box of food. "The Patio? You going to eat this?"

Three bonfires burned as I pulled into the beach access lot. I parked next to Sheriff Cook. He rested his rump on the hood of his car.

"Busy night, Sheriff?"

"Your drifter assaulted a couple of patrons at the Sand Dooner. Bruce Carver had to step in to stop him. He's going to have a nice scar on his chin."

"Just you here to arrest him? No deputies?"

Cook pointed to one of the bonfires. "Two down at the bonfire. Three more in the shadows. Your boy has been a nuisance since he arrived. It's time to box him up and send him to the next town."

Edmonds washed down a chunk of slab burger with a swallow of cola. "Got news for you, Stan. Your nuisance is my son. You knew when you brought that television man to talk to me."

Cook tipped his hat back. Rubbed his thumbnail into his thinning hair. "The hell I did, Pete. All I knew was he looking for you."

Out of the night a voice roared. "Sinners! You desecrate this sacred ground!"

One of the deputies drew his gun. "I think he's here now."

"Hold on," I said. "Give me an opportunity to bring him in."

Martin continued his oration.

"You are all trespassers against the hallowed resting place of this mighty—Uncle Jimmy?"

"Hello, Marty."

"Mom sent you, didn't she?"

"You know Annie. Impetuous. Now she wants you home."

"I have no home, Uncle Jimmy."

"Sure, you do."

"I don't!"

I could feel the silence along the beach.

"Marty. There's someone here I think you might want to see."

"Who?"

"Your dad."

"Heinrich is here?"

"Not Heinrich."

"I don't understand."

Edmonds moved up behind me. "He's talking about me, son."

"You're the guy who lives in the trailer."

"Not much of a step up from an old bus," Cook said under his breath but loud enough his deputies could laugh.

Edmonds ignored Cook. "Let me help you, son."

"You can't help me, mister. I've done horrible things. I set fire to homes. I struck old men and ladies in the mouth with my M-16 and wiped the gore off on their clothes. I chased children. Children. All under the command of my superiors when I should have been following dictates of peace and compassion. Now my own family abandons me, hoping I return to the jungles I once called home."

Marty punched the whale. "I wish this leviathan would open its mouth to eat this vile slab of repulsive flesh."

"Son," Edmonds said. "A dead fish can't give you any answers. I'm not even certain I can but at least I'll listen."

Flashlights illuminated Marty Drexler as he put his hands on both lips of the whale's great mouth, straightened the bend of his prosthetic leg, bent his back, strained his arm muscles, and tried desperately to pry open the jaw.

"Let me back into the belly. Let me back into the belly of the beast!"

He brought out his knife. Maybe to cut his way into the whale, maybe to defend himself. A woman at one of the bonfires screamed. A volley of shots exploded, hitting both Martin Drexler and the whale. When the shooting ceased, only Cook held a smoking gun. I grabbed Cook by the front his shirt and rolled him into the sand.

"You didn't have to kill him."

"He was erratic! You heard his confession."

"I heard the rantings of a troubled young man."

"He pulled a knife, damn it. I did what I had to do."

"Do me a favor. When you call his mother, be sure to tell her that."

"Hey," one of the deputies said. "Jonah ain't dead."

Edmonds held Marty's knife to Cook's neck. "Call an ambulance now. He dies you die."

I took hold of Edmond's wrist. "Tell you what, Pete. Marty's going to need you to not be in jail."

Edmonds surrendered the knife.

I don't know how Cook had managed it, but of the six rounds he fired, only one struck Marty and that one got him in the prosthetic leg, snapping the knee-joint and knocking him to the ground. The other five slugs hit the whale.

* * *

An hour later I used the pay phone at the Sand Dooner to call Annie down in Los Angeles.

"Jimmy! Did you find him?"

"I did."

"Is he—"

I could hear the relief in her silence.

"He's fine, Annie. " More silence. Neither of us spoke for several hard moments. "But he won't be coming home anytime soon. He has a couple of assault charges pending."

She sighed on her end. Softly swore. "Damn it."

"I'm sure you'll have Lamont Sanders clean it all up for you."

"He wouldn't have come home, regardless. You know that, Jimmy. He wasn't my son anymore. I don't know that he ever was."

"He wasn't Heinrich's son, I know that. Did Heinrich know?"

"He always knew. He was in love with me and said it didn't matter."

"Looks like it did."

"Send me a bill for your trouble, Jimmy, and I'll send you a certified check."

I hung up and went back to the bar where Carol waited for me.

"Go well?" Carol asked.

I drank my beer. "It's done."

"The job or you and Annie?"

"They're one and the same."

"You all right?"

"Me? I'm fine. Let's get out of here."

"Walk on the beach?"

She poked me and I laughed. "It's a top-down kind of night."

I was back in my San Francisco office watching the local news when a story came on about the ill-fated removal of a dead whale near the Salinas Dunes. The local sheriff, fed up with waiting for the Army Corp of Engineers to handle the matter, had taken it upon himself to dispose of it. The sheriff packed sixteen crates of dynamite around the dead whale. All sixteen crates detonated simultaneously off a single push of a plunger box.

Instantaneous devastation had followed.

Wooden signs were sand-blasted clean. Scores of spectators were burned by molten whale blubber. The sheriff's patrol car was flattened when a sizable portion of the whale landed on it.

And that, at least to me, was what the studio writers called poetic justice.

BAD VIBRATIONS

C.W. Blackwell

Not seconds.

Not minutes.

Time flows instead with each semi-truck screaming down the highway, each air horn blast and flick of the high beams. It's measured with each painful inch I crawl, elbows ratcheting in the hard sand, Army-drill fashion, with every spatter of blood from my car-wrecked mouth. The Mustang lies in a ditch behind me, tangled up in barbed-wire fencing. A cockeyed headlamp shines skyward. Ahead of me, sand dunes stretch along the bay shoreline where I'll bury myself until morning, hoping the men who ran me off the road don't circle back with dogs and lights. Maybe it's not the first case that ever gave me bad vibes from the start, nor the first where I ended up horizontal and bleeding—but damn if it wasn't the first time I'd been ejected from a '66 fastback at highway speeds in the dead of night on account of some federal goon squad.

The whole mess had started a few weeks ago on Montgomery Street in San Francisco, just a stone's throw from the beating heart of the American counterculture. If Haight-Ashbury was the heart, the blood it pumped was LSD, flowing through hilly streets and alleyways and into North Beach cafes and Tenderloin dives.

It flowed across bridges and ferry ways into college towns like Berkeley and down the Redwood Highway to Santa Cruz and beyond. And it had certainly reached the two-hundred block of Montgomery Street in the Financial District, where my new client had just come down from an acid-fueled hell ride.

"It's mind control," said Burt Flanchon. He sat cross-legged on his office chair wearing nothing but swim shorts and a fisherman's cap, an unlit cigarette wagging when he spoke. "They've finally found a way."

I looked for a place to sit, but he'd stacked every surface with reams of blank typing paper. Instead, I lit a cigarette and folded my arms, looking over this nervous little man before me. With my stars-and-stripes-painted jeans and tie-dyed button-up I thought I'd be the most underdressed, but I was clearly wrong.

"You didn't mention mind-control over the phone," I said.

"Would you have come if I had?"

"Probably not." But that wasn't true. I needed the money, and I knew Flanchon was good for it. Concert promoters were raking it in these days, and he'd found himself in the center of a gold rush, booking everything from Big Brother and the Holding Company and the Grateful Dead, to some of the big British invasion groups. "Got any ideas who's trying to"—I almost couldn't say it—"*control your mind?*"

"Sure, I got ideas. Hoover, the CIA Aliens, maybe."

"Sounds like you've really narrowed it down."

"Let me ask you something—Teddy, is it?"

"That's right."

"Have you ever had a bad acid trip, Teddy?"

I shook my head. "Nothing but sunshine and rainbows, man."

"Neither had I, until this stuff showed up." Flanchon lifted his fisherman's cap and removed a sheet of blotter paper encased in a cellophane bag. Rows of happy face stamps ran up and down the sheet on perforated squares, with one tab missing at the corner. "If Dante Alighieri dropped this shit, he'd add a tenth circle of hell."

"Where'd you get it?"

"From the guys—Jerry and Phil. Last night, we canceled the Winterland show because of it. It turned us all into schizophrenic maniacs. Like someone was invading our thoughts—and you know what? Maybe they were, man. But before you ask the next question: no, we don't know how it turned up. We've got our own chemist, a guy named Owsley, so it makes no sense how this stuff keeps getting into the mix. That's why you're here."

"This has happened before?"

"Twice before. All in the past six weeks."

"Must be hurting your bottom line."

Flanchon pointed to his bare chest. "I've lost my shirt, brother."

"So, when's the next show?"

"Two weeks, down in Monterey." He motioned to the wall, where a yellow concert poster with bold, black letters hung with pushpins. It advertised a three-day festival called Monterey Pop. "It's a benefit concert, but I've got a piece of the film rights. If it goes off the rails, I'll be cooked. You feel me?"

I nodded, still awed by the superstar lineup.

"Jimi Hendrix, huh?"

"You've heard of him? The kid can play. He's going to blow everyone's whiskers back. Unless of course he ends up in the bad trip teepee with his mind picked apart by little green men. You dig?"

"Yeah," I said. "I dig. By the way, what's with all the typing paper?"

"A diversion to confuse the mind-readers," he said. He got up from the chair and crouched among the pillars of paper, tapping his temples. "You can't read a blank page, man. Think about it."

With Flanchon's retainer in my front pocket, I grabbed a newspaper and headed up to North Beach for a late breakfast at Mel's Diner. The fog sat heavy on the city, and I watched it drift through the streets as I drank coffee and caught up with the day's news: riots in Boston, American F-105 bombers over North Vietnam. I found a promo picture of the Beatles supporting their new album *Sergeant Pepper's Lonely Hearts Club Band*, and by the looks of it, they'd finally bought a ticket on the LSD train.

Mel's wasn't my favorite diner, but it had a good view of Owsley's apartment from the front patio. Just an old brick row-style building with a rainbow-colored front door and peace signs painted on the bay windows. After a while, a blond college girl in a bathrobe opened the front door and wandered onto the sidewalk, squinting into the fogged-out sky. She watched the traffic on Columbus Street as if expecting a ride, then she picked a flower from a young primrose tree, tucked it behind her ear, and wandered back inside.

As I took another sip of coffee, something else caught my eye.

A man sat in the restaurant patio next door, eyes hard on Owsley's place. Square as can be, like he'd just leaped out of a Sears, Roebuck and Company catalog. Gray wool suit. Dress shirt and tie. Brow-line glasses. When the blonde closed the front door behind her, the man noted it on a pad of paper and returned to his meal. He glanced up at me and I dove back into the newspaper.

Maybe just another private dick.

Maybe one of Hoover's men.

Either way, I knew I'd just earned another week's retainer.

I paid up and tipped the waitress, slipped the cook a few bucks so I could use the rear exit. I didn't want the square to get eyeballs on me when I left. Anything I could do to stay off his little writing pad. The backdoor led into an alley between the diner and an auto repair shop, the odd combination of bacon grease and shop grease mingling in the air. The fog was just starting to break up, ragged vapors curling over the rooftops into the bald blue sky. The idea was to circle around to the bus stop a half-block down so I could keep an eye on both Owsley's place and the square without being made.

Coming out of the alley, I found it was too late.

The square grabbed me by the shoulders and shoved me backward. I lost my balance and tumbled against a dumpster with the lids clammed open. He came at me hard, but I'd regained my footing enough to dodge the blow. His knuckles clanged into the dumpster's steel housing, and he pulled back, howling.

I came up swinging.

One blow to the gut and another square to the chin.

He staggered back but didn't fall. After he regained his composure, he removed his glasses and carefully folded them into his pocket.

"Who do you work for?" I said, more of a demand than a question.

"Win this fight and I'll tell you," he replied. He pounded his meaty palm and shifted his stance like some old-timey boxer. "Just to warn you, I don't lose fights to hippies."

I took him at his word and rushed him with a barrel hug into the brick wall. All I wanted was to knock him down so I could get a good running start, but the man just wouldn't drop. Instead, I took a sharp knee to the chest. He wound a handful of my hair, whipped my head back and pummeled me with the butt of his palm. Once, twice—on the third strike he let go and I went down hard. Another blow like that and I'd wake up in the E.R.

"Mind your own business, Hippy," he said. He straightened his coat, slipped on his glasses, and then he was gone.

I got to my feet, staggered two blocks up Greenwich Street where I found an open alcove to an apartment complex. I folded into it, the world slowly coming back into focus. After spitting a few mouthfuls of blood, I flipped open the badge holder I'd pilfered from the square's pocket.

Ronald Paul Vickers, San Francisco Field Office.

FBI.

At least it wasn't aliens.

* * *

I hid out in my Tenderloin apartment, mostly icing my swollen face and making calls to Flanchon's musical acts. I wasn't getting very far. The guys were reluctant to talk to me over the phone, suspecting some kind of law enforcement ruse. Given Agent Vickers's surveillance of Owsley's place, I couldn't fault their suspicion. What I wanted to know was whether the FBI was running a garden-variety drug detail or if they had their hands into something more sinister.

My split lip and black eyes steered me in the latter direction.

I took my chances and paid Owsley a visit just after sundown a few days later. I dressed more inconspicuously than before in plain jeans and a sweater, my hair tucked up into a brown newsie cap. If Vickers still had eyeballs on the place, I wasn't about to give him an easy ID.

A minute or two after knocking, a woman's voice called from the other side of the door. I explained that Owsley was expecting me—I had Flanchon's office call ahead—and after another minute the door unlatched and swung open. By the looks of it, I'd overdressed yet again. The blonde stood before me, wearing nothing but a necklace of primrose she must have picked from the tree out front. She told me her name was Moonflower and she'd dreamt that a Capricorn would visit her this week.

"Lucky guess," I said.

"Not lucky," she said. "It was a premonition. I'm clairvoyant."

"That right?" I gave her the once-over. "Can't you envision where your clothes went?"

"That's a choice, man. I'm also a naturist."

She had me intrigued. "So, tell me, Moonflower—is Johnson going to win in sixty-eight?"

"Don't count on it," she said. "What's he to run on? War and civil unrest?"

"Is that your analysis or another premonition?"

"My analysis is that he's politically vulnerable, and let's agree—it's mostly due to strategic miscalculations and plain hubris. I think everyone understands that. My premonition is that RFK will try to outflank either him or Humphrey on the left during the primaries. My hope is that we all wake up soon and realize that love is the answer to all our current and future societal issues and that war and materialism have only brought us despair."

"I can dig that."

"I bet you can," she said, straightening the bill of my hat. "You're a Capricorn in the Year of the Goat. Everything's groovy for you, Baby."

Owsley appeared at the end of the hallway wearing some sort of Bedouin tunic and laboratory gloves. "You Flanchon's guy?" he said. "Teddy T?"

I went to shake his hand, but he held them up in a gesture of caution. "I wouldn't touch these gloves unless you've blocked off your schedule for the next twelve hours."

Owsley told me to call him Bear, and he led me into a small room lit with bug zappers. A lab bench ran the length of the walls, laden with foil-capped beakers and Bunsen burners. Miniature refrigerators in the corners of the room. On the concrete walls hung posters for local rock shows, mostly featuring the Grateful Dead.

"It's a little creepy back here, but you get used to it," said Owsley.

"You have a bug problem?"

"A drug problem?"

"I said a *bug problem.*" I nodded at the bug zappers.

"Oh, no man. Regular light degrades the LSD, so I have to use those."

"Sounds like you have it all figured out."

"I'm the best there is. It's science, you know. You have to be precise and methodical."

I pointed to a ruled journal open on the lab bench. "Is that why you keep so many notes?"

"Man, I log everything. You have to. This stuff is so pure, it gets into your system whether you want it or not. You get used to it, but that's why you have to keep track. I'm always a little high."

"So where do you think the bad acid is coming from?"

"Well, not from me, if that's what you're saying."

"I didn't say that. But someone's distributing the acid."

"That's just it. It's not even LSD," he said it sadly, with a shrug.

"It's not?"

"No, man. First, I thought it was some hack trying to elbow into the market, just pushing out bad shit. But I studied it. The pH is too high—*way too high*. The chemical composition is all wrong."

"So what is it?"

He looked me over, that ninety-yard stare like he stood with one foot planted in another dimension. "What happened to your face?"

"There's a federal agent surveilling your apartment. He took offense when I spotted him."

"What a bummer, man. I'm sorry. He's been out there all week."

"You're not worried he'll arrest you?"

"A little. I'm moving to Denver later this month. This whole scene is going down the tubes, man. You know, it started with the KGB, then CIA. Everyone wanted a truth serum or a mind-control drug, something they could use to interrogate enemy spies. When LSD first broke out of the lab, who knows what they thought would happen. Ask Kesey, maybe he knows. I'm sure they didn't expect it to open everyone's minds and start a cultural revolution. So, they course-corrected, dig? Now they're putting out an evil version of LSD to kill the entire movement before it threatens the establishment. Bad vibes, man. Bad vibes."

"You really think this stuff comes from the government?"

"Is a frog's butthole watertight?"

Moonflower appeared in the doorway and casually leaned into the jamb.

"Bear, it's happening again," she said.

"Where?" Owsley and I both responded at once.

"The Matrix. Sounds like another bad one."

I folded my arms and tossed Moonflower a sideways glance. "If only you could have seen this coming."

The Matrix was a small club on Fillmore, well-known as the home base of Jefferson Airplane. It had grown in popularity with the rest of the hippie scene and now attracted national acts like the Doors, who were performing when the bad juice hit the audience. By the time the taxi dropped me off, the cops had the place mostly buttoned down, save for a handful of roaming showgoers in the shadows. I saw a few ambulances take off with lights and sirens, patrol cars spinning white and blue strobes on the avenue.

Around back, I found the main act's roadies loading gear onto a charter bus. When I came out of the shadows with a lit cigarette, they stopped and studied me very intently. They relaxed when they saw my face.

"It's not him," said one.

"Who did you think I was?" I asked.

A stocky kid with shaggy hair squared off with me, hands on his hips. He ignored my question. "Look, mister. We don't allow anyone back here. The show's over."

"I work for Burt Flanchon," I said. "He wants to get to the bottom of things."

I held out my card, but he didn't take it.

"This ain't Flanchon's gig," he said. "You want Helms."

"Flanchon and Helms have a mutual interest. What happened here is what shut down Winterland last week. It'll shut down Monterey Pop if we don't stop it."

I gave the roadies a few details to stir up intrigue. Gossip makes for good currency, especially when it comes with a heavy dose of government conspiracy. It didn't take long to turn them. I had a joint hidden away in the bill of my hat and I lit it and passed it around, all of us joking like old buddies. A few minutes later, the stocky kid led me through the back door of the Matrix and showed me to the dressing rooms.

I thanked him, and he gave me a strange reply.

"Morrison," he said.

"What about him?"

"That's who we thought you were. You kind of look like him."

"He hasn't left for LA?"

"No, man. He's in the wind. I think he took that bad shit, too. They told us to keep an eye out for him."

The dressing room door was unlocked, and I found the room empty. It looked like what you'd expect from a big-time rock band on a Saturday night in San Francisco. Lipstick on the mirrors. Empty cigarette packs on the floor. The skunky smell of sweat and sativa—then again, maybe that was me. There must have been a hundred empty beer bottles crowding every surface. Someone had turned the drawers and rifled the closets—no doubt the cops had already done a sweep.

I flicked at a crowded ashtray, kicked over a shard of bottle glass.

Then—I saw it.

A pink and purple flower crushed into the linoleum.

Primrose.

By the time I gave Flanchon my report on the Matrix, Moonflower—just like Morrison—had gone MIA. But while Morrison turned up the next day in Golden Gate Park wearing nothing but a Viking helmet and a wool poncho, Moonflower couldn't be found. With the festival only a week away, Flanchon gave me the keys to his '66 Mustang fastback so I could set up shop down in Monterey and run interference in case she turned up there. I hadn't left the city all year, so I didn't mind the drive. I took Highway 1 along the coast, through beach towns and strawberry fields, past little artichoke stands on the side of the highway. Just south of Castroville, the Monterey Bay cut into the coastline, a deep crystalline blue like something from a Greek Island travel brochure.

I checked into the Monterey Hotel, an old stucco building on Alvarado Street that could have been a holdover from the Spanish Conquest. The room wouldn't knock your socks off, but it had what I needed: a warm bed and a view of the street. I kicked off my boots and stared at the ceiling, trying to piece it together. If Moonflower was brewing bad dope in Owlsey's laboratory, his disciplined lab protocols surely would have tipped him off. He logged every ounce of raw materials that came and went. And if he was somehow in on it, what was his motivation in wrecking the counterculture he helped to create? Was the FBI angle just a nutso conspiracy theory after all?

I spent the next few days driving back and forth to the Fairgrounds where stagehands hustled to set up the PA system and piece the stage together. At first, only a few teenaged kids milled around the place, some camping out in tents or laying on bedrolls. But the crowd trickled in with each passing day, often by the busload. The vibe was mostly groovy, and the small-town cops appeared pleasantly amused with these strange and joyful hippies with their colorful clothes, long beards, and acoustic guitars. It felt like something important was taking root here, something transformational.

The San Francisco scene had crested the dam.

The hippies were on the march.

I wandered from tent to tent, taking my time and soaking up the scene. Word had already spread about the bad acid, so all I could do was amplify the message. *Don't eat the smiley-face tabs, kids.* I caught up with Jon Phillips from the Mamas and the Papas—also one of the principal organizers of the festival—and he brushed off my client's concerns as needless negativity.

"This isn't Winterland," he told me, in between phone calls. He seemed mostly worried about the logistics of the international acts. Flight schedules, charter buses. "There won't be any bad vibes here, I promise you. You tell Flanchon that his movie is getting made, come hell or high water."

It occurred to me that Phillips didn't know how high water could get.

The first night of the festival came and went without incident, and by the second night, I was beginning to feel that perhaps Phillips was right. I'd been to plenty of shows, but the enormity of Monterey Pop in both crowd size and enthusiasm filled me with a sense of awe. I couldn't help getting swept away with the music and positive vibrations, and by the time Joplin belted her encore performance on Sunday night, I'd stopped worrying about demonic acid and government conspiracies and melted in with the crowd.

The first sign of trouble came with a thirty-minute lag after Buffalo Springfield's set. When I found Phillips backstage, he looked frazzled, barking orders at anyone within earshot.

"Hendrix is missing," he said. "The Who is tuning up now, but Hendrix is our headliner. We need to find him."

"Where have you looked?"

"I don't know man, everywhere. His trailer, the bad-trip teepee. I saw him hanging with some blond chick earlier and now he's just gone."

The words hit me like a punch to the gut. "What was she wearing?"

"The blonde?" He gave me a strange look, then: "Absolutely nothing."

I made the parking lot thirty seconds later, searching up and down the rows of charter busses and camper vans. Only a few minutes of sunlight remained, shadows reeling over the lot. Crows gathered in the cypress trees, calling and chanting. When I came around the back of a double-decker tour bus, the door folded open and a woman descended the stairs in a hurry. She wore a long coat and had her blond hair folded up into a velvet hat.

She froze when she saw me.

"A little overdressed, aren't you, Moonflower?" I said.

"I knew you'd catch up to me eventually," she said.

"I bet you did." I walked to her slowly. "Where's Hendrix?"

She shrugged. "Who knows? I'm not his manager."

"You slipped him the bad dope, didn't you? Just like Morrison and the Dead? Why?"

She glanced at the Fairgrounds just as the Who stormed into the first few riffs of their set. Her eyes glistened and she folded her arms defensively. "They made me, Teddy. I didn't have a choice."

"Who made you?"

A form descended from the bus behind her, taking each step slowly.

Wool suit, brow-line glasses.

"I thought I told you to mind your own business," said Vickers.

"As long as Flanchon's checks clear, this *is* my business, G-man."

"Choose your next steps carefully, Hippy," he pounded his palm like he had the first time we met, as if hoping for a rematch. "It's a crime to impede a federal investigation."

"Isn't it a crime to poison innocent people with bad dope?"

Vickers took off his glasses and polished them on his shirt. "Did you say *innocent people*?" He laughed, a sort of callous and cold-hearted laugh. "I think you mean communist sympathizers. Why don't you climb aboard, and we'll talk it over? I'll tell you all about our little operation."

"Do you have Hendrix?"

"Come see for yourself."

Moonflower waved her hands. "Look out, Teddy!"

Two squares had snuck up behind me on either side.

I didn't hesitate.

I spun, dropped the closest one with a hard blow to the cheek. He doubled over the trunk of a Ford coupe and toppled to the dirt. The second square rushed me, pinning my arm behind my back and guiding me toward the tour bus. I shinned him with the heel of my boot, and he wheeled back, cursing. I grappled him and we went to the ground together, throwing punches and elbows. He hit me twice in the kidneys and I almost folded, but I held on tight.

No way in hell they were getting me on that damn bus.

I rolled the square onto his back and gave him a few headbutts to the nose before he softened up. He gave me a funny look, blood coursing down his cheeks, then he gazed over my shoulder. I looked up in time to see Vickers grab me by the shirt collar. He lifted me and tossed me against the side of the tour bus. I tumbled to the ground.

I took a hard kick to the gut.

Then another.

"Stop it," cried Moonflower. She threw herself at Vickers and he easily pushed her aside, but it gave me a chance to roll underneath the bus. I kept rolling. When I got to the other side, I picked myself up and ran, gasping for breath. The Mustang wasn't far, maybe twenty yards or so, just close enough to dive in and key the ignition before the goon squad knew what was happening. I hammered the pedal and screamed out of the parking lot in a surge of dust and hot rubber, pitching sideways onto the main road toward the highway.

The sun had set. Orange strata over Monterey Bay. I weaved through traffic, gunning the straightaways whenever I found them. All the way to San Francisco with my foot to the floor if that's what it would take. I'd go straight to Flanchon—he'd protect me. Then to the newspapers if I had to. No way I'd become a casualty in some hair-brained government plot to kill the hippy scene. I was going to blow the lid off this thing, Baby. Blow it all sky-high.

But the FBI had fast cars, too.

The steering wheel jumped in my hands when the first car rammed me from the side. I swerved and corrected, but the next plowed straight into my rear bumper. Then another blow. They crowded me from every angle, headlights off, the glow of the dash lights pasting their evil, bureaucratic faces. I cut the wheel, aiming for the Seaside offramp.

Then, gunfire.

One, two, three shots.

These boys weren't playing anymore.

A tire blew and the Mustang jolted into the shoulder, then it pitched across the highway into the oncoming lane. Big rigs and small cars alike, high beams flickering on and off in my windshield. I cut the wheel again, closed my eyes and felt a cold weightlessness as I soared through the air.

Sunrise.

The sound of crashing waves.

Sea lions barking from some distant pier.

I rolled onto my side, brushed the sand from my face. Something was broken. My jaw, maybe. My arm, definitely. I tested my weight on my right foot, but the left hurt too bad. Maybe there was just enough left in me to shoulder down the beach to Monterey, enough to fold into a phone booth and dial Flanchon, tell him we made it to the very last act before the wheels fell off the bus. Surely they had enough footage to make a movie, maybe even a good one. Something historic to mark what might be the pinnacle of the sixties music scene.

I shuffled past the early-morning fishermen with their waders and white buckets, casting into the surf. Maybe they thought I was a drunk, some burned-out hippy whose time had come and gone before he even knew it.

I scanned the dunes for squares.

Nothing.

Just the morning fog pulling back to the sea.

Sure, it was a rotten case. The kind that goes sideways fast and never quits. I thought of Moonflower, and what kind of screws they must have turned to get her to betray the cause. I thought of poor Hendrix, with his head full of bad acid. But a part of me wondered if he found his way to the stage somehow, if maybe he knew how to exercise the demons and send them back into the flames like a shaman straddling two worlds, a master of both. Maybe he pulled it off not only to save himself, but to save the crowd—*to save the whole generation.*

And if they caught something like that on camera?

What a truly remarkable act that would be.

KICK OUT THE JAMS

Steve Liskow

She's dressed like you'd expect a spoiled brat from Grosse Pointe to dress: frayed cut-offs with threads hanging down, sandals, and a T-shirt with a clenched-fist graphic over her breasts. Her blond hair would reach her waist if she wore it down, but tonight she's got it up and a bandanna covering it above silly little sunglasses with heart-shaped lenses. Never mind that we're inside and it's eight-forty, so the sun's below the skyline outside. She still looks *good.*

She passes a joint to Kelton and pulls out her Zippo. Again, never mind that we're inside with about eighteen hundred other people. Kelton drags until the tip glows like an orange eye, and even in the dark and the crowd I can feel him holding back a laugh. Maddie wants to be a bad girl, but she doesn't know how. Unfortunately, the people she's with know enough to give her daddy nightmares, which is why he hired me in the first place.

Saturday night at the Grande Ballroom with a bunch of guys in tie-dyed shirts and ragged jeans, watching and listening to the sound of Fuckin' DEE-troit. The MC5 is onstage now, kicking out the jams, the sound too big and ballsy for the small stage under the proscenium arch, Rob Tyner sweating like a horse and the band churning up the mix behind him like a cement mixer in heat. Tim Buckley will be on later, if anyone can still hear him.

I'm spending too much time watching Maddie get beatifically stoned while Kelton and the other guy slide their hands under her tee and give that clenched fist extra knuckles.

Another joint works down the row. I take a hit and pass it on. I don't mind a little, especially if it's free, and if I pass, everyone will notice. Not good when you're trying to blend in. My hair is longer than when they dumped me from the Detroit PD in January, and my red-, white-, and blue-striped bell-bottoms have that lived-in look around my butt. I've got a baggy seersucker shirt over my wife beater, not because it's chilly in late July, but because children in the Summer of Love don't carry heat, not even in Detroit.

The MC5 slams through Chuck Berry's "Back in the USA" to finish their set. They wave at the crowd, which is roaring even louder than their amps, and Tyner wipes his face with a towel before leaving the stage to the guys who move amps and microphones around for Buckley.

Maddie sucks on a joint big enough to tuck into my pants. She passes it off to the other guy, Randall. He knows John Sinclair, who co-owns the Grande and heads the White Panthers. He's the main reason Maddie's daddy hired me. Charles Rohr is old Automotive Money, and revolutionaries give him ulcers.

Maddie has this big smile, like a dinner plate with blue eyes, her eyelids heavy as the trunk of my Malibu, and Randall and Kelton look like they're trying to sell her on something, but I can't get close enough to hear more than "party" and "Nam."

Buckley comes out and everyone cheers. Maddie sways back and forth with the music, her eyes closed and her hands up like she's fondling a cloud. I maneuver between two dudes in tie-dye and a girl in a grannie dress and no bra and get close enough to hear Kelton say something about 12th Street. They move toward an exit and I manage to follow without drawing attention to myself, which is hard when we're the only people leaving now that the headliner has come on.

Outside, they side-step through the traffic on Grand River

Avenue and I slide into my car and wait for them to ease out of the lot across the street. Hot summer night, everyone's out, so it's easy to slide four cars behind Maddie's, a Mustang with a Bad Mad vanity plate. I follow down Woodward and over to Chene, toward East. Yeah, we're definitely on the way to 12th, right on the edge of Highland Park. Highland Park is like ninety-nine percent black, so Maddie and I will stick out like flashers on a Crown Vic. Easy to follow her, hard to stay invisible.

It's almost midnight when they pull up in front of a print shop that's closed. I see light in the windows on the second story, though, and park in an alley around the corner. I hot-foot back in time to see the three of them go up a flight of stairs. Voices and loud music leak through an open door before it closes behind them. The sign says, "United Community League for Civic Action."

I tap on the door and nobody answers for a minute. When I try again, a Black guy about a foot taller than me looks out.

"Whatchu want?"

"Scully told me about the party. Him and Rashid."

"Who the hell's Scully. Or the other guy?"

"Who are you if you don't know them?" I demand. He's still puzzling that one when I push into the room. Sixty or seventy people jam the space and there's a bar over to my left where one guy is pouring shots and another one is tapping a keg. Everyone has a drink, and you could wear the sweat and smoke as a mask. Where the hell is Maddie? Two guys in uniforms are by the bar, both with combat ribbons, and they already look a little out of focus with everyone offering them another glass. I wonder if they just came back from a McNamara Fellowship and that's why there's a party.

A record player on the bar is blaring out "Can't Help Myself" by the Four Tops, loud enough so I feel the bass in my gut. A few people are dancing, but more are staying close to the soldiers. I move around the room, avoiding eye contact and looking for other doors.

"Hey, Sugar."

A chick with an afro big as a basketball and a chest not much smaller grabs my arm. "Let's dance."

"I'm not much of a dancer, but...."

"I dint ax if you was any good, white boy. Blanche wants to boogie."

Her pupils are pinpoints and her breath would dent a fender. When she dances, she raises her hands high over her head so her sweaty T-shirt sticks to her nipples. Her hips shimmy like maracas, and I can't look away. I'm no dancer, but even I can get down to Motown. Besides, it's safer to let someone think I'm with her than to wonder who let the honky in.

The song changes to "Bernadette," and Blanche doesn't even slow down. I'm panting from keeping up with her, and there's still no sign of Maddie.

There. Another door, behind the bar. I let myself get caught up in the other dancers and move with another girl in a red Nehru jacket much too big for her. She's not wearing anything under it. Maddie could learn something about how to dress from these chicks.

I edge closer to that door and wait until the guy at the keg turns to hand someone another beer. I cut behind him, slide through the door, and close it behind me.

I'm in a room with a bed, heavy blinds on the windows, three Black guys, and Maddie. They all look at me like I pissed on their birthday cake.

"We're busy here, white boy." His eyes look like he's already soaring over the Ambassador Bridge. Maddie pouts at me, then at the other guys again. One of them has a bag of pills, and she's clutching her purse with both hands.

"Righteous shit, man," she says. "I told you. And it's two hundred."

"Not widdout a test." The tall guy in shades looks big enough to play tackle for the Lions. Maddie's sunglasses look funny, but his look scary, maybe because he's twice her size.

"You think we just off the farm? We gotta be sure you not selling M&Ms."

She shakes her head. "Um, like not a chance, brother. I gotta make something on the deal, you dig?"

"You still make something." The guy reaches out his hand and Maddie pulls back. He reaches for her purse with one hand and clamps the other one around her upper arm so tight she gasps in pain. Below his grip, the skin of her arm turns even lighter.

"Let go of me, Boy."

He squeezes harder and her face loses all its color. I can feel the night going off the rails.

"Hey, Man. Let's be cool. The music is loud, and the booze is free. Let's all just have a good time."

They turn toward me, one big, the others bigger, and none of them on my side. The guy holding Maddie jerks her off her feet and she squeals, dangling like a rag doll.

"You bastard. Put me down."

He slaps her and I almost feel my own head ring. He reaches up and hooks the neckline of her T-shirt and pulls down hard. The clenched fist vanishes and her bare chest gleams like a Cadillac grille before my eyes, headlights and all. He tosses her onto the bed and I pull out my gun.

"Back off," I tell them. "Now."

The guy slit-eyes my piece, a .38 snubby.

"Fuckin' cop gun. You got no business here, piggy."

"It's my business now, Jack. Back up against the wall or I'll blow your guts out."

"You don't got the balls," he says. "They's seventy, eighty people out there, they tear you ass apart you pull dat shit here."

"Won't help you, though, will it?"

He's still thinking for an answer to that when Maddie rolls off the bed, her breasts swinging and a red handprint on her cheek. I want to give her a standing-eight count while she gropes for her purse.

I slide my left hand out of the sleeve of my big shirt.

"All of you, lie on the floor and put your hands in your pockets."

They do. I switch the gun to my other hand and hand Maddie my shirt.

"Cover yourself," I say. "We have to get the hell out of here."

"Assholes," she says. Her voice shakes like a little girl's holding back tears. "Bastards."

I drag her to the door and yank it open. I stuff my gun hand into my jeans pocket and pull her into the main room. The Four Tops are still pounding away, and Blanche is dancing with some other guy who never takes his eyes off her chest. The girl in the red Nehru jacket looks at us.

"Yo, we getting down now, for sure."

"Far out," I say. "Be cool."

Maddie winces at the loud music and I wonder if she's got a concussion.

She scans the room.

"Where are my guys?"

"They can catch up with us."

We're almost to the door when that enormous guy who stopped me before looms in front of us.

"Nobody knows you, motherfucker. You're outta here."

"We're just going," I say.

But he's already swinging. I try to roll with it but I'm next to the wall so there's nowhere to go. I bounce off that wall and my head rings like the Ford plant down in Rouge. I end up flat on my back and my eyes watch five of the guy reach down and pull me to my feet before he heaves me out the door. I grab the railing so I don't go down the stairs headfirst, and the door echoes when he slams it behind me. My teeth feel loose.

Maddie leans over me and her faces overlap. She disappears again and I roll onto my stomach and fight back nausea. I get to my knees and hold on to the newel post to stand up.

Maddie rejoins me and trots down the stairs.

"Bastards," she says again.

She vanishes through the door while I'm still stumbling down the stairs. I remember she and I have separate cars and I'll have to follow her. No telling where she's going now, but I'm pretty sure it's not back to the Grande.

When I open the door, what passes for fresh air in the Detroit summer fills my head. I suck in carbon monoxide and garbage and lean against the wall. A streetlight drops its cone on Maddie, and I see her bare chest under my shirt.

"You should button up," I say. My voice rattles in my skull.

"Who the hell are you, anyway? Do I even know you?"

"Not really."

She looks up and down the street and I feel my brain settling back into place. A few cars cruise the street, but they always do in Detroit. I can still hear the music upstairs.

"Son of a bitch," she snarls. Her eyes gain focus as we breathe. "They took my stash."

"You've still got your money, so don't worry about it."

"What money? They were supposed to pay me. Son of a bitch."

She looks up and down the street again and her face lights up when she sees a phone booth. She strides over to it, digging in her purse.

"You got change?" Her rich daddy's polish is gone, and rage turns her into a rabid Tinker Bell.

I pull out a few coins and she grabs a dime.

"Operator, give me the police."

I can't figure out what she's doing, but I don't have long to wait. When someone picks up at the precinct, she looks up at the lit window.

"Ninety-one-twenty-five Twelfth," she says. "They got music loud enough to wake a dead man, and most of them are drunk."

She hangs up and starts toward her car. Her Mustang is primo around here, and someone might already be looking to jack it, so I trot after her.

"Let's make sure your car is okay."

"Why wouldn't it be?"

"Do people around here know you?" I ask. "Or your car?"

She lets that sink in. There's nobody in sight and I walk all around the car. The tires appear untouched. She unlocks the door and slides in.

"Thanks for the dime and stuff."

"Sure."

She backs down the alley and I trot to my own car, a half block down in the alley across the street.

When I reach it, I'm still holding the rest of my change in my hand. I dig into my pocket for my keys and realize for the first time that my pockets feel too light. I remember Maddie bending over me after that big guy clocked me.

The little bitch took my gun.

If she called the cops about this party, they may show up soon. And if she was crazy enough to take my gun, she probably used it back there. My gun, registered in my name, with my fingerprints on it.

By the time I pull out into the light traffic, Maddie's taillights are nowhere in sight.

I zigzag around blocks for fifteen minutes before I decide it's a lost cause. When I turn the last corner, two Crown Vics sit by the curb near the print shop. I couldn't get back inside even if I were invisible, which I'm not. There's even a chance that someone in one of those cars would know me. I only left the PD in late January, six months ago.

I U-turn and head back toward Grand Avenue and points west. Maddie has an apartment in Ann Arbor, so maybe she went back there. That's probably where she got the pills, too. Speed is big on a campus like U of M, and that's where she first met Kelton. He wasn't a student, but he and Randall both came over from Eastern, where they were recruiting for the SDS. That was what got Maddie's old man worried enough to hire me.

Once I hit I-94, I stand on the pedal. When I reach Maddie's parking lot, her Mustang is in its space, the only thing that's gone right the whole damn night. By now, my teeth don't feel like they'll fall out if I talk, either, another step in the right direction.

I ride the elevator and knock on Maddie's door. No answer. It's three a.m., so maybe she's crashed. I slide my Sears credit card between the door and frame, feeling the latch slide back. I step into a dark room and let my eyes adjust so I won't trip over the furniture.

I follow a hallway, walking near the wall so none of the boards creak. Deep breathing drifts from the far end and I hope Maddie didn't bring a guy back with her. She didn't have a lot of time, but all she had to do was unbutton my shirt.

She's alone. I flick on her bedside lamp. When her eyes burst open, I slam my palm against her lips.

"One sound and I will break your neck." I say it quietly. Recognition dawns and her eyes open even wider. I pull her to a sitting position and the sheet falls off her chest. She sleeps naked.

I take my hand off her mouth but clamp my other hand around the back of her neck. She smells both musky and sweet, her hair a golden tangle around her face.

"Where's my gun?"

She frowns and her face fills with consciousness inch by inch. She's even more beautiful when she's out of it, but right now I've got bigger things on my mind.

She blinks and rubs her eyes.

"Um, back there. I left it after...."

"You did what?" I want to strangle her.

"Hey, cool your jets, Man. It was hot. I stuck it in my waistband, almost branded myself. I didn't know guns get hot when you shoot them."

"You actually shot someone?" I'm watching a really bad movie, the Marx Brothers meet the Purple Gang, with Sandra Dee playing the lead.

"Those bastards who took my stash."

"Tell me you took the money and got your pills back, too."

She shakes her head. "That gun, I didn't know they were that loud, either. It scared me. I shot until it was empty, then I ran. Everyone in the front room was dancing and drinking and I don't know if they heard...."

"Jesus Christ, Madison."

She frowns. "How do you know my name?"

"I'm a PI. Your father hired me because Kelton and Randall are bad guys, and he was worried about you."

"Daddy. Worried about me. Right."

I shake her a little and watch her hair fly around.

"You shot someone and left my gun there?"

"There won't be any fingerprints, don't worry. And they'd be mine, right? But I wrapped the handle in your shirttail—"

"I want that shirt back, too."

She nods toward a cloth bag on the other side of the room. "Laundry. I was going to wash it and then throw it away."

I drag her out of bed and across the room to empty the bag onto the floor. Underwear, T-shirts, a mini-skirt, and my big seersucker buddy. I pick it up and see the burn mark on the tail. Gunshot residue. Of course, it protected her hand, too.

"I need to get that gun back," I tell her. "Forget fingerprints. The gun was registered, and the cops can trace the serial number back to me."

"Your fingerprints aren't on it, though."

It's like talking to a car when you run out of gas.

"Get dressed," I tell her. "We're going back."

Her hands come up, fingernails slashing at my eyes, and she rakes my forehead before I can block it. I clamp her wrists together and half-carry, half-heave her across the room, forcing her face down into her pillow. Light through the window throws a cold gray stripe across her ass.

I hold her face in the pillow and speak softly into her ear.

"Listen very carefully. You're going to get dressed. The cops have found my gun, they're probably already looking for me, and if they think I killed a guy—"

She mumbles something into the pillow and I pull her face back so she can repeat it.

"Three guys. Those assholes who—"

I shove her face down again.

"If they already think I killed three guys, I've got nothing to lose. You make a sound, I'll break your neck and flush you down the toilet. Understand?"

When she doesn't say anything, I slap her ass and she whimpers.

"Understand?"

"Umm-hmmm."

She finds underwear, another T-shirt and what might be those same cut-offs, dressing without looking at me. When she's ready, I lead her downstairs to my car. I wish I had handcuffs because I'd love to lock her in the trunk until we get back to 12th Street. Fortunately, my Malibu's a two-door, so I stuff her in the back seat.

"I'm going to drive like a bat out of hell," I tell her. "You try anything funny while I'm driving, and they'll scrape us up with a spatula."

She curls up in the seat and looks scared for the first time.

I get off at the nearest exit and I'm still two blocks from the party when I have to stop. Hundreds of people block the street, and they're all looking toward my destination, where red and blue flashes light up the whole area. I turn around and turn on my radio. CKLW, broadcasting from Windsor, Ontario, is playing music, as usual, and I hope for news.

The eastern sky has a slight rim around it, so I decide to dump Maddie at her family's house and let them keep an eye on her. Her car is forty miles away in Ann Arbor. I've been up nearly twenty-four hours and been punched in the head. I need a shower, some aspirin, and a bed.

I pull into Charles Rohr's driveway, wrap my hand in Maddie's hair, and lean on the doorbell. After my second ring, a light comes on.

Rohr wears a bathrobe that probably cost more than my entire closet, and he blinks when he sees us.

"What are you doing here? What is—?"

I swing Maddie into the vestibule.

"Keep her here," I say. "Don't talk to anyone and don't mention that she's here. And don't ask her anything, either. The less you know, the better."

"But—"

"I'll call you," I tell him. "I'll take her off your hands again, but I need to see which way the wind is blowing."

"Don't believe him, Daddy." Maddie sounds about ten years old now. "He's making it all up."

"I haven't said anything I have to make up," I say. "Keep her in her room and don't let her use a phone. Especially that. No telephone."

I go back to my car before he can say anything. It's another half-hour to my apartment and by then CKLW has reported that the police raided a blind pig on 12th and the local residents are demonstrating and refusing to go home. The mayor is calling for assistance.

That's all they say.

I take a shower and fall into bed for a few hours, finally getting to my office around noon. By then, I can see smoke in the sky near Highland Park, and the radio stations are talking about riots spreading out from around Brush Street and John R. The cops are battling thousands of demonstrators and it's getting nasty. The stations don't mention any gunshot victims, so maybe Maddie was bullshitting me. That sounds too easy, though.

Sure enough, around three thirty, my phone rings.

"Richard Lyle, private investigations."

"Hey, Hippie. It's Patterson."

Patterson was head of my precinct before I got canned. He was the one who first told me to cut my hair.

"What's up, Pat? No parking tickets to write?"

"We got an interesting thing here. You know the shit's going down on the West Side, right?"

"I've had the radio on, yeah. Is it as bad as it sounds?"

"Worse. Listen, you own a Smith and Wesson Police Special?"

I take a deep breath and try to sound calm.

"Oh, you've found it then?"

"Found it?"

I take another deep breath.

"It was stolen out of my car last week. Up in Warren. Someone smashed my window and went through my glove compartment while I was following a guy on a case. When I came back, they'd stolen the gun, a few maps, and an umbrella I had in the back seat."

Patterson doesn't say anything for a minute.

"You report it?"

"Yeah, up in Warren. I talked to a cop. Umm, Miller? Mason? Something like that. But if you're asking, you've found it, right?"

"Our guys found it in a raid this morning. That blind pig, as a matter of fact. All five rounds discharged and no fingerprints. We saw a few slugs in the wall of a room off the main space."

"Shit," I say. "Anyone hurt?"

"Not that we know of yet. There's a ton of people in hospitals, but we haven't got any reports from the raid."

"Christ," I say. So Maddie emptied my gun and missed everyone in the room. Maybe. I force myself to breathe more easily.

"I guess that's good news, though, isn't it? Nobody hurt."

"Yeah, looks like. But I saw your name on the registration, thought I'd check with you."

"Sure. Thanks."

He takes another deep breath. "You sure you reported it?"

"Yeah," I say. "Warren. Mason or Miller, I think. Late Tuesday night or Wednesday morning."

I hang up, my hands shaking. *God damn you, Maddie.*

I lock up the office and buy a fifth of Jim Beam and a fifth of Cutty Sark on my way home. I'm tempted to call Maddie at her parents' house, but I don't want to say something over a phone where someone else could be listening in.

By that night, the mayor has called for help and Governor Romney is asking President Johnson to send in the National Guard. The cops have arrested more than a thousand people and they're busing them to Jackson State Penitentiary because the local jails can't handle it.

Tuesday, I'm listening to my radio on the way to my office. CKLW is playing "Light My Fire" by the Doors when the radio goes silent. A minute later, the DJ comes on.

"Okay," he says. "We've been asked by the Detroit Police not to play that song anymore. But they requested this one, so we'll put it on. Lee Hazelwood and Nancy Sinatra. Here you go."

It's "Going to Jackson," talk about a hint. By that night, the fires cover seventy blocks and the firefighters can't get through the demonstrators to put them out. Johnson is still stalling on the National Guard and Romney accuses him of playing politics with a burning city.

For the next two days, I sit at my office without a single person coming in. The smoke fills the sky, and I can smell the burning—near Highland Park, another section on Woodward, the whole freakin' city. The good news is Patterson hasn't called me again. He's probably buried in so much shit he's forgotten about my gun.

Friday, I'm on my way home when "Light My Fire" comes on the radio for the first time in three days. I've heard "Jackson" about two hundred times, and I never liked the song anyway.

I crack a beer and look out my window. The smoke is thinner.

Half an hour later, my phone rings.

"Hey, Man," Maddie says.

"Hey, Babe," I say. She sounds like she worked out what she was going to say, but now she's forgotten it all.

"I guess it's about over. I guess I owe you one, too."

"Maybe."

"Listen, a guy I know, he can get me into the Grande tomorrow night for the SRC. You want, I can get you in, too."

I like the SRC.

"Your dad letting you out?"

"I told him I was calling you, he thought that was okay."

"All right."

Her breath comes through the phone and finally she says what's really on her mind.

"This whole thing was my fault, wasn't it? My phone call?"

"Don't let it turn your head," I say. "But maybe don't mention it to your dad, either."

She breathes again, like she needs practice.

"About seven?"

"Far out."

Saturday, the Quackenbush brothers fill the Grande with their organ and guitar sound, Scott Richardson's voice soaring above them. They're really on tonight, and everyone is letting loose after six days of fire and crazy. The whole town still smells like smoke, and probably will for weeks. What we need is about a month of heavy rain.

When the SRC leave the stage, Maddie looks at me. She's got her hair down tonight, and her jeans are tight and low on her butt. She's still got those silly little sunglasses, too, but they don't bother me now.

"Someone told me both Kenny and Jack are dead."

That's Randall and Kelton. They were holed-up in a garage off Woodward and tried to shoot it out with a tank.

"I heard that, too."

She clears her throat.

"Um, my car's still back in Ann Arbor. Maybe we can go back there after."

"I don't know," I say. "After last week, I'm a little afraid of you."

"No gun, I promise."

"From what I hear, you couldn't hit the broad side of a barn if you were leaning against it," I tell her. "But that's not what I'm afraid of."

The MC5 steps on stage, Wayne Kramer and Sonic Smith tuning their guitars as Rob Tyner leans into the microphone.

"Brothers and sisters, are you feeling all right tonight?"

Eighteen hundred voices yell back. "Yeah!"

Maddie turns to me and in the dim light I think she's blushing.

"Well, last week, you had me naked in bed. That's like half the battle."

That's what I'm afraid of. Tyner turns to the band, then leans into the mic again.

"I can't hear you. Do you feel all right?"

"Yeah! Yeah! Yeah!"

"All right. So right now, it's time to...*kick out the jams, Motherfuckers.*"

The opening riff hits like the tanks on Woodward Avenue. Everybody in Detroit knows the song. Someday, maybe these guys will get a record contract and radio stations all over the country can censor it.

Maddie raises her hands and moves her hips to the music.

"I was thinking, you get naked, too, we're the rest of the way there."

She moves back against me, and I'm not afraid anymore.

DESERT GIRL WAITING

Robb White

Not even my ex haunted my thoughts like she did. I used to think about her in bars, lying on the couch in my office after nightmares kept me away from home, and anywhere I saw a bar of sunlight slash through a dark cloud. My obsession: a twenty-year-old missing girl I never met in life.

Detective Jerry Pruel called me at my office on Mahoning. Another night on the couch, another bleak dawn in grimy Youngstown.

"You still working her?"

Her. Staci Van Dever. Missing college coed.

"What have you got?"

Pruel's a homicide bull in Youngstown PD, close to retirement—he says—but I doubt if he'll ever pull the pin. He likes being murder police. "The sound of some hippie's head cracking beneath my baton makes me happy," he says. Jerry believes in a hard-nosed justice, delivered with boots in some back alley, especially when it comes to those "peace-loving freaks." The only reason cops like Jerry allowed me to drink in their bar is because of my tattoo: *Non Gratus Anum Rodentum*. The tunnel rat's motto: "Not Worth a Rat's Ass." Pruel practically adopted me right there.

Being short with a twenty-three-inch waist was no advantage in sports but ideal for squeezing into narrow tunnels on search-

and-destroy missions.

"What's in that rag this morning that has you looking so glum?"

Pruel had a linebacker's gracefulness despite his bulk. I never heard him approach until I looked over the top of the *Vindicator* and stared into his cop's eyes. Many suspects made the mistake of looking into those washed-out blue eyes, mistaking them for kindness.

"The Tet Offensive is worse. LBJ's doing the backstroke in his Vietnam toilet and he's drowning in turds."

Pruel liked to mock me: "Hey, hey, LBJ, how many kids have you killed today?"

"War's over for me."

Easy to say. Not so easy to believe. The nightmares come, the night sweats.

Someone in the booth behind us snickered. Jerry swung his big head around and glared at them. Turning back to me, he said "punks" like hawking a gob of phlegm from his throat.

"Holbeck's getting out day after tomorrow."

"Christ."

"Thought you'd want to know."

Holbeck wasn't due for release from Youngstown Max until next month. Jerry's contact there said the joint was full of Hell's Angels and a new gang. The recent transfers, all Irish bikers sporting swastikas and shamrocks, were mixing it up with the Angels—stabbings in the chow line and in the yard. I'd never heard of anyone confronting the Angels in prison.

"They must be tough, these new guys."

"Call themselves Aryan Brotherhood or some bullshit. The Angels will make short work of them."

In between bites of his breakfast, Pruel offered scuttlebutt that claimed Holbeck told his cellie he was leaving for Arizona because he wanted to check out "some rare desert cactus." Pruel wouldn't know what *horticulturalist* meant without a *Webster's* handy, but he knew a shit-bird like Holbeck knew as much about the desert flora as the Bolshoi Ballet.

Jerry was getting too little sleep. Mob hits between the Pittsburgh and Youngstown crime families had kept cops busy ever since "Cadillac Charlie" Cavallaro and his son were blown to bits in their garage.

Pruel believed in the war, loved LBJ, hated commies, and despised "longhairs and college punks" protesting the war. Anything less than my full-throated support warranted a lecture. Losing access to a gold mine of information no private eye can get on his own was too big a price.

"Tell me you'll have him under surveillance."

"Keep dreaming, bucko. Cap says we don't have money or manpower for that. If he takes off for Arizona, he won't be Youngstown's problem anymore."

He checked his wristwatch. "Twenty-four hours, he's all yours."

Living next door to a girl who goes missing isn't evidence. Being in proximity to three who go missing isn't coincidence. The new DA, according to Pruel, was a pansy who wouldn't take anything to court that didn't come with eight-by-ten glossies of the killer holding a bloody hatchet.

Holbeck moved around the city like a nomad, never staying in one place long, often beating his landlords out of a month's rent. Staci's parents gave me keys to her place and her car, a '64 Buick Skylark, after the cops dusted for prints, and I spent hours interviewing her friends and classmates—twice as many and twice as long as the cops did—and it had all added up to zilch-point-shit so far.

My hand shook. I spilled coffee bringing the mug to my lips.

"Goddamn it."

Jerry looked at me hard with those hard cop's eyes.

"You okay?"

I ignored the question. "Two former girlfriends claim he beat them black-and-blue."

"Hey, I'd love to see that fucko strapped into the chair down in Lucasville."

Giggling from the booth behind. Jerry whipped his head around again and gave them the benefit of his spiky gray flattop, and the auger stare beneath it that could bore through cement. He looked at each face, one at a time.

"You fairies wanna keep it down?"

One boy said, "What's your bag, man?"

Suppressed snickers from the other two.

"Faggot, I come over there, you'll be sorry."

"Cool it, Dominic," one of his friends said. "He looks like fuzz."

"*Fuzz* is right, punk," Jerry growled. "I've got more fuzz on my testicles than you three have on your baby faces."

No point in telling Detective Pruel to let it go. I waited, sipped coffee.

"C'mon, Donny," the friend in the Pete the Penguin sweatshirt said, "this place is a bummer."

One boy lingered long enough in front of our booth to scowl before moving on.

Pruel had fought at the Chosin Reservoir during the Korean War in brutal six-below-zero conditions. Get him drunk enough, he'll show you the patch he carries in his wallet that says: *One of the Chosin Few*.

The skin beneath his eyes looked bruised. He'd missed spots while shaving. Jerry shaved with a masochistic zeal in defiance against all the hair being sported on men's faces nowadays.

"Makes you feel like a real shit heel."

"What does?"

"You. Going off to war to fight for spoiled trash like that. You risk your life in that shithole jungle while your wife is banging her professor."

"I let it go, my marriage and the war."

Some booby traps you couldn't see coming—pits that opened beneath you as you crawled in the black tunnels, punji sticks sharpened to dagger points fixed at the bottom, tips laced with poison. Like the venomous spiders and snakes they placed in the tunnels. Worst were the buried wires you tripped, wires attached to grenades or firearms. Or opening a letter from home while you're on bivouac that said the woman you thought would love you forever had found "a perfect soulmate."

"Gotta run," he said, slurping the last of his coffee. "Lots of criminals to catch."

I'd pick up the tab and leave the tip. Debt paid.

I graduated in the lower third of my class at Cardinal Mooney. Most of my friends' parents kept copies of *Field & Stream*, *Reader's Digest*, and *Cosmopolitan* on their coffee tables. Some of their dads even displayed *Playboy* to show how "hip" and "cool" they were. I've always been a reader of the odd stuff the magazines don't know about.

You won't find a single magazine like those in my place, but you will see textbooks on abnormal psychology and copies of *Psychology Today*, a recent discovery. Last month's issue featured a new concept in police investigation being explored by Scotland Yard concerning the phenomenon of "serial murder," to use the article's words for it. Certain killers murder out of psychological compulsion, "fantasies." Not like, say, Charlie Starkweather, the "thrill killer." A serial murderer needs to kill in a ritualized way, and he needs to do it *the same way* every time.

Law enforcement in this country, the FBI especially, have no experience with this kind of murderer. The *Vindicator* speculated about reasons the girls might have gone missing, such as "dropping out to join a hippie commune," based on one girl's journal entry. In Staci's case, because police noted her bedside Bible highlighted verses on Satan and the name "Anton LaVey" was penciled next to one verse, she might have been kidnapped by a Satanist cult.

Staci Van Dever didn't run off to join a hippie commune; she wasn't picked up by a bunch of drugged-out youth in a painted

VW bus to go roam the country. She was normal, middle-class Youngstown. The cops grilled her ex-boyfriend mercilessly. Pruel told me the kid had a "nervous breakdown" after fourteen straight hours in interrogation and had to be carried out of the building. Every male she knew—including Staci's father—was asked to take a "lie detector test."

Pruel laughed. Youngstown doesn't have a lie detector, but the cops figured anyone who refused was a suspect. I was convinced they were barking up a wrong tree. Watching through his bedroom window, Darrell Holbeck had monitored Staci's comings and goings. Something about her and those other two girls satisfied whatever dark impulses he carried around inside.

Holbeck was raised by the state until he was thirteen, when an aunt took a chance on him, which lasted all of three weeks; he was a classic social misfit. If my textbooks were on target, he was deeply, psychologically disturbed far beyond using girlfriends as punching bags.

His reference to going out West to view cacti was as phony as his convict sincerity to the parole board. Scotland Yard's expert on criminal behavior said serial murderers often liked to view their kills, often returning to the bodies to relive the excitement. Killers who stalk the same kinds of victims time and time again are acting out deep-rooted fantasies. They like to collect things from victims. These "trophies"—scraps of clothing, hanks of hair, even bits of flesh—remind them of their murders. "Jonathan Elliott," the writer noted, "strangler of five street prostitutes from the Midlands, often masturbated when he felt one of the items from his cache of 'murder memorabilia.'"

I called his parole officer as soon as I left the diner. It would cost me three hundred for him to make the contact with Holbeck before his release.

"Look, none of this better come back on me, dig? Pruel vouched for you, his word's good enough for me. But I ain't gonna get my dick caught in my zipper if this goes kerflooey."

"I'll fall on my sword," I said, using one of old Sister Regis's expressions at Cardinal Mooney High for the "noble Romans" she admired.

"What, me worry?"

He looked blank, reminding me of the retarded kid on the cover of *Mad*.

The bar across from the Southside Boxing Gym was quiet in the mornings and that's why I'd chosen it. Holbeck didn't hesitate when I suggested we stop off for a couple brewskis.

A guy with a Fu-Manchu moustache and blue-tinted round glasses, wearing elephant pants and a silk shirt, was playing a local hustler at the pool table. The hustler wore long sideburns, blue jeans, and a white tee; he kept a pack of Luckies rolled up in his sleeve. The changing times were on display between the two opponents.

I cautioned myself not to lay it on too thick. Cons are hustlers; they don't like to be hustled.

"My cousin didn't mention you were coming for me."

Jimmy Choate was Holbeck's lowlife cousin from Boardman. Choate corresponded from Chillicothe where he was doing time for strongarm robberies. My bribe to Holbeck's parole officer paid for two phony calls: one to Mickey Donafer to warn him away from the prison tomorrow because cops would be waiting to bag him on an open warrant. The other was to Choate to say his cousin's ride after his release from Y-Max was arranged by a former cellmate of Donafer.

"Yeah," I said, "Mickey had him a little problem, see. He had to skip town last night."

"How do you know Mick?"

"We did time in Mansfield."

Holbeck laughed. "That shithole."

"Two years for writing rubber checks," I said. "Donafer rang me up and said he saw a plainclothes hanging out around his apartment, so I came in his place."

I couldn't read Holbeck well enough to see if he bought it.

"I'm surprised."

"Why are you surprised?"

"My cousin Jimmy's picky. No offense, man, but you look more like the type he'd make grow out your hair, wear a dress, and change your name to Mary."

"I'm tougher than I look."

"You must be. Jimmy's a maniac."

Holbeck was my age but looked much older: crow's-feet around the eyes, a jailbird stamp from keeping his head on a swivel in a predatory landscape. His grin was rare and never reached his eyes.

More questions followed, some couched in observations about sports, women ("poontang"), and current events—that is, from a criminal's point of view. All of it a test. The prison grapevine knows more about life outside the walls than the average square john knows from his newspapers and TV.

The big question was still lurking behind the small talk. I added boilermakers to the beers to help the charade along. Holbeck had no trouble handling liquor. He said he'd kept his brain cells fuzzed with pruno inside.

He threw back his third whisky. "Whew, like an angel pissing on my tongue."

"Been awhile I take it, huh?"

"Shitty prison pruno made in the toilet with potato peels rots your guts and brains." He had Pruel's gimlet stare.

He faced the door, kept looking out the plate-glass window.

"That building across the street." His lifted eyebrows asked the question.

"Southside Gym," I replied. "I saw Don Fullmer sparring in there once."

"Coons coming and going through the door like shit through a tin horn. I figure they must be giving away Cadillacs. Whole city's turned into a dinge box."

I tossed a fresh pack of Pall Malls in front of him and lit one of my own. Calculating my next move, I said, "Going to try my luck in California. Steel mills won't hire me since I clocked a foreman at Republic for riding my ass," I told him.

I blew a stream of smoke from both nostrils, kept my face blank.

"LA's got some mighty fine pussy," Holbeck said.

"What I hear, too."

"Blondes on every corner. Blonde downstairs, too, not like these Youngstown gash."

"Know what you mean, man."

The bait dangled in front of us for what seemed a full minute. Something told me not to say another word.

"I hate fuckin' Greyhound buses," Holbeck said. "Full of fat Black mommas and their squalling babies, shitty diapers. What say I ride with you as far as Arizona?"

"You pick up half the gas and meal tabs," I said, "you bought yourself a seat."

There, said it...

The sound of pool balls clicking on the table drew my gaze.

Fu Manchu leaned against the jukebox, popping quarters into the slot. Up to now, all the music had been Johnny Cash and Roy Orbison. The giddy lyrics to "Mony Mony" poured from the speakers. All the music I'd heard in Nam was about sex, drugs, and war. This sounded more like frenzied teenaged lust.

"I can do that," Holbeck said, tossing back the last of his whisky.

My heart, a crazy bongo in my chest, seemed loud enough for him to hear.

Thenk yew, Jesus.

Holbeck wouldn't say where he was staying. We arranged to meet at seven a.m. where I dropped him, the Sunoco station across from Youngstown State.

Holbeck was too cagey to be won over by a few drinks and a

ride to the Land of Fruits and Nuts, as he called it. My car is spotless, an old habit from the Army. I placed some fur magazines around the floorboards and a couple on top of a case of Iron City on the back seat. Bags of banana splits and boxes of lemonheads on the dashboard added to the slovenly effect. An opened carton of Pall Malls lay on the passenger seat. I replaced my cassettes of the Doors and the Byrds with some shitkicker music from the drugstore near Isaly's, across from my apartment. I cued Elvis's "Suspicious Minds" to midway and set it in the eight-track player. Photos of Holbeck's cell told me he wasn't likely to be popular with his cellie, whose neat bunk area and shelving were in stark contrast to Holbeck's debris-strewn side. A convict who fouls his nest is a rare bird. I hoped the props would relax his own suspicious mind.

Mentally, I had a lot to engage with—not least of which was a ripe passenger to be endured for twenty-four hundred miles. When Holbeck showed twenty minutes after seven, he wore the same clothes he'd walked out of prison wearing, and he hadn't shaved. The leathery smell he gave off reminded me of something in my serial-murder article: some serial murderers exude a fierce body odor, causing the author to speculate about certain body chemicals as "madness qualifiers." I imagined Detective Pruel's opinion of this theory, one that the Brit author wouldn't appreciate. "Killers kill," he told me once, "because they're stupid fuckups. Don't give me any of that pissant, college-boy psychology crap like 'Mommy didn't potty-train-me, boo-hoo.'"

Most scumbags brag about their deeds. I knew everything about Staci Van Dever's short life. Somehow, I had to find the right buttons to push to get him to go into that cesspool in his mind where he stored up the memory of her and bring it out into the light.

I had to make someone with the cunning of a Norwegian rat trust me with his life.

***

Three days on the road with a cigar-store Indian. He chain-smoked and stared out the window at the passing scenery while I jawed at him, tried to get him to open up. Nothing worked. Sports, an easy one, you'd think: "The Tigers look good for the pennant again." He fiddled with the radio knobs, laughed at Bible stations and their fire-and-brimstone preachers. Ten minutes later, as we crossed the Ohio River, he said. "I don't watch baseball."

The same went for the Celtics, "Broadway" Joe, and Joe Frazier. *Nada*, zip.

"They say they're going to put a man on the moon next year."

"You believe that horseshit?"

If I tried to prod him, he'd turn up the music. If he didn't like what was playing on the radio, he'd sing along with Elvis on the tape. The only strong reaction I heard from him in five hundred miles was to curse whenever a folk song came on.

"Don't care for Bob Dylan I take it?"

"Stupid, all of it. Who cares about dead sailors at the bottom of the sea?"

Forget politics, too.

"They say Bobby Kennedy's likely to beat Tricky Dick. I hear he's going to be in Los Angeles by the time I arrive."

"I hope he gets a bullet in the head like Martin Lucifer Coon."

His admiration was limited to big-time thieves like armored-car robbers and bank stick-up men. His worldly goods were contained in a sailor's duffel bag he kept between his feet. The first night we stopped outside Durango, Colorado, he took it inside.

"That bag'll be okay in the trunk," I told him.

"It comes inside with me," he mumbled, not looking back.

I'd heard enough teenaged slang hanging around psychedelic bars and hippie crash pads to get a hefty dose of the bad vibrations and body fumes that Holbeck gave off. I believed he packed more than dirty clothing in that bag, too. He took a long gander at the cash in my wallet at the last truck stop. Before we crossed the state line from Gallup, I expected him to make a grab for my money. Letting him rob me was the only strategy I had.

Back on Route 66, Holbeck turned talkative; he got twitchy, rubbed himself, couldn't stop yapping about his past capers, guys he'd done time with, prison scams he'd worked on guards and other cons. Traveling through small towns like Winslow, Two Guns, and Winona on the edge of the Painted Desert brought out something in him. Or else, as I was convinced, there was something waiting for him in the desert. Most people feel themselves shrink in that vast, barren landscape of buttes and cacti. Not Holbeck. His ego expanded. Its harshness spoke to him.

"We need to make a stop," I said.

"You said we'd hit Flagstaff by sundown."

"The air-conditioner filter must be clogged. We'll be sweating like pigs."

The humidity had been brutal when we'd left the motel that morning. The heat was building to another hundred-degree day.

"Fuck me."

"Not many stations between here and the Black Mountains," I said. "I'll get a grease monkey to look at it."

"Shit, piss, fuck."

My real motive was to get a look inside that bag he protected like the crown jewels.

"Ain't nothing between here and the Pacific Ocean but a barbed-wire fence and a lobo wolf," Holbeck whined. "And a buncha drunken Indians."

"Next town we come to. Seligman, about eight miles."

"I guess a cold Co'Cola can't hurt nothing," Holbeck replied, turning chatty again. "Maybe we'll spot some college girls in granny dresses with no bras. Tits bouncing around. Makes me feel all tingly inside."

Despite the half-moons of sweat under my arms and the shirt clinging to my back, hearing him speak of girls for the first time since we left Youngstown made me queasy.

On the outskirts of Seligman, a green Texaco sign loomed into view. I pulled up to an open bay where an exhaust system from a copper Grand Prix lay on the cement, its top blistered and flaked by the sun.

We got out and stretched.

"Betcha your chassis is all rusted to shit and back," the mechanic called out.

All I saw was a human head peeking up from the hydraulic lift's well like a gopher popping up from its burrow.

"Sorry?"

"Your license plate. Ohio. Winter salt ruins the bottoms. Out here, it's sun rot from the top down."

Holbeck turned to me. "You and your new pal have a nice chat. I'm gonna take me a long piss."

He walked inside and said something to the mechanic, who thrust an arm in the direction of the rest room. As soon as he was out of sight, I went around to the passenger side and opened the door. Hunching low, I grabbed his duffel bag and pulled it open.

Musty clothing, which I shoved aside, a deck of nudie playing cards, and a triple pack of Trojans. I felt along the sides until my fingers touched the raw edges of a slit. Sticking my hand inside, I felt fabric.

Women's bras—red, black, and one lacy white. Different cup sizes. The red one was Staci's. Her name was stenciled on the side the way college dorms have you do for the laundry.

I groped along the other side—something hard. The gun, a Smith & Wesson .38.

Revolvers jam like any mechanism, never mind the myth you get six shots with six pulls of the trigger. Pruel always mocked me as "a gunless gumshoe," although he was impressed when I field-stripped his weapon blindfolded on a bar bet. Any tunnel rat could do it. You can jam one, too, by bending the moon clip to prevent the cylinder from opening. With that mechanic's toolbox and one uninterrupted minute, I could bend the ejector rod or mess up the hand and teeth of the cylinder star. But Holbeck could come out of the john any second and catch me rooting in his duffel bag.

Replacing his kit, I shoved the bag back down in the well of the floorboard and set the crumpled cigarette pack behind it exactly as he'd left it before exiting the car. His arrogance kept him from assuming anyone besides himself could have the same awareness of a baseline normal in observation.

I regretted my caution when he left the bathroom five minutes later. We stood around smoking and watching the mechanic tinker with my air conditioning.

"Sorry, man, compressor's all busted," he said, "and we ain't got the replacement for that model."

Holbeck spat a hawker on the pavement and flicked the cigarette stub at the display of motor oil near the pumps.

"*Shee-yit* almighty fuck, let's go," he commanded.

I gave the mechanic a fiver for his trouble, got a "far out, man" for thanks, and we hit the road again. Holbeck's bad temper improved. My hands, wrists, and shoulders ached from non-stop driving. Holbeck hadn't spelled me at the wheel since we crossed the Mississippi.

"Say, you mind we take a short detour?"

After an hour of driving in silence, other than hot air whistling through the vents, his question raised the hackles on my neck.

"How short?"

"A couple, three miles down the highway."

The blue-tinted range of the San Francisco Peaks belied the blast furnace heat we drove through and teased with its crisp mountain air. White-capped Humphrey's Peak mantled in Ponderosa pine contrasted with the tan desert where miners once dug for silver, gambled, and drank whisky. It brought to mind all those cowboy movies I grew up with.

"You'll see a dirt road coming up past a cemetery. Follow it."

"What are we looking for?"

He grinned like the Cheshire Cat. "Something I want to

check out. Pass me a smoke. Never mind. I got a fresh pack in my bag."

I knew he didn't. I knew I was in trouble.

"We ought to stay on schedule—"

"Turn when I tell you to turn."

The gun barrel poking in my ribs was all the persuasion needed.

"Find anything else interesting in my bag, fucker?"

"Interesting, like women's lingerie?"

"Ha, that red one now, a pair of mighty fine Double-Ds went into it, I can tell you. Firm, big dark nipples like pencil erasers."

Fear surged hot bile into my throat.

"See that cattle fence? Cemetery's ahead and a dirt road on the left. Take it."

My mind raced at a good clip until I forced myself to breathe, slow down, *think*.

Deeper into desert terrain colors shifted from dull beige and brown to reds, purples and golds as the sun began dipping in the pale blue sky. The tires kicked up the gritty yellow dust that blew into the car through the vents.

"Close the windows."

"We'll suffocate."

The barrel swiped my ear lobe, drew blood.

A polite request and a gun will always do the trick. I rolled up my window.

"Now keep your trap shut."

I hadn't joined the PD like many returning vets. The tunnels had ruined me. Cops are paramilitary, and if you can't be a team player, you'll stand out like a dog's balls. Fighting a war underground means you're on your own. Every yard you crawl over seems like a hundred yards in that thick blackness. In Cao-Doi, the tunnels are the size of the Carlsbad Caverns. In places along the Ho Chi Minh Trail, you feel like you're stuck in a pipe that's getting narrower the farther you go. I was planning to re-up just before the Cu Chi tunnels near the Mekong Delta, where I got stuck when part of the tunnel collapsed behind me. Three hours later, dizzy from sucking dirt-clogged air into my lungs, I kept my .45 close to my chin, alert to movement behind or ahead. The double tap on my boot sole told me it was a fellow rat. That taught me patience, not to panic.

The gun rested in his lap, the barrel pointed at my stomach. The M1911 was standard issue in Vietnam. That and a short-barreled shotgun went with me into the tunnels.

I drove past the same cacti I'd seen in my cowboy movies: Prickly Pear, Golden Barrel, Organ Pipe, Saguaro. Tumbleweeds banked against desert palm trees. Sweat half-blinded me. I couldn't risk wiping my face. Holbeck faced the windshield; he watched me through slit eyes, as still as a rattler in the broiling landscape outside.

"That shack three hundred yards on the right, aim for it."

A humpbacked gray blob in the heat haze shimmered in the distance and took on a lumpish square shape as we approached; the car bounced over the hard-packed ruts. Darrel's grip on the gun tensed. The track had narrowed and disappeared and left us in a landscape as barren as the Moon's.

"Don't get any ideas," Holbeck warned.

"I'm fresh out."

It could have been some miner's cabin, maybe a settler's. Long abandoned, it had weathered and shrunk over long decades in the sun. No glass over the windows, a ramshackle door leaned off its hinges.

"Park and get out. Leave the keys in the ignition."

I did what he said.

"Try anything funny and I'll gut shoot you."

"I'm not feeling funny, Holbeck."

"That's good, Mister Hot-Shit Private Investigator."

"How long have you known?"

"Before we left town, Ace. My cousin got word to me just as they handed me my bus ticket and the commissary payout. That parole officer sold you out, Boy."

"What now?"

"You still want to know what happened to Miss D-Cup?"

"I can guess."

"Step into that cabin. Slow. Remember there's a gun pointed at your liver."

Light invaded from every slit in the boards. The place had junk and trash in the corners, even graffiti on the walls: *Jamie D. Sucks Cock. Draft Beer Not Students. Mary F. Gives Great Head.* A broken table was the only piece of furniture. Dopers had been here—a smoke-blackened bong lay on its side.

"Cozy," I said.

"Move them boards in that corner."

A scorpion scuttled behind the planking when I did. A shovel with a chipped and rusted blade lay hidden.

"I'm digging my own grave? Fuck you."

"Drag that shovel by the tip and stay ahead of me. I see the blade come off the ground, you get a bullet."

He directed me to an arroyo invisible from the shack's door.

"What now?"

"Your little desert flower is down there."

The footing down the slope was tricky. I made sure the blade clattered over the gravel, even though Holbeck wasn't the jumpy kind. I wanted him to see how obedient I was.

"That crop of rocks yonder. Go round to the other side. Halfway, start digging."

The ground was solid rock, impossible work for a beat-up shovel. I was surprised when the blade went all the way in. Deserts get little rain. When it did, the wash turned into a flash flood and carried a top layer of sandy grit along banks.

In minutes, my clothes were soaked with perspiration. I hadn't drunk water since we left the garage that morning. My hands shook.

Three feet down I hit something soft—a blue tarp.

"Go on, dig her up out of there."

I scooped out muck, twigs, and sand around the perimeter and pulled the tarp free. He'd knotted both ends like a giant Tootsie Roll.

"Stand back," Holbeck ordered.

He slit the tarp lengthwise with his boot knife. I prepared myself for the stench of decomposition. What was left of her lay intact. The black residue of blood and liquified organs had dissolved beneath her. Most of the soft tissue was gone. Two cue-ball-sized sockets where her eyes had been. I recalled the eight-by-ten glossy of Staci in a bouffant and floor-length chiffon dress her mother showed me at the house. Hanks of black hair clung to the skull.

"Pretty, huh?"

"How?"

"Oh, I had me some fun, I can tell you. Took the same highway we did to get here. Made a few extra stops along the way so I could take my time. When we got here, she begged me to kill her. I'd had enough by then. She was startin' to stink up my car."

"My car smells like a body farm because the only bar of soap you ever saw was the one you dropped in the prison shower for the Aryan Brotherhood."

Holbeck's eyes narrowed and the gun rose to level at my forehead.

"Rattlesnake! At your foot!"

He jerked instinctively, spun around too late to recover his aim. I flung myself to the ground and rolled. Slugs whistled past my head, burning a channel of sizzled air past my ear. My left leg was swinging at the back of his knees at the same time he pulled the trigger again. That bullet slammed into the dirt where I had been a moment earlier.

He went down backward. I threw myself on top of him, digging my knees into his chest. His body weight worked against him because of the slope. I had one hand clamped around the wrist of his gun hand so he could do nothing with it.

I leaned over his face and dug my thumb into his eye socket. He dropped the gun and tried to claw my face.

A streetfighter, no training, just brawn and aggression, but he outweighed me by fifty pounds. I clamped my heels into his ribs as though I were a bronc rider. His adrenalin surge almost threw me off. I released his wrist and flattened my body; he battered the back of my head with his fist, but his blows were ineffective. With both thumbs, I gouged his eyes and felt one pop free to dangle on his cheek, held in place by a gristly cord. The other escaped being pulped when he twisted his head and I grazed it, scraping his cheek, and tearing off my thumbnail.

His screams warbled through me. With a great effort, he threw me off. I scooped up the gun and rose in one motion.

I almost shot him in the head there and then. I placed the barrel to his forehead. He urinated in his pants and babbled incoherently. I made him sit up, kept the gun on him while he spat curses at me.

Ordering him to his feet, I watched him stumble blindly, waving his hands in front of him. He tried to find me with his claws for hands, telling me he'd tear my throat out.

We played a hideous game of Blind Man's Bluff in that gulley for long minutes. I kept circling out of his reach; he'd lunge and fall, get up, and attempt to find me again. When he realized the hopelessness of it, he sank to the ground.

"Are you done?"

"I'll kill you, I swear I'll kill you—"

"Listen to me. I'll take you to a hospital if you tell me where the other two girls are."

The desert came alive at dusk with sounds of nocturnal life moving around in the sage and yucca bordering the arroyo. In an hour it would be too dark to see him a few feet away.

"I'll make you...eat your shit...before I kill you."

"You'll need at least one good eye to do that, Holbeck. The hospital—yes or no?"

Groaning, mumbling, words slipped from their moorings in a

rambling monologue that made no sense unless you were inside his brain. Then he motioned to where the girls were buried.

"Show me."

"There's one, the other's behind that tree."

Hurt though he was, his big hands could snap my windpipe. A wounded dog is a dangerous dog.

"Don't react when I touch you," I said. "I'm going to point you in the direction of town. It's about three miles judging from the lights on the horizon. If you get to the highway, someone will take you to the hospital."

He wobbled on his feet.

I stepped around behind him and turned his shoulders toward the desert.

"If you start walking now, you'll make it in an hour."

"You said...you said you'd take me—"

"I lied."

Without another word, he took a step, then another like a toddler learning to walk on his own. In seconds, the desert swallowed him up.

How long he walked, or how far he got, I wouldn't know until the state troopers and Coconino County Sheriff's investigators located him three days later. I stayed at a roadside motel watching daytime talk shows and old cowboy movies before reporting to the Flagstaff police. They didn't believe me at first but Staci's corpse in that filthy tarp in the wash lit a fire under law enforcement, and I found myself being detained as a material witness.

Both bodies of the two other missing girls were recovered where Holbeck had showed me. I gave lengthy reports to a Detective Sergeant Olsen, who grilled me as a suspect more than a witness. Five minutes in his office and I'd seen enough Vietnam memorabilia to know he was a jarhead from the First Marines and had seen action at Chu Lai. That was before the war turned to shit and LBJ was still promising the American people he was going to nail that coonskin to the wall.

"So this rattlesnake just happens to show up at the right time to save your life?"

"Yes, sir."

"Lucky rattlesnake, wouldn't you say?"

"Yes, sir."

"This Holbeck, he was going in the wrong direction from town. What made him go off like that?"

"Don't know, sir."

"Five miles stumbling in the dark, then he collapses. The ME said he must have dragged himself through the scrub another fifty yards. Coyotes pulled his intestines out. Ants ate clear through to his brain."

"Yes, sir. A hard way to go, sir."

"Thing is, Mac, our ME said his face was messed up bad. But I never heard of coyotes or mountain lions devouring a man's eyeballs first. Like gourmands ordering oysters before the entrée, wouldn't you say?"

"What's a gourmand, sir?"

Staci's parents were prepared for me when I arrived. When the air in a room feels charged—something says, "Bad news coming." The mother wept, her father cursed: "By God, I hope he suffered, that evil son of a bitch!"

I sat in their living room admiring the décor, the gleaming black piano Staci once practiced on, the family photos on the wall. A friendly poodle tried to crawl into my lap until Staci's mother chased it off. When the silence became unbearable, I said my goodbyes.

In the parking lot on Mahoning, I sat in my car smoking. I decided to find a bar instead. I wanted to be around people having a good time and listening to the "groovy" music Pruel hated. Night would come to Youngstown no matter what I did or didn't do.

BUILDING SOMETHING BETTER

Andrew Welsh-Huggins

The drive down 15A took me through a town called Rush, which was good for a laugh since these days I was going nowhere fast. Farm fields tall with corn and golden with wheat carpeted the rolling hills as I continued south, marveling at all the green even as I wondered what the hell I'd gotten myself into. Don't get me wrong. The late July countryside was a relief after the monotony of successive overnight stints filling in on security shifts up at Kodak's main campus. And I'd awakened late this morning, realizing that if I spent a single minute more than necessary in the tiny one-bedroom I rented on the second floor of a wood frame off Monroe Avenue in Rochester—with its depressingly empty other side of the bed—there was a good chance someone was going to get hurt. Probably me, but who's counting? It's just that, as much as I was coming to loathe the city, being out in nature like this wasn't exactly in my comfort zone.

A few minutes and several more miles of fields later—some dotted with black-and-white cows and tangy with the smell of manure—I caught sight of a water tower in the distance. Five minutes after that I was inside the village limits of a town named Lima. Crossroads of Western New York State, the sign said. Good to be known for something. I caught a red light at the four corners of downtown. While waiting for it to change I took in a Presbyterian church, a fire station, a pharmacy, a hardware store, and a bunch of other storefronts. Fast forward to winter and you'd have a miniature *It's A Wonderful Life* heavy on dairy farms. I pulled across Main Street and maneuvered my Impala into a space beside the American Hotel. I was considering whether to bring along my .38 just in case when two teenage girls in polka-dot blouses and freshly pressed bellbottoms, ice cream cones in hand, strolled down the sidewalk. They smiled at me. I smiled back. Don't be a fool, I thought, locking the gun in the glove compartment. A bigger fool, I said under my breath as I walked inside.

The hotel restaurant was crowded, most seats taken at the bar and the tables full. I looked around, wondering how I'd find my new client. No need to worry. A man rose from a back table almost immediately and approached.

"Mr. Hollister?"

"Call me Jerry. You're—"

"Brian Morgan. We spoke on the phone. Thanks a lot for making the trip." He gestured at his table and I followed him back, aware as I did that several pairs of eyes tracked my progress across the room.

A waitress stopped by the table right away. I asked for a bottle of Genny Cream to keep the one Morgan was having company. She dropped a menu in front of me and told me to take my time.

"They do a good job here," Morgan said. "Best soup and sandwich in town."

"Good to know," I said, wondering how many other places the small town had.

"Don't take this the wrong way, but you're…younger than I expected."

"Is that a problem?"

"I guess not. Just that I've never seen a private eye before. I mean, a real one, not one of those TV guys."

I nodded. He wasn't the first on my short clientele list to

point out this discrepancy. Like Morgan, most of the men who hired me struggled to hide their disappointment, both at my age and the length of my hair, which currently brushed the collar of my shirt. Hands down, it was the longest of any man occupying space that afternoon in the American Hotel at the crossroads of Western New York State. By contrast, most of my female clients struggled to hide their enthusiasm for the same two factors. Some struggled less effectively than others, as I'd learned the hard way. I thought about boring Morgan with my resume—a long two years in Vietnam, followed by an even longer two years as a Rochester cop—but decided to skip it. Instead, I said what I usually did: "T-V gets most of it wrong."

"Ain't that the truth," he said.

Before I could reply the waitress appeared with my beer. I asked for a burger and fries and let her talk me into a cup of tomato soup. I waited until she walked away again before getting down to business.

"On the phone. You said your wife's missing?"

His face turned serious. "If that's what you call walking out on her husband and son, sure."

"What do you call it?"

"Irresponsibility." He shook his head. "I gave her a good home, provided for her, handed her a generous allowance every week. And this is how she rewards me?"

"Why don't you tell me what happened."

Morgan took a drink of beer and launched into his story. He ran a small but growing insurance firm in Canandaigua, a city about twenty-five miles east perched at the top of a Finger Lake by the same name. He had met Joan—she went by Joanie—when she answered an ad for a secretarial position. She was a good worker with a head for numbers. They got along. One thing led to another. They got married. They bought a house in bucolic Lima. She got pregnant almost right away.

"Is she still your secretary?"

He gave me a funny look. "Of course not. I made her...Well,

she stopped working after the baby was born."

I registered his slip—*I made her*—but didn't pursue it. "I take it something happened between the two of you?"

What happened, Morgan explained, was that the previous fall a couple had purchased the house next door to them. They had a son, Donovan, who went to college in nearby Geneseo. I knew of the small city but told him I wasn't aware of a college there. It wasn't saying much. With my grades I'd been lucky to get out of East High, and you can forget about anything after that. Even the Army intake guy shook his head at my transcript.

"Perfect place for an arts and crafts degree," Morgan said dismissively. "Which is what this guy was getting, apparently. He came home for breaks with a long beard and longer hair, reeking of pot. Total hippie. But for whatever reason he and Joanie took to one another. I'd come home after a hard day, catch them talking in the backyard when she should have been making dinner. Before I knew it, I was finding goddamn Confucius books around the house—full of crap about Eastern Religion. Then she stopped going to church. Said it 'just wasn't her thing.' And then, the way she kept herself. She always dressed nice, you know? Real pretty. But she stopped wearing make-up. Her hair got long, too—almost down to her waist. And no more skirts and blouses for her. It was either jeans and T-shirts or these loose dresses like some kind of peasant would wear. No bra, either—you could see her tits poking out, just like that." He reddened and apologized for the comment.

I waved it off and waited for him to finish the story, though it was obvious where it was going.

Morgan said he came home from work a month ago to an empty house. His wife was gone, and the baby was at a neighbor's. It took no more than a walk next door to confirm with Donavan's parents that he was gone, too. The only thing she left behind was a note. He handed it to me.

I'm sorry. I need more. This wasn't what I signed up for.

"'Wasn't what I signed up for,'" Morgan said bitterly.

"What the hell's that supposed to mean?"

I thought back to his accidental admission earlier, that he'd made her quit her job after the baby. I said, "Do you have a picture of your wife?"

He handed me a snapshot. I took in an attractive blonde, orange band lifting long hair off her forehead, with eyes as blue as the sky I'd driven under on my way here today, and a sprinkling of freckles on her nose. All-American. Girl next door. Pretty as a picture. And also, a good ten years younger than Morgan, whose shortly cropped black hair was already showing some gray at the temples. Even I could figure out she was probably much closer to Donovan Whoever's age than her husband's.

"Donavan's parents found an envelope with a return address in Springlake—just a PO Box," Morgan continued. He explained that the small town was another twenty miles south on 15A. "All they knew is he talked about some farm down there. That he had big plans that didn't involve 'the establishment.' I drove down, looked around, even talked to the sheriff. He told me the hills are lousy with back-to-landers out that way, but he hadn't seen either of them or heard anything about a farm. Said he'd keep an eye out. Nice enough guy but he wasn't real optimistic. Haven't heard a thing to this day. I wasn't sure what to do next. Then a buddy of mine had some business in Rochester and saw your name in the yellow pages."

I asked my next question carefully. "What exactly do you want me to do after I find her?"

"Bring her home, of course."

"What if she doesn't want to come?"

He stared at me as if I'd suggested he write up a combined car and house policy for the Politburo.

"She's got a husband. A baby. A house. Why wouldn't she come back? That's what people do. They take responsibility for themselves and others."

* * *

My lunch came. I handed Morgan my notebook and he scribbled directions to the sheriff's office in Springlake. I ate quickly, the rest of the meal spent listening to Morgan bitch about the country going to hell in a handbasket. Afterward, he handed me fifty bucks as we stood on the stoop of the hotel outside. I could tell by the way his eyes fell on the money he expected a return on his investment. To assuage his concerns, I let slip I'd been a cop for a while after Vietnam and was used to helping solve people's problems.

"Why'd you quit?" he said, suspicion in his eyes.

"Wasn't really my style."

Hollister, what the fuck are you doing?

I'm seeing if this guy is all right.

Not like that you aren't—

I shook my head, told him I'd do my best, and headed for my car. As I drove out of town, I saw the two girls I'd seen earlier, the ones who'd smiled at me, standing behind a low garage at the corner of an alley. They stared as I passed, and it didn't take a private eye to spy the small bottle of booze they struggled too late to hide. I quickly looked inside my glove compartment, then relaxed when I saw my gun was still there. Leave it to me to forget that Bedford Falls turned into Pottersville, I thought, opening it up as I passed the town limits.

The drive to Springlake was more of the same, but now fat nimbus clouds smudged with a touch of gray rolled across the sun like piles of laundry you just can't get clean, diminishing some of the sunny beauty of the day I'd experienced coming down that morning. I turned on the radio but only caught a couple lines of "Puff, the Magic Dragon" on an AM station before static drowned it out.

Lima was a metropolis compared to Springlake, which sat at the bottom of a long hill just below the southern marshes of Conesus and Hemlock, two of the smaller Finger Lakes nestled at the top of the Bristol Hills. I saw the sheriff's office a block south of downtown but detoured first to Porrazzo's, a tavern two doors down. A couple of guys wearing fishing caps and stone faces sat at the far end of the bar in the dimly lit room, smoke signals rising from their cigarettes in adjoining ash trays. I gave them a couple seats' breathing room. A girl who didn't look that much older than Joan Morgan strolled up, eyed me for a second too long, and asked what I wanted. I ordered a Molson and a bag of Fritos.

"Not from around here?" she said, returning with the beer a minute later.

"That obvious?"

"You don't live here and you ain't fishing. Just a guess, but still."

"You guessed right." She had dark hair pulled back in a ponytail and wore a pair of cut-off jeans shorts and a red checkered blouse—and a bra to boot. Her face was pretty, eyes big and brown, but she also had the look of someone who'd seen some shit, and maybe done some of it too. I retrieved a business card, a five-dollar bill, the snapshot of Joan Morgan, and pushed all three toward her.

"A private eye, huh?" she said, reading the card. "Like in the movies?"

"As far from that as you can get." I asked her about Joan and a guy named Donovan.

"Haven't seen her around," she said carefully. "Face like that would stick out."

"How about Donovan?"

She looked about to reply. But then, to my surprise, her hand moved fast across the bar, knocking my beer into my lap.

"Oh, shit, I'm so sorry," she said loudly.

"What the hell?"

"That one's on me—and the next one, too. I'm real sorry, mister. Here, clean yourself up and move on down a bit." She handed me a dish towel and I wiped the beer from my jeans as best I could. I took a seat two stools down, but she tut-tutted and told me to keep going. Finally, crisis averted, she returned as promised with a fresh Molson. I repeated my question about Donovan.

"We get all types down here. Can't say I heard a name like that."

"You sure?"

"Sure as I can be, Mr. Jerry Hollister," she said, dropping her voice as her eyes flicked briefly to the fishermen at the other end of the bar.

"All right then. How about you?"

"How about me what?"

"You know who I am. Who are you?"

"Everybody calls me Katie."

"And why's that?"

"Because that's my name," she said, face as solemn as a Rochester winter sky.

Over at the sheriff's office, a pear-shaped lady with upswept hair eyed my business card as if I'd slapped an invitation to a Students for a Democratic Society rap session in front of her.

"Donovan, you said?"

"That's right. And the girl's name is Joan Morgan. Just wondered if the sheriff might have heard anything."

"He expecting you?"

"Don't think so. I just happened to stop by."

"He's a little busy right now," she said doubtfully. "Might be a while."

"Is that so?" I said, eyes drifting around the empty lobby. But I knew the drill. I'd seen the same lack of cooperation many a day in the eyes of supply clerks in Long Binh Post outside of Saigon. I gave her my biggest smile and said, "Won't be but just a minute."

"Have a seat and I'll see what I can do."

I sat and picked up a year-old copy of *Life* magazine. "Negro Revolt: The Flames Spread," the cover headline read. I set it down and stared at my boots instead. Five minutes passed and then ten, and then the door next to the receptionist's window opened and a man in uniform emerged.

"Mr. Hollister?"

"That's right."

"Sheriff Marks. Why don't you come on back?"

A minute later I was seated in an office down the hall. *Canadice County Sheriff Phil Marks*, the brass plate on the door said. Several plaques of commendation hanging on the wall of the large office confirmed the information, as did the framed photo of him shaking hands with Governor Rockefeller. Marks had thinning hair, a standard-issue trimmed mustache, a bit of middle-aged spread and a skeptical look as he fingered my card.

"Private eye, huh?"

"That's right."

"Don't see a lot of that down here. How's a guy get into a gig like that?"

I thought of the *Life* magazine in the lobby. "Dumb luck," I said, which earned a small laugh. "I was on the job for a little while. Up in Rochester. One thing led to another."

"Mind if I ask what happened?"

"Just wasn't for me."

"Too bad."

"I suppose."

"Listen up, Hollister," the older cop said, grabbing the terrified boy by the arm and dragging him down the alley. "We're not taking any shit, you understand?" He pulled out his baton and raised it high in the air.

"What are you doing?"

"Shut up, if you know what's good for you."

I jumped as if shocked at the sound of wood meeting bone.

"Suit yourself," the sheriff said. "You're here about Joan Morgan, is it?"

I gave him the *Reader's Digest* version of her husband's story, concluding with his account of a long-haired wanna-be farmer named Donovan.

"Yeah," he said when I finished, a frown on his face. "Sounds familiar."

"So, you know him?"

"Not this particular guy. At least I don't think so. But I know the type. What I told Mr. Morgan. We started seeing them more and more, two, maybe three years ago. Hair down to their assholes—that's the guys I'm talking about—stoned half the time, decked out in nothing but tie-dye when they're wearing anything at all. Living in tents or cabins they build themselves back in the hills, raising chickens and shit, driving beater vans down to the lake late at night. Not what we're used to in these parts, you know what I mean."

I nodded, thinking it didn't sound like a half-bad life. I said, "But no sign of this girl?"

"None I could see. We asked around, and I've got my deputies on the lookout. But we're a small force as it is. You don't mind me asking, what's your intent, if you find her?"

"Good question. Her husband wants her back. But she's of age, so he may just have to be satisfied knowing she's safe."

"Safe being a relative word these days."

"Meaning?"

"If she's caught up with a guy like you describe, she's probably getting high half the time and getting balled the other half, pardon my French. Probably not what Mr. Morgan expected when he tied the knot. But unfortunately, it's hard to prove the first one and the second one's not illegal. I'm sorry. I wish there was more I could do. I wish to hell these people would pack up and go someplace else. This used to be a real nice community. But I guess times are changing." He spoke the last words bitterly, as if he were taking the invasion of hemp, long hair, and tie-dye personally.

"I appreciate your time, Sheriff," I said. "I might ask around a little, just to help Mr. Morgan out."

"Be my guest. I hope you find her. Can't imagine how

Morgan's feeling. Hard-working guy and now this. Not the America I grew up in, I can tell you that."

He showed me down the hall, shook my hand and wished me luck. Outside, I crossed the street and leaned against the Impala, digging in my pocket for a pack of cigarettes, trying to decide my next step. It was helpful having the sheriff's blessing to look around, though his own inability to find Donovan or Joan wasn't promising. But this far from my crummy apartment, going door-to-door in a small town seemed like the more appealing option for spending the rest of the day. I lit up a Marlboro, took three long drags, tossed the remainder onto the street and stubbed it out with my boot. I was debating which direction to start walking when I saw a piece of paper tucked under the driver's side windshield wiper that hadn't been there before. I looked up and down the street, retrieved it and read the short note written in a loopy, feminine script.

Scottville Road, third turn on the left after you pass the cobblestone house on the edge of town, then the second right after that. Look for the pheasant. Be careful.

P.S. I'm off at 11.

I read the note again and then tucked it into my right rear pocket, staring at the front door of the bar as I did. I thought of those big, brown eyes, those cut-off jeans shorts and that red-checkered blouse. Next, I thought about the way those eyes had strayed just briefly to the guys at the end of the bar. I considered the number of ambushes I'd heard about in-country that started with a woman's smile in a bar and ended with body parts blown across a market square. I weighed the odds of whether I was being set up. Fifty-fifty, I figured. With nothing better to do, I decided to risk it.

The left turn past the cobblestone house took me onto a narrow, asphalt road barely big enough for two cars. Rows of grape vines climbed the slope to my left, while thick hardwoods marched downhill on the opposite side. I found the second right easily enough, about a mile down, and soon was bumping along a gravel road that wove its way through thicker and thicker woods. I was trying to figure out what the hell Katie had meant about a pheasant when I spied it on a tree as I passed an almost invisible drive—a rough-hewn plank nailed to a tree with a hand-painted picture of a pheasant in full red and brown plumage. "Welcome to Pheasant Farm," the writing below it said. I stopped, backed up and turned down the lane. I made it only thirty feet or so when I ran into a gate blocking my progress. The lock and the chain wrapped tightly around the post looked serious, as did the "Absolutely No Trespassing" sign hanging from it. So much for peace, love, and good karma. I backed up, returned to the gravel road, and drove a hundred yards or so until I found a place to pull off on the side. I thought about the sheriff's dismissal of the situation as nothing more than a bunch of half-naked hippies cluttering up the landscape. Then I remembered the girls sneaking booze back in Lima. I reached for my gun.

Absent the no trespassing sign, I might have tried a head-on approach by walking down the drive. But something about the sign's emphatic warning inspired me to take the scenic route instead. I crept into the woods, brushing away memories of patrols through a different, wilder set of foliage, and set off toward Pheasant Farm. After a few minutes, I arrived at a large limestone outcropping. I peered around the rock and looked down at a clearing in the woods ringed by a couple of trailers, a yurt, and a teepee. It would have looked authentic if this were the High Plains and not Iroquois country, but they don't teach history like they used to. After a minute or so I heard voices. I lowered myself and duck-walked closer, taking refuge behind the wide trunk of a vine-engulfed oak tree.

At first, I didn't see anyone. Then, crossing from the right, someone left the yurt and emerged into view. I wasn't that far away, but no matter what, it was easy to tell her gender because she was naked from the waist up. A moment later a second woman appeared from the opposite direction, also topless, followed closely by a bearded young man, both shirtless and barefoot. The three stopped and chatted a moment. The guy said something that made the girls laugh. Then a change fell over them. They stood up a bit straighter as someone else appeared. A tall man with a scraggly beard, Maharishi Mahesh Yogi style. Not my cup of tea, but I'd always been more of a Stones than a Beatles guy. Bare-chested, bare-footed, and wearing a set of billowy, loose-fitting pants like something out of *The Arabian Nights*. He was holding the hand of a blonde, also topless, but with a more serious look on her face than either of the other girls.

I had little doubt that the bearded guy was Donovan. And there was no question the girl whose hand he held was Joanie Morgan.

The trio—the two girls and the guy—listened respectfully for a few minutes, then nodded and headed out of my view. Donavan and Joan turned the opposite direction and moments later disappeared inside an A-frame on the other side of the clearing.

I sat back and considered my options. It seemed obvious from the evidence at hand that Brian Morgan's worst nightmare had come at least partially true; his sunny wife with magazine-cover looks was prancing around half-naked with the college kid from next door. My first instinct was to stroll into the little settlement and see if I could talk Joan into coming home, or at least let her husband know where she was. It might be ugly, but I would have fulfilled my contract. I stood and prepared to head down when a branch cracked behind me and I heard someone clear his throat. I turned and didn't like what I saw. Standing above me was yet another bearded young man naked from the waist up. But it was the shotgun in his arms, leveled at my chest, that really caught my attention.

"Take out your gun and drop it on the ground. Slowly."

Reluctantly, I did as I was told.

"Now turn around, hands on top of your head, and start

walking. Be careful. There's a bunch of roots along here. Easy to trip on and then you don't know what might happen."

So much for avoiding a trap, I thought, thinking of Katie and those big brown eyes. I followed his instructions and stumbled downhill, toward the compound. A few minutes later we reached the yard. He told me to head for the A-frame I'd seen Donovan and Joanie disappear into.

Inside, the air was thick with the smoke of incense and the smoke from another kind of mind-altering substance. Confirming my suspicion: what looked like several bales of tightly wrapped marijuana were stacked along the side of a far wall. A lot more than was necessary for recreational use, that was for sure. In front of them, the man I made as Donovan sat in a chair of hewn logs that, if I didn't know better, I'd have said was a homemade throne. Beside him stood Joanie, who'd covered her breasts with a shawl and was eying me with a look rapidly darkening, like the clouds on my drive down, from bliss to danger. The guy with the shotgun handed Donovan my gun and explained how he'd caught me snooping in the woods.

"Who are you?" Donovan said.

"A courier. I'm here to pick up a package."

"A package?"

"The one standing next to you."

"And who would that be?"

"Joan Morgan." I turned my attention to her. "Your husband's worried about you."

"My name's Chicory now," she said. "And he can go screw himself."

"Be that as it may, maybe we could have this conversation when there's not a guy with a twelve-gauge behind me. Why don't we take a little ride back to town and discuss our options?"

"I don't think that's going to be possible," Donovan said, glancing at the bales of marijuana. "It's not our way to accept rides from strangers."

"You mean a stranger who might let the wrong people know

about the real reason you're hiding out in the woods down here? I'm trying to imagine the street value of what's sitting there beside you."

Donovan looked ready to say something. But the next person to speak was Joan aka Joanie aka Chicory. "I'm sorry you went to all this trouble for no reason," she said. Looking past me, she said to the man behind me, "Take him down to the love field and handle things there. We'll deal with his car later."

A tense few seconds passed. My head reeled at the turn this had taken. I braced myself for a move, since a trip to the love field didn't sound like one worth going on. But I never got the chance to spring into action. A sound behind us as the door opened. I registered the surprise on Donovan's face as I turned and saw Sheriff Marks, gun drawn.

"Hold it right there," he said. "You're all under arrest."

"What?"

Joan, a new look on her face. One of betrayal.

"Lower the shotgun or I'll shoot," the sheriff said, and that's when everything went to hell. I had no sooner registered the fact that my captor, standing behind me and to the left, had been holding his shotgun by his side, the barrel pointed downward and well out of danger's way, than the sheriff raised his .45 and shot the man in the back. I dove to the side just as the sheriff's gun went off again and an ugly red crater appeared in Donovan's chest. He slumped in his throne as blood streamed onto his billowy pants.

As I stared from the floor in disbelief, the sheriff pointed his gun at me. "Drop your weapon."

"I don't have a weapon. What are you—"

But I got no further as another gunshot rocked the A-frame's interior. I jerked back involuntarily, and then watched as the sheriff staggered, a crater in his own chest, before dropping to his knees. I turned and saw Joan with my gun in her hand, angry eyes pinned on the bloody lawman. But just as quickly the look on her face changed—was it impatience I saw in those blue eyes?—and she bent over the stricken Donovan, who was slipping farther and farther down in his chair as small red bubbles appeared on his lips. I didn't need an invitation. I rolled, grabbed the shotgun from my fallen captor, racked a shell into place, and took a stance as I leveled the barrel at Joan Morgan.

"Drop it."

"He promised," she said in a flat voice.

"I said drop it."

As if in a trance, she lowered the revolver.

"Who promised what?" I said.

Leaning over Donovan, she said something I couldn't make out. I told her to repeat it.

"We were building something better here. He promised he'd help."

"Who did?"

Her reply was to stare at the sheriff bleeding out on the floor, his chest rising and falling rapidly.

"You've ruined everything," she said, and raised the gun in my direction.

For the fourth time inside of two minutes, an explosion filled the inside of the smoky A-frame.

Pheasant Farm might have been a proletarian utopia, but it still had a phone, no doubt courtesy of proceeds from the bales of green stuff whose discovery had nearly sent me to the "love field." I had the operator connect me to the state police. Once the dispatcher figured out that I wasn't pranking her, she said someone would be there as soon as possible. While I waited, I rounded up the rest of the compound's inhabitants at gunpoint. I sent the two girls into the A-frame and told them to stop the bleeding on anyone still breathing and locked the three guys I encountered into a trailer and told them not to try anything funny.

Half an hour after that I was cuffed and sitting in the back of a New York State trooper's Crown Vic as what seemed like a small army of law enforcement descended on Pheasant Farm. Outside, the summer sun started its slow descent over the Bristol Hills. Eventually, a ramrod-straight statie with a lieutenant's patch on his uniform dragged me out of the car and told me to start talking. I did and then demanded a few answers of my own. Eventually this war of words concluded with me cooling my heels in a cell back at the sheriff's station, armed with the knowledge that my shotgun-wielding captor and Joan Morgan had both survived but with serious injuries. The sheriff and Donovan were dead. At ten-thirty that night, a sour man who couldn't have been much taller than my grandmother and who introduced himself as the Canadice County district attorney, informed me of what I'd already guessed. Sheriff Marks had been helping Donovan distribute West Coast weed all across the Finger Lakes. Fortunately, the brains of the operation had survived and could be prosecuted.

"Joan Morgan," I said.

"That's right," the DA said, surprised. "How'd you know?"

"Her husband said she had a head for numbers." Now there was a follow-up call I wasn't looking forward to. "Plus," I continued, "the look on her face when she drilled the sheriff. She wasn't upset that he'd shot her lover."

"What then?"

"Hell hath no fury like a woman whose business partner has just been killed."

It was almost eleven when I finally walked out of the sheriff's office. I was headed to my Impala, ruing the long drive home, when I heard my name called. I turned and saw Katie locking Porrazzo's front door.

"I told you to be careful," she said.

"Indeed, you did."

"Were you?"

"That remains to be seen," I said. "The fishermen. In the bar this afternoon."

"What about them?"

"They were in on it, weren't they? Why you spilled the beer on me, made me move down."

"Busted, marshal. It was the only way to warn you. Them and the sheriff were always tight as ticks."

"Not anymore, they aren't."

"Good riddance, then."

"I'll take your word for it," I said. "Too bad you're closed. I could use a drink right about now."

"Porrazzo's is closed," she said. "But I'm open for business."

I would have put Katie in a mobile home or maybe an apartment in a chopped-up Victorian on the edge of the village. Instead, she had a nice little cottage set close to Conesus Lake, with a great view of the moon floating on the water like a hand-hammered wafer of gold. I admired it from her bed, afterward, as I took a drag of my Marlboro and brushed my hand down her thigh.

"People are saying you used to be a cop."

"Are they?"

"News travels fast around here," Katie said. "Especially after a day like today. So, were you?"

"For a while."

"Why'd you quit?"

Speechless, I stared at the teen's bloody head, and watched my fellow officer's face twist in fury as he turned his back to me and raised the baton for another blow. July 23, 1967. "The Flames Spread."

One year ago today, I realized.

"Don't," I gasped.

"Fuck off," he said. "Were you soft on gooks, too?"

And that was that. Without another word, I grabbed my own baton and brought it crashing down on his head from behind. Once, twice, three times. He never knew what—or who—hit him.

"Please," the Negro teen said as he watched in terror while I beat the cop who'd beaten him.

"Scram," I said, wiping my baton down and turning and walking away.

I said, "It just wasn't for me."

"Like the private stuff better?"

"Always," I said, setting the cigarette into the nightstand ashtray and pulling her back into my arms.

CASE #5 FROM THE FILES OF THE MOON DOG DETECTIVE AGENCY

Mark Thielman

The twisted rings of barbed wire reminded me of Khe Sanh. I hadn't expected to see them in Chicago. August sunlight glinted off the steel edges while the oppressive heat accumulated between the downtown buildings. The heat reminded me of Vietnam. At least I wasn't slipping and sliding on red delta mud. And Charlie wasn't shooting at me. So, on the whole, I still preferred Chi-town to being in-country.

A potential client and I had agreed to meet at his office a few blocks from the International Amphitheater. The 1968 Democratic National Convention would begin there soon. Mayor Daley had ringed the amphitheater with fencing and police. The place was a fortress. I'd overslept and then street closures had slowed me further. I'd humped it *didi mau* to get there on time. I really wanted to land this gig. The rent was due in ten days and I was short. I wore my best T-shirt beneath my jungle jacket. I'd dressed to impress. I had even intended to shave, but oversleeping made me choose between pretty and punctual. The walk had left me sweat-soaked. Good thing I'd chosen punctual. A guy can only be so pretty in a damp T-shirt and fatigue jacket.

The small ground-floor office had practically no furniture. The three suits inside all looked at me when I entered the room. Then they looked at each other. Their eyes expressed their doubts. I didn't let it faze me. I get that a lot. They formed a line, all seated behind the room's single table. I spun a chair around and dropped myself into it on the other side. We faced each other across the table. They'd kept the back door closed but had a window open and a box fan pushing air into the room. The fan made a slight hum, like somebody outside was shaving with an electric razor. I adjusted my chair to get the maximum breeze. I had a T-shirt to dry.

"One of you gentlemen called needing a private investigator," I said.

They looked at one another again. The guy sitting on the right made a slight nod. Now I knew who the boss was. All three had their hair cut short and Brylcreemed flat. They each wore a dark suit, white shirt, and tie. One guy's tie had dots rather than stripes. I guessed that was why he got seated on the left.

"I called you," the liberal said. "We need a man for a special job."

"My mom always said I was special."

The boss frowned.

Middleman started talking. "We need someone who can follow orders. You don't look the type."

"I spent most of sixty-seven following all kinds of orders," I said. "You want someone who can take orders and wear a uniform, swing by the McDonald's. That guy will throw in French fries. You want someone who can get a job done, tell me the gig."

The boss eyeballed me again. The others stared too, but only because he did. I waited, resisting the temptation to blow him a kiss. After a long moment, he shifted his gaze to the man in the middle. The boss gave another quick bob of his head.

"We're with the Democratic Party," Middleman said.

"That explains the hug when I came in."

He ignored me. "The convention starts in five days."

My turn to nod. "My McCarthy button is on my other jacket."

He still ignored me. "Protesters arrive every day. They predict ten thousand of them. Every LBJ-hater in the country with a paper sign and gas money will show up."

"I walk around downtown," I said. "You can see and feel them. The city is on edge."

"Yippies, The Mobe, Black Panthers, Students for a Democratic Society, Mothers for Peace—they are all arriving."

I shouldn't have been surprised that the left-winger knew the names of all the groups.

The boss circled his hand. Clearly, he wanted them to get to the point. We had that in common.

"We don't much care about the protesters," Middleman said. "The police and the National Guard will handle them. But there is a report that the Yippies plan to put LSD into the convention's water supply."

"Damn Youth International Party," the left suit said. "They ain't youth or international. They're just a party. They get off stirring up shit."

"Imagine the field day Nixon's boys would have if they succeed," Middleman added.

"Where did you hear this rumor?" I asked.

"We've got intelligence," Middleman said.

I was skeptical, but I didn't comment. Like I said, I needed the money. "Why me?"

"We checked you out." Middleman ran his finger up and down. "Behind all this flower child crap you wear, you're a patriot. You're honorably discharged. And...." He did the finger thing again, "You look like a hippie. You can infiltrate the enemy."

"And Joe Mannix was busy."

Again, they ignored me. I was getting used to it.

"We need written updates...daily," Lefty said.

"Hard to be undercover if I have to come down here every day to deliver a report."

"We'll give you a PO Box address. Mail 'em," Lefty said.

The suits across the table looked at me. I didn't really like these guys calling a bunch of kids who were using their constitutional rights to stop an undeclared war the enemy. But I didn't want anyone dropping acid without their knowledge. LSD should be a choice. I weighed my options.

The boss reached inside his jacket. His hand returned holding an envelope. He fanned the bills inside. I saw three hundred dollars. He tossed the money on the table and looked at the center suit. The boss wore a small smile, just the tiniest upturn at the corners of his mouth.

"There's a hundred for today and tomorrow. Plus, another C-note for expenses," Middleman said.

I knew a little something about lures. When I was in-country I got stationed at Firebase Bravo. Bulldozers cleared the brush to create a better field of fire for the GIs. The engineers intentionally left a few stands of trees. They wanted the VC to use that cover because we had our weapons pre-sighted for that brush. The money lay on the table. I knew it was a lure. The boss knew I knew it was a lure. The smile told me that he didn't care. Neither did I. I scooped up the envelope and stuffed it into the pocket of my jungle jacket. "I'll mail you something tomorrow."

Walking away, I felt a little dirty. Normally, the Moon Dog Detective Agency works for the people. My last case, I staked out the Liberation Food Bank to see who was painting graffiti on their outside wall mural. I caught the kid. The client paid me in sweet corn and fresh tortillas. As a bonus, they threw in an ounce of reefer because I'd done the job quickly and hadn't hurt the kid, merely scared him into practicing his craft on the Chicago Bank and Trust building instead of the food bank. Cash in hand wasn't something I was used to.

I pointed myself toward my apartment. I wanted to stash this bread before I did something stupid. Along the way, I bought an ounce of Acapulco Gold from D-Ball. I used some of the expense money. I figured that a job like this might require some non-linear thinking. The weed was a tool in my search for the truth. I considered trying some just to help me plan my strategy for this case, but I rejected the idea. I promised my clients that they'd receive my first report the following day. It ought to say something besides, "got stoned." First impressions are important.

In my platoon, there had been another kid from Chicago. A true-blue flag-waver named Ricky. After we were discharged, he kept his hair short and joined the Chi-town PD. He went by 'Richard' these days. I considered phoning him to see if law enforcement had any reports about the Yippies. But the department probably had him busy manning the ramparts. I might play that card if my information needs got a little more specific.

I climbed the stairs to my second-floor apartment. On the landing, the Korean kids who lived next door were playing two-square. They asked me to join them, but I politely declined.

When I'm working I like to carry a few things. I collected a screwdriver, my sunglasses, and a whistle. A flat-head screwdriver makes a handy multi-purpose tool. A knife will accomplish the same, but these were dangerous times to be carrying an obvious weapon. Sunglasses add mystery. People can't tell where I'm looking. They also can't see when I'm stoned. The whistle—well, the VC used them to communicate in the deep jungle. It worked for them. A sharp blast also mimics a traffic cop, a useful tactic if I've got to get somewhere fast.

After collecting my kit, I headed back out, past the kids, and went walking. My path made a wide circle around the International Amphitheater. I'd caught the Beatles there in '66, just before I shipped out. I remembered the inside of the place. Security looked tight. I searched for chinks in the armor. I considered how a Yippie might sneak inside the place. Then, I pointed myself toward Michigan Avenue. I walked up to the Conrad Hilton Hotel. That's where the Dems would be stashing convention delegates. Cops were everywhere, but its perimeter looked easier to penetrate than the convention center. Before I could study the situation any further, I felt the hairs on the back of my neck start to tingle. I didn't turn around. My gut told me that one of Chicago's finest had started eyeballing me. I'd stayed alive for the past year by trusting my instincts. An odd smell carried on the breeze or the snap of a twig might mean approaching VC. Go with my gut, I'd learned. The ounce of Acapulco Gold felt heavy in one pocket. My expense money dragged in another. I knew what conclusion the cop would draw if he searched me. Without looking back, I started walking before he got the idea.

My feet carried me by Saks Fifth and the tony shops along Michigan Avenue. With money in my pocket, it was easy to imagine myself as the capitalist pig I'd been accused of supporting.

I hadn't found a sign announcing the "Future Home of Yippie Secret Headquarters" by the time I reached Lake Shore Park. There, the sun shone, and the water glistened. I felt footsore, so I rested. I considered some non-linear thinking. Again, I resisted. I still didn't have anything to report.

I headed toward Humboldt Park. I knew a Puerto Rican guy who hung out there. He dealt in information. He'd sell the police tips on Latin gang activity, and then resell the tip about a pending raid to the Young Lords. Everybody knew, nobody minded. The gangs would lay low, the police got to run their raid, and no one got hurt.

I found Cha-Cha by the boat house in Humboldt Park. We hooked thumbs in a dap. As we came together, his nostrils flared.

"You're living the high life," Cha-Cha said.

I explained what I wanted, avoiding the implied question.

Cha-Cha pursed his lips and thought. He looked a little like a fish pulled up from the lake. "You give me the weed, I'll get you the information."

"What weed?"

His eyes focused on my pocket. He laughed. "You smell like Grade-A reefer."

If his current gig didn't work out, Cha-Cha could work border crossings for US Customs. I removed the marijuana from my pocket. I let it dangle like a hypnotist's watch. Before Cha-Cha could grab it, I pulled my hand back. "I need the information tomorrow."

He nodded and wrapped his hand around the bag. I didn't let go.

"And you can't tell the Yippies I'm looking."

Cha-Cha's face fell, but he nodded. I released my handhold and the Acapulco Gold disappeared into his jeans. His eyes brightened. "Let me see your forearm."

I pushed up my jacket sleeve.

With a ballpoint pen, Cha-Cha scribbled a number on my skin. "Call me tomorrow, one o'clock. It's a pay phone. If it's busy, wait five minutes and call back."

"A pay phone?"

"Harder for The Man to bug your calls. Don't want to give away what you can sell," Cha-Cha said before turning away.

I watched my weed disappear down Humboldt Drive. I should have stayed longer at Lake Shore Park.

That night I mailed the PO Box a nice postcard of the mastodon skeleton at the Field Museum. On the back I'd written, "Nothing to report."

The next morning, I walked among the crowd of protesters camping at Lincoln Park. Even from blocks away, a guy would have to be in a coma not to sense the growing excitement. Music blared. Organizers led classes in self-defense, first aid, and snake dancing. Police watched everything. I listened to some Hendrix blasting over tinny speakers, got some spirit beads from a shaman, but learned nothing about LSD in the water.

"Took some doing, but I got your info," Cha-Cha said when I called him.

I heard street noise behind him. "Give," I said.

"I called a guy who put me in touch with another guy. He said he rented the space for the Yippies."

"And you believed him?"

"Imagine you're a capitalist tool landlord," Cha-Cha said.

"Spare me the Marx and Lenin, just get to the point."

"I am. Imagine you've got a business space to rent. You want to make money. Would you rent to Abbie Hoffman and the Yippies?"

"Not likely," I said.

"Course not. Police raids, phones bugged, tear gas stinking up your place. Every day you rent to them is a day you risk getting your property busted up. So, this Butch-waxed crew-cut guy claims to be a businessman. He rents it. Landlord happily hands him the keys. He looks like he'll fly the flag and always pay the rent on time. Then I hear the straitlaced guy slides the keys over to Yippies. Even if the landlord starts trying to evict them today, he doesn't get a court date till after the Democratic Convention is over."

I admired the ingenuity. "Hippies going undercover. What'd this guy look like?"

Cha-Cha exhaled a burst of air. "I told you, short hair and straight looking. He looked like The Man."

"This is Chicago. The city is full of people like that. Anything else?"

I could practically hear Cha-Cha shaking his head over the phone. "In this business, you don't spend much time studying faces. Makes people think you're a snitch."

"But you are, Cha-Cha."

"I'm a broker. Snitch is an easy way to end up in Lake Michigan instead of beside it."

"Got anything else about the guy to broker?"

"He talked funny," Cha-Cha said.

"Accent? Like he was from the South, New York, France?"

"No man, just *funny* funny."

I gave up trying. "Where's this hideout?"

Cha-Cha gave me the address. I wrote it down on my other forearm, although I didn't need to. I'd walked by the address the previous day.

The small storefront looked out on Michigan Avenue. The Yippie headquarters would be the hole in the center of a capitalist doughnut. On one side sat Saks department store and on the other a boutique jeweler. It wasn't a bad spot for the hippie underground, I thought. The cops wouldn't immediately think to look here; instead, they'd focus surveillance on the poorer neighborhoods in town, looking for some peacenik hooch playing Country Joe music. In my mind I ticked off the reasons why this location made sense. The Conrad Hilton stood close by. Northwestern Memorial Hospital lay just east down Huron in case the confrontations with the police really got out of hand. Finally, Lake Shore Park, a convenient rally point for protesters, sat just on the other side of the hospital.

I took up a position across Michigan Avenue, which allowed me to do recon on the store front. The owner had the rolling grates pulled down to protect his property. No one came or went. The store remained dark. About forty-five minutes in, my neck started to tingle. I couldn't really stay any longer. Michigan Avenue traffic was sparse, and every shopkeeper stood on high alert for trouble. They watched me with suspicion. My spirit beads did nothing to alleviate their concern. I looked around. Another guy watched the place. He tried to seem casual, but he failed. He looked a little like Jethro from the *Beverly Hillbillies*. I assumed the merchants association had hired him to protect the businesses. I flashed him a peace sign and walked slowly west on Huron. Then, I ducked down the alley and went to the service entrance for the Yippie office.

I pounded on the door with my fist. "Delivery," I used my firebase voice, the one loud enough to be heard over artillery. No one answered. I jimmied the door with the screwdriver. After the door popped, I wiped the screwdriver clean and dropped it in an empty trash bin. If I got caught here, I didn't want to have an obvious weapon. Cops were on edge. The guns might come out quickly.

That didn't mean I wasn't packing. In the small of my back, I carried a newspaper. I rolled it up tight, real tight. At home, I keep a spindle and crank apparatus for just this purpose. Wound tight enough, a newspaper can hit like an iron bar. But the prosecution has a lot more trouble persuading the jury you've got a deadly weapon when they use the same tool to housetrain a puppy.

The metal grates covering the windows threw jagged shadows across the two desks in the small space. The light was sketchy, especially along the walls of the store. I could see well enough to know that I'd found what I was looking for. I've been in a few command centers for anti-war protests since returning stateside, but never one aimed at disrupting a national political convention by poisoning the water supply. Usually, they operate out of some guy's garage. If I ordered a headquarters from the Sears catalog, this is what it would look like.

In the corner was a stack of protest signs. Another bundle of signs lay against the far wall. Standard slogans, "Make Love Not War" and "Give Peace a Chance" shared space with "Bread for the Workers." These Yippies were pro-peace, pro-food, pro-love. Against the same wall as the bread sign, they also had a sledge-hammer. I guess they were pro-busting stuff, too. I opened several empty desk drawers before hitting the jackpot. The top drawer of the second desk held a .38 revolver and two small pieces of blotter paper. Either one of the Yippies needed protection for their fountain pen, or I'd just found the proof my clients were looking for.

I picked up the gun, holding it with my shirt to keep it free of my fingerprints. The serial number had been filed off. I put it back. I didn't like the idea of leaving a loaded gun here, but I didn't want to be caught with it. If the Yippies found their gun missing, they'd know someone had been here. The blotter acid was a different story. I took it with me. That was my smoking gun.

I made a last pass through the office to confirm I hadn't missed anything. The Yippies didn't look committed to a long stay, just like Cha-Cha had said. I figured they'd split as soon as the convention finished. The place still smelled as clean as a stateside barrack. I slipped out the back door and reset the lock.

Back home, the Korean kids were playing some new game on the landing. This one involved the boy throwing the ball at his sister's head. I smelled their dinner cooking. From inside, mama-san screeched at her children. I assumed she was telling the boy to quit trying to decapitate his sister. I only know a little Vietnamese, enough to order a beer. Angry Korean didn't sound like any word I recognized.

I hurried past the kids and unlocked my door. Inside, my phone rang. I grabbed the receiver. Before I could say hello, the earpiece exploded.

"What kind of bullthit report is thith?"

"Hello," I said. "Who's this?"

"This is the idiot who paid you cash for results. I expect better than a bullthit postcard."

Or at least that's what I surmised the boss said. He was so angry he was spitting. Apparently, when he gets worked up, he drops his esses.

"I'm hoping to have better info by this afternoon," I said.

"Deliver your report here tomorrow. If you can't do better than thith, your ath ith fired."

"How about I go talk to these guys? I've got connections in the counterculture. Maybe I can persuade them—"

"No!" the boss said. "You got paid to do a job. Do it. Be here, noon tomorrow." The phone disconnected.

I explained to the dial tone three cogent reasons why my intervention was in everyone's best interest. Satisfied that I had won the phone company over to my way of thinking, I hung up.

Pulling out my Smith Corona, I pecked out a two-page report detailing my efforts. Then I folded it like a paper football and dropped it into an envelope.

I was nearly ready for tomorrow's meeting. From my wallet, I pulled the two pieces of blotter acid I'd recovered from the Yippies' headquarters. I looked at them. My professional ethics dictated that I guarantee their authenticity. I thought about the reefer I'd had to give up getting a lead on this case. In a way, I reasoned, the suits owed me for the expense. Persuaded, I dropped one piece of blotter paper on my tongue. The second one I put into the envelope. Then, I dropped the needle on Jefferson Airplane's *Surrealistic Pillow* and settled myself on the bed.

It didn't take long. Soon the patterns on the walls began to shift and move. They flowed like a lava lamp, little blobs of color suspended in space. I felt myself transported back to Southeast Asia. I wasn't slogging beside rice paddies on patrol. Instead, I was hanging out in Bangkok on R & R. Delicious smells emanated from the food stalls. Some of the buildings had jungle snakes on display in cages. They hissed like I remembered, only the sound wasn't threatening. Instead, angels sang in my ears. I'd never had a better leave.

When my mind returned to my room, my front door stood open. Outside, the neighbor kids still played. The mama-san's cooking aromas wafted into my room. The smell of rice lingered in my nose. Sitting on the bed, I drank some water and thought about my LSD trip. The drug opened parts of my brain I didn't think existed. I had become more aware of smells and sounds.

Maybe it came from my trip to a different astral plane. Maybe I paid attention to my senses. Either way, suddenly, the answer became obvious.

I woke up early the next morning, my mind clear of all the static that usually interferes with the clear reception of my thoughts. I knew what I needed to do.

I changed a dollar of my expense money for a handful of dimes and stood at the payphone. The desk officer at the PD disconnected me twice before I finally got through to Richard. He sounded harried, like he'd been going too long without enough sleep. Still, he listened while I told him a few things. He promised to talk to the detectives. We agreed to meet later.

A crowd of people filled the secondhand clothing store where I stopped. Not everyone had brought enough threads to Chicago. The racks of denim and work shirts were pretty picked over. The executive collection, however, still had lots to choose from. I found a blue blazer, white shirt, a tie with dots, and a porkpie hat.

I held the tie up to my T-shirt while I paid. "Too liberal?"

The cashier looked at me like I had become a white rabbit. Wearing my Army khakis and this getup, I looked and felt positively Brooks Brothers. I piled my hair up under the porkpie.

Next, I stopped to see D-Ball. At first, he was reluctant to make eye contact. He didn't recognize me. Even when he did, he didn't relax. Likely, he thought it would hurt his business to be seen associating with a guy dressed like this. But D-Ball took my money. Suburban dwellers have vices too. They just don't get arrested for them as often.

I looped around the International Amphitheater. Workers busied themselves hanging bunting and Humphrey signs. There weren't enough balloons in Chicago to mask the barbed wire. But everyone was polite to a respectable citizen like me. The cops didn't look twice. One even offered to give me directions.

I made the short trek to the meeting spot. Before going in, I circled the block to see if anything had changed since my last visit. I paused at the back door, and then came around to the front. The same three guys were there, still in their same seats, this time in shirt sleeves. They still had the box fan going, still making its low hum. Everybody had cigarettes burning. Tendrils of smoke rose from their ashtrays until the fan's jet stream caught them and they disappeared.

Lefty glanced up. "We're closed, sir,"

"Too bad. I thought we'd be friends since we got matching ties." As I spoke, I took off my hat and shook out my hair. I slipped off the blazer and hung it on a coat hook, then fished an envelope from the inner pocket.

"Oh, it's you," he said.

All three looked up with newfound recognition.

I freed my neck from the tie, dropping it in the trash. Finally, I felt like I could breathe.

Boss checked his watch.

"We weren't sure you'd show," Middleman said.

"You guys paid for a job. I'm here to deliver." I patted the envelope with the palm of my hand.

"You got it?" Middleman asked.

I nodded, tapping the envelope again before taking a seat on my side of the table. "I got the location of the Yippie headquarters. I inventoried the office's contents. I even know when the Yippies will be there."

Lefty and Middleman looked at each other and smiled. They turned to the boss.

"When they gonna thow?" he asked, still trading his S in on a later model.

"Never," I said.

All three men stared at me. Middleman stabbed at me with an index finger. "Stop being a wiseacre."

I held my hands up, signaling surrender. "Never kid a client. It's bad for the professional reputation. I got the location. I found a gun, some acid, and a big sledgehammer and protest signs. The place looks like a set for a hippie movie. Chicago police will have no doubt that leftist agitators used this office for their looting and rioting."

Lefty started nodding.

"You know what I didn't see?"

Middleman shrugged his shoulders. The boss started to scowl.

"Scraps of paper, bits of wood. All those protest signs made with no trash. The bin in the alley was empty. Someone created signs someplace else and left them there to be found. Then I started using my other senses. I didn't smell marijuana smoke or old food inside. The place was spotless. I got hippies sleeping in Grant Park and nobody is using this office as their hooch? It don't make sense."

The boss's upper lip curled like it had been snagged with a hook.

"You know what else don't make sense," I continued before they could answer. "Why real Democrats wouldn't want the protesters to stand down. Humphrey don't want riots during his convention. When I offered to talk to the Yippies, you ordered me not to. So, who benefits from a riot? Jewel thieves maybe. The kinda people who'd bust through one wall to clean out a jeweler and another wall to hit the Saks department store."

The boss surprised me. He leaned back in his chair. He smiled. Or came as close as he ever could. He made the circle gesture with his hand.

"Police will be busy on the streets. You three got time for your crimes. And afterward, a report from a private investigator gets mailed to the PD identifying a radical headquarters. Yippies take the blame. Incidentally, I thought the 'Bread for the Workers' sign was a nice touch. Tells the cops what they plan to do with the money."

The boss nodded. "My idea."

"You're careful to pick words without S sounds," I said. "Hides your lisp. At least until you get mad. Then you talk kinda funny, funny."

The boss sneered. "You peath of thit."

"Did you hire that big lug to stake out the place? Probably got my picture there."

"Haven't developed the film yet," said the boss. "A win/win. If we got your front, you get blamed. If we got your back, we got more proof that hippies were in the building. What are you going to do?"

I could see in his eyes that he knew I could never use Cha-Cha as a witness. His information is golden on the streets but worthless in a court of law. I could never prove these guys were there.

They had me. If I went to the police about this, I was more likely to get arrested than they were.

I nodded in defeat. "It does explain why we couldn't meet inside the amphitheater. I asked at the gate. No one knows you."

"What are you going to do?" the boss asked again. He practically laughed when he asked.

I stood and handed him the envelope. "I'm going to deliver my report. It says that I found no evidence that the Yippies had any connection to the address on Michigan Avenue."

He wadded up the envelope and threw it on the floor. "Delivered."

"Then I'm going to keep your money. You paid for two days, you got two days." I turned toward the door, took a step, and looked back. "Keep the coat and tie. I paid for them out of the expense money." I held up my fingers. "Peace."

I walked outside. Just down the street, I found a hot dog cart. I bought a Chicago dog with everything and a Pepsi. I munched on the pickle spear. The vender and I were discussing the weather when the police hit the front door. A few minutes later, I saw Lefty, Middleman and the Boss led away in handcuffs.

I finished my hot dog and waved at a patrolman. He headed my way.

"What did you find, Richard?"

"Just what my anonymous tip said. We located LSD hidden in a blazer pocket, inside the lining on a necktie and in an envelope on the floor. The one guy, talks with a lisp, tried to hide the stuff by wadding it up. He'll catch an extra charge for tampering with evidence."

"They say anything?"

Richard shook his head. "Just the usual stuff. Innocent. Set up. Not my drugs. If they were innocent, why do you suppose they tried to run out the back when we came in the front."

I shrugged. "Dunno."

"Funny thing," Richard said. "The back door was wedged shut with newspapers rolled up as tight as a steel rod."

I didn't say anything, just looked toward the amphitheater. "Guys like that, based here. Think what they could do if they slipped their LSD to some of the convention delegates."

Richard nodded. "That's exactly what the narcotics detectives were saying. I'll probably get a commendation out of this."

"You deserve it," I said. "It's good police work."

Richard shook my hand. "If I can help you sometime, I owe you."

"See if you can get them convicted before the election," I said. "They aren't the kind of guys who need to vote."

HEIR APPARENT

Neil S. Plakcy

"Mr. Clay, you have to help me. I've been to three other private investigators and none of them will work for a faggot."

The man across from me was in his fifties and bore a striking resemblance to Liberace, from the wavy brown hair plastered in place with hair spray to the spangly jacket and the multiple rings on his fingers.

My office was a single room above Mr. Ho's, a Chinese restaurant on Washington Avenue. The window unit air conditioner behind me had only one setting—frigid—but it was that or open up to the Miami Beach heat and humidity.

"Why do you care if this boy is cheating on you, anyway?" I asked. "Haven't you heard? This is the swinging sixties, the era of free love. There's no reason for two men to settle down the way the straights do."

"But I love him."

"Oh, God."

I had finished my two years of internship as a private eye a few months before, and after a difference of opinion with my employer—he discovered that I liked to fuck men—he fired me and I put up my own shingle.

Work had been slow to come, and I made up the difference as a bouncer in a bar a few blocks from my office. I'd been a Master-at-Arms in the Navy, so I had the build, the experience and the temperament to keep drunks in line.

The thought of working for Leonard Fitts put the wind up me. He was just the kind of guy the straights pegged as a homosexual, and that made it more difficult for guys like me. But I needed the work, so I sighed and said, “Give me his name and everything you know about him. And a hundred-dollar retainer.”

He handed me a page of pink notepaper that smelled like a whore’s boudoir. The young man’s name was Efrain Perez Duarte, he was twenty-two and lived in an apartment about a dozen blocks south of my office.

Gay men tended to cluster on Miami Beach, in the cheaper apartments south of Fifth Street, mixed in with Jewish retirees from the Northeast. The wealthier ones, like my client, lived farther north, in old Spanish-style houses on large lots, where they sponsored pool parties for the younger, cute set.

Sadly, I didn’t fit in with either group. At twenty-eight I was too old to be someone’s plaything. I had a square jaw and my nose had been broken while I was in the Navy, and I was built like a brick shithouse, tough and muscular. I ran along the beach and boxed at a gym south of Fifth Street.

I lived only a few blocks from Efrain Perez Duarte, but that was where the resemblance stopped. I had my own place, a studio apartment with a built-in Art Deco bar, while he lived with a couple of other boys in a rooming house.

“What do you want me to do?” I asked Fitts. “Take pictures of him with whoever he’s cheating with?”

Fitts shuddered. “I’d rather be proved wrong, but yes, photographs will do.”

He handed me a check for the hundred bucks, and as soon as he left my office, I walked down the street and around the corner to my bank, where I cashed it. You can never be too careful with clients.

It was a hot, sunny day in mid-September, and the palm trees dripped with moisture from the morning’s rain. The pavement was already dry, but occasional puddles bounced sunlight into my eyes. Long-haired boys in tie-dyed T-shirts held hands with girls in miniskirts whose arms clattered with bangle bracelets. Frankie Valli sang "Can't Take My Eyes Off You" from speakers above the record store on the corner.

I retrieved my car, a 1958 lime-green Chevrolet Bel Air, from its parking place in the alley behind Mr. Ho's and cruised south to Efrain's neighborhood, passing the broad open spaces of Flamingo Park, where I occasionally joined pick-up basketball games. The streets were lined with two- and three-story 1930s apartment buildings, a collection of Art Deco jewels someone had forgotten to polish.

I crossed Fifth Street, passing the gym where I boxed, and after the broad avenue the neighborhood changed. These small hotels and apartment buildings primarily catered to elderly Jews from the Northeast. Many of them sat out in front of their buildings in lawn chairs, while others hiked over to the broad expanse of sand that fronted the Atlantic to do the same thing. Some clustered around wrought-iron tables on terrazzo terraces to play mahjong, bridge, or canasta.

Tinny transistor radios played songs in Yiddish I couldn't understand while the sun beat down mercilessly. The air smelled of automobile exhaust and salt water, but to these retirees it must have seemed like heaven.

A half-block away from Efrain's building, a hotel had gone out of business and had its windows boarded up. I cruised around for a while, getting the lay of the land, then had to hustle to get to the job that paid my bills—managing drunks at the Cockpit.

You had to know the Cockpit was there to find it. A single-story building on 32nd Avenue, it sat right along the line between Miami and its western neighbor, Coral Gables. The Miami cops rarely made it to the farthest border of the city, and the officers of the City Beautiful pretended their realm ended a block before it—unless either of them was looking for the chance to make some headlines by arresting a bunch of fags with their cocks out.

There was no name outside the building, only a drawing of a single-engine airplane over a darkened window. A casual drinker might have been fooled into thinking it was somehow connected with the airport, just down the street. That is, until you walked in.

A horseshoe-shaped bar filled the center, with an exclusively male clientele on the barstools. Booths lined the side walls for a bit more privacy. It was usually a quiet crowd, unless two queens went at it over the attentions of a young man, or one of the older regulars had a couple too many beers and began yelling every homosexual slur he'd heard in his life.

I checked ID at the door and handled the extreme cases. My years in the Navy had taught me how to handle sloppy drunks, big men who'd received Dear John letters, and most garden-variety violent situations. I could disarm men with knives, talk suicides off the ledge (usually metaphorically), and with one look intimidate most men.

It wasn't a bathhouse—there was a perfectly good one on Miami Beach. But men being men, they still got up to antics in the john, or by playing footsie in the booths. As long as they didn't disturb the peace, I left them to their business. Many of them wore wedding rings and the sad, faded look of office workers trapped in lives not of their choosing. Who was I to complain if they got a little nookie?

I was offered my share, despite my crooked nose, by those who appreciated the muscles in my arms or the bulge in my pants, but I didn't want to soil my own nest. A guy who was interested in me had to wait until the end of my shift and then follow me back to the Beach or, in rare cases, down to Peacock Park in Coconut Grove, where the occasional grope in the darkness took place.

On this night, the sound of Spanish filled one corner of the Cockpit. It wasn't that unfamiliar; after Castro took over Cuba in 1959, the wealthy Cubans fled to Miami. This group were all in their forties, old enough to have had the prime of their lives destroyed by a cigar-smoking farmer's son.

I had picked up some Spanish during a stint at Subic Bay, and I'd been polishing it at the gym, where most of the men I boxed with spoke that language. I could understand enough of what the men in the corner were saying to know they were commiserating about appropriated sugar cane plantations, stolen mansions and frozen bank accounts.

One of the men caught my eye. He was a couple of years older than I, slim and darkly handsome, wearing a well-tailored suit and a sharp hat. My grandmother used to say, "A man without a hat is like a lamp without a shade," and there's something about me that's a sucker for a gent in a topper.

Of course, there was nothing either of us could do about it—I was at work and so, apparently, was he, and though we traded a few hungry glances, he left with his fellows around eleven, and I stayed at the Cockpit until my shift was over at two.

The next morning, I staked out a place on the front patio of the shuttered hotel across from Efrain's rooming house. I set myself up with my own folding chair, a light Indian cotton shirt over Bermuda shorts, with a porkpie hat to shield my dome, and my camera in a satchel at my feet.

I was young for the neighborhood, but by hunching over I didn't attract any attention among the early risers who grab prime positions in folding lawn chairs on patios and porches, and often on the beach as well. When the sun goes down, they retreat to their buildings for bridge, canasta, and poker, and turn in early.

On my way home from Subic Bay, I'd stopped over at an Army base in Garmisch-Partenkirchen for a few days of leave so I could learn to ski. What I discovered quickly was that my face burned fast in the alpine sun, so when I moved to Miami Beach, I started using Piz Buin sun crème to protect my skin.

I dabbed some cream on my nose and lower arms and sat there for two hours before Efrain emerged from his building in snazzy white cotton shorts and a white T-shirt with a large multicolored peace sign. He wore dark-green flip-flops and carried a beach towel. He was accompanied by a friend dressed similarly.

I knew exactly where they were going, and I didn't bother to follow them. Instead, I drove up to Twenty-First Street, parked, and walked over toward the beach. I was sitting in my lounge chair once again when Efrain and his friend approached, heading for the section of the beach that was most frequented by men of our kind.

It was already crowded with men of all shapes and sizes. Wizened old men with wrinkled arms lay on towels beside overweight guys in bikini bathing suits. Sprinkled between them were young men like Efrain and his friend, with bronzed skin and flat stomachs. It was a feast for the eyes.

The two stripped down to bikini suits, laid out their towels, and sunbathed for nearly two hours. They both had dark enough skin that sun crème was not necessary, and the glint off their tanned flesh was enough to make a grown man's mouth water. Or maybe it was the glow of a gold chain around Efrain's neck, with some kind of love token hanging from it.

A few minutes before twelve, Efrain stood up, dressed, and bid his friend goodbye, accompanied by *besos* on each cheek.

I watched him come toward me, holding my breath that he hadn't marked me. But instead, he walked straight past me, and eventually I picked up my chair and followed him down to Lincoln Road, the main thoroughfare for Miami Beach. He walked into a tall office building, but I didn't want to jump into the elevator with him.

Instead, I stood in the lobby and watched the arrow over the elevator swoop in its circular orbit until it stopped on the twelfth floor. Then I walked over to the building's directory and scoped out those on twelve.

There were only two offices listed. Campo Real and Bernstein Real Estate. Since I doubted Efrain was in the market for property, that left his destination as Campo Real, which translated as Royal Field. As Cuba was a land of sugar plantations, I had to assume that was the name of a property or a trading company.

I stationed myself outside at a café on Lincoln Road with a big glass of iced tea and waited.

I could only stretch the tea out for so long, though, and Efrain was still inside the office building an hour later. When the Cuban waitress came over to present my check, I asked her in Spanish, "Do you know the term Campo Real?"

She shrugged. "Is name for many companies," she answered in English.

"Cuban?

"Was a big property near Cienfuegos," she said. "They say Batista owned it once, but who knows."

She took my dollar and I told her to keep the change. Cienfuegos. City of a Hundred Fires. The paperwork Leonard Fitts had given me said that Efrain was born there. I had asked Leonard if Efrain worked and he said something vague about the boy having family money. I doubted that; I would have bet you that hundred-dollar retainer that Leonard was supporting him.

Was Campo Real the source of the "family money"?

One of the mantras I'd learned as a Master-at-Arms was "where there's smoke there's fire." A cliché, sure, but usually when we investigated a situation involving sailors, it held true. Men who acted shiftily had something to hide.

I knew I did. When I joined the Navy, I had no idea I was a homosexual. I grew up on Maryland's Eastern Shore, and even though big cities were close, they were a world away. We didn't even have a television until I graduated from high school and started working at the chicken processing plant nearby and bought my parents a small black-and-white set for Christmas.

My body knew a long time before I did. As soon as I hit puberty, I became acutely aware of the young men growing up around me. They were all Christian and god-fearing as I was, so there was no playing around. We were taught that sex was reserved for marriage, and that anything other than the missionary position was immoral and unethical.

It wasn't until I was in boot camp, surrounded by young, horny guys away from home, family and girlfriends, that I heard my first fag jokes and came to understand what they meant. But it was still a long time before I became what my supervisors would call a practicing homosexual.

I got up to stretch my legs, walking in short circuits around Lincoln Road, watching the door of the office building. I heard snatches of news from transistor radios carried by beachgoers—fresh battles and more deaths in Vietnam, an upcoming concert by Jim Morrison and the Doors, a health update on the astronauts who had walked on the moon.

That passed another hour. Was he still inside? Had I missed him? I started to get nervous around three o'clock. I didn't know what to do. Stay where I was? Head up to the twelfth floor and see if I could find him?

I had been on long stakeouts before, when I was still an apprentice, but I always had my boss to check in with and ask questions of. Now I was on my own.

My instinct told me he was still inside, though I didn't know why. It was doubtful he was working there; even in the swinging sixties a responsible young man did not show up for work in an office building in a sweaty T-shirt and shorts.

What else could he be doing? I walked and fussed for another half hour until Efrain came out of the building. He was accompanied by the fellow I'd made eye contact with the night before at the Cockpit.

That was interesting. Had they been upstairs fooling around the whole time I was sweltering outside? That irritated me, at least in part because I'd marked that man as mine, and I didn't like to share.

They parted in front of the building, but without the *besos* Efrain had given his friend—a very Anglo handshake instead. Curious. Why would lovers shake hands when they could have easily gotten away with cheek kisses and perhaps even sweet endearments whispered in ears?

Not that I was an endearment kind of guy, you understand. But I'd seen it often enough.

I followed Efrain on foot until it was clear he was on his way back to his apartment. Then I hustled back to my car and drove down there in time to catch him walking inside.

I was still parked across the street when a new cherry-red Chrysler 300 Convertible 440 with a V-8 TorqueFlite engine pulled up. I may not be able to afford a decent car, but I know one when I see one. I was impressed until I realized the driver was Leonard Fitts.

Efrain danced out the front door of the building like Tinkerbell after all the applause and hopped into the convertible without even opening the door. Then he leaned over and kissed Leonard Fitts for all and sundry to see.

Was it all an act? Or did he have a very different relationship with the hombre from the Lincoln Road office tower?

I hadn't been hired to follow Efrain when he was with Leonard Fitts, so I left them alone and drove back over to the Cockpit.

I wasn't on duty that night so my only reason for going there was to see if I could spot Efrain's handsome friend again. I wasn't sure what I wanted to do with him though—quiz him? Or throw him down on a bed and fuck him until he cried out for his *mami*?

It didn't matter, because he wasn't there. I ordered a Florida Special, a light beer out of Tampa they kept on tap, and the bartender, a bald guy in his fifties, asked me what I was doing there on a night off.

"Can't a guy have a little fun?" I asked.

"It's just I've never seen you here not working." I knew he was interested in me, but I'd politely declined his advances in the past. "Always thought you had some cutie locked up with you over on the beach."

"No cutie." I was about to say that I liked my men older and more dangerous when Efrain's friend from the twelfth floor walked in.

I caught his eye, then took my beer over to a table by the wall.

Five minutes later, he was there in front of me with a highball glass in his hand and a bulge in his trousers. "May I join you?" he asked, in a smooth, Spanish-accented baritone that ran an electric wire right to my groin.

"It would be my pleasure." When he sat, I held out my hand. "George."

"Alex," he said. "Well, Alejandro, but there's no need for us to be formal, is there?"

The purr in his voice really got to me. "Not if things go the way I'd like."

He laughed, showing beautiful white teeth. He wasn't quite as tan as Efrain, but his skin was a few shades darker than mine, and he had opened the top two buttons of his shirt, showing off some dark curly hairs I knew would end up between my teeth at some point.

"Do you work here every night?" Alex asked.

I shook my head. "Tonight's my night off. Free to do as I please."

"Excellent." Then he leaned in close to me. "And what do you please?"

I abandoned any thought of getting information from him about Efrain. "A man," I said carefully. Even though I'd seen him here the day before with his friends, there was still the possibility he was trying to entrap me.

"That is good," he said. "I, myself, am a man."

I moved my leg under the table to rest against his, and again felt that electric shock. Hell, I wasn't interested in small talk; I wanted him. I leaned in. "My place is over on the beach. Are you any closer?"

"Do you know Segovia?"

I cocked my head. "In Spain?"

"No. Segovia Avenue, in Coral Gables."

"If you give me directions, I can find it."

He pulled a Publix cash register receipt from his wallet and turned it over. "Take Coral Way west and bear left at City Hall," he said. "Then turn left at the roundabout." He scribbled a street number on the paper and handed it to me. "Do you like rum?"

"I do," I said, and I could hear the yearning in my voice—not for the liquor, but for him.

"I will have a glass ready for you, then," he said. Then he got up and left.

I waited for a moment or two for my stiffy to settle down; I didn't need to put on a show for the bartender or anyone else who was watching. I downed the rest of my beer and walked out.

I was disappointed that Alex wasn't waiting for me in the parking lot, but I pulled my car out and followed his directions. His house was a single-story Spanish-style bungalow with arched windows and an orange tile roof. I parked in the driveway, swallowed hard, and walked up to the door.

Alex had shucked his shirt and shoes, leaving him barefoot in his business slacks, and true to his word, he had a tumbler of rum in his hand. I took it from him, sniffed it, and let the scent fill my nostrils.

While he closed the door behind me, I took a sip of the rum, which ran through my veins like fire. Then I kicked off my shoes and turned to him.

He kissed me like a man who knew what he was doing, and I was happy for once to let someone else lead the way. We stood there awkwardly holding our drinks and kissing, without our bodies touching, until he pulled away and said, "Come into the living room."

I followed him and put my drink down on a terrazzo-topped table. "You're a bit ahead of me," I said, and I shucked my shirt and pulled off my socks.

He came over to me then and we embraced, skin to skin. Pretty quickly, we were both naked and in his king-sized bed, where we engaged in a variety of positions over the next few hours, cementing our compatibility.

It was after midnight when we got up. We both pulled on

boxers and walked into his tiny kitchen, where he made us Spanish-style omelets with sliced potatoes and spicy sausage.

"Are you a chef?" I asked, as he served the omelets with flair.

He shook his head. "A businessman. I grew up on my father's sugar plantation in Cienfuegos. When I was not exploring in the hills, I spent time in the kitchen with our cook, and she taught me everything I know about food."

"Sounds idyllic."

"It was, until the bastard Castro took office. Then everything changed."

I didn't move to eat, not wanting to disturb his story, though I was salivating.

"A year after Castro seized power, he decided my father was a threat. He seized our plantation and took my father into police custody."

I held my breath, knowing there was no good ending to the story. "They killed him quickly, at least," he said. "I was already here so there was nothing I could do."

"I'm sorry," I said.

He picked up his fork. "Eat, *por favor*."

I ate. The eggs were light and fluffy, the potatoes meltingly smooth. The sausage added just the right sharpness. I complimented his cooking, and he brushed the words away, staring into my face.

Then I decided it was time to prod a bit, to see if I could discover what his connection was to Efrain Perez Duarte.

"Are the Cuban men you were meeting with last night in similar circumstances as you?" I asked.

"So you noticed us."

"I noticed you."

He smiled. "I am flattered. I thought you did, which was why I came back tonight."

He had not answered my question, so I tried again. "Rarely get a group of businessmen in like yours," I said.

"Which is why I suggested the bar," he said. "None of the

men with me had ever heard of the Cockpit, and most of them believed it was something to do with the airport when I suggested it."

"Cubans aren't noticeably friendly toward *maricons*," I said, using the nasty term I had picked up on Miami's streets.

"Not unless they serve a purpose," Alex said. "In this case, camouflaging us. We could not go to a Cuban restaurant, or an Anglo bar, without attracting too much unwanted attention. The Cockpit provides a good place to hide."

"And you're not worried about getting caught up in a raid?"

He smiled. "One of the men with me last night is a senior officer in the police department. No, we were not worried."

He finished the last of his omelet and said, "And now? Do we return to the bedroom? Or do you have somewhere else to be?"

I assumed Efrain would be sacked out with Leonard, so I said, "The bedroom it is."

I stayed with Alex until six, when my internal alarm clock went off, and I crept out of his house like a thief. He knew my first name and where I worked, if he wanted to see me again.

And I knew where he lived.

I drove back across the causeway as the sun began to rise in the east, sending painfully bright shards of sunlight against my windshield. Then I went for a long run along Ocean Drive and the beach, followed by a hot shower to wash away the sweat and cum and set me up for the day.

I was ready to leave for another day of surveilling Efrain when I called my answering service to check for messages. There was an abrupt one from a man named Frank Coyne. "I'm Leonard Fitts's attorney. Call me as soon as you get this message."

Coyne was a prominent figure on Miami Beach. Like Leonard, he was gay and wealthy, though considerably more discreet. What kind of trouble had Leonard gotten himself into? Been pulled over by the cops when he was in his convertible, in a clinch with Efrain?

I returned the call and was connected to Coyne in a moment.

"Where were you last night?" he demanded.

My first reaction was to tell the man to go fuck himself, and my second was to tell the truth. Instead, I opted for clarity with a hint of opacity. "I met a friend at the Cockpit in Coral Gables at about seven o'clock yesterday evening. We were apart for about twenty minutes while I followed him to his house, where I remained until six this morning. Why is that important?"

"Because someone killed Efrain Perez last night, and the police have arrested Leonard Fitts. I was hoping you were watching Perez."

I explained that the last time I'd seen Efrain, he was getting into Leonard's car. "I was hired to find out if Mr. Perez was cheating on Mr. Fitts," I said. "Once they were together, I stopped the clock."

"I understand, but it's bad news for both of them. If you'd been watching you'd give Leonard an alibi, and you might have been able to save Efrain."

He let that sink in for a minute.

"I've heard good things about you, Mr. Clay," he said eventually. "You're sharp and tough and you can get in places other PIs might not be able to. I'd like to hire to you collect any information you can on Efrain and why someone might want to kill him."

"What do the police say?"

"There are two theories at present. The first is that Leonard got angry with Efrain, probably over cheating. Typical homosexual spat that got out of hand, ending with Leonard killing Efrain and dumping his body in a canal off Dade Boulevard."

My mouth went dry. If called to testify in a case like that, I would be forced to reveal that Leonard had hired me because of his suspicions.

But that's why Coyne wanted to hire me, to protect my conversations with his client from discovery.

"However, according to the police there was significant blood found at the site. No blood in Leonard's house or car. Which leads to the second theory. That he was a young homosexual, dressed provocatively and prowling the streets at night. That someone picked him up for sex, and then killed him."

"What does Mr. Fitts say?"

"That he took Efrain out to dinner and then back to his home for some intimate conversation, accompanied by a large quantity of wine. He was too drunk to drive Efrain back to his apartment, and wanted to call him a cab, but Efrain insisted on walking."

"How far?"

"About three miles," Coyne said. "Efrain insisted he wanted the exercise, and that he had walked that distance many times over in Cuba."

"What time did the police find the body?"

"About three a.m. Consistent with Leonard's story."

I thought for a minute. "Dade Boulevard. That's not a typical area to pick up men."

"I wouldn't know," Coyne said frostily.

"But the cops would. So that's one hole to poke in their second story."

"You have a better idea?"

"I have to speak to a source. But I'll come by your office first to sign on with you."

"My secretary will have the paperwork. I have a meeting with the president of Dade Bank that I can't get out of."

A subtle way of telling me he was an important man. But then, I already knew that. The only unimportant men in this case were me and Efrain Perez.

And Perez was dead.

Coyne's office was in the Pierce Fenner and Smith building on Southeast First Street in the middle of downtown Miami's growing financial district. Very nicely paneled and carpeted, though I didn't see much more of it than his secretary's desk, where I signed the appropriate paperwork and received another hundred-dollar retainer.

My bank was going to get to know me well if business kept up like this. I drove back over to the beach, deposited the check in my business account, and then walked to the office building on Lincoln Road where I had seen Efrain go the day before. I stopped at the information desk where a Black woman in a peach-colored business suit reigned.

"Do you have a directory of office clients?" I asked.

"Who is it you're looking for?" she asked, with a hint of a southern accent.

"A gentleman named Alejandro. I believe he works on the twelfth floor."

"Mr. Reyes," she said. "Campo Real. Suite 1201."

She pronounced it the English way rather than the Spanish. I thanked her, rode the elevator up to the twelfth floor and walked into the office of Campo Real.

I gave my name to the beautiful young receptionist, and when she asked, I told her I was there about Efrain Perez Duarte. She nodded, made a call, and spoke softly in Spanish. When she hung up, she said, "Mr. Reyes will be right with you."

I caught a glimpse of surprise and then anger in Alex's eyes when he came to fetch me. We didn't speak until he had ushered me into a large office with a desk and chairs to one side and a sofa and coffee table to the other.

He sat behind the desk, looking powerful in his tailored business suit. Knowing that I had seen what was under that suit the night before pushed some of the power back to me, though.

"Why do you come to my office? And what do you know of Efrain?"

I didn't like his tone, but if it hadn't been for my case, I'd never have considered confronting a one-night stand in his office.

I handed him my card, which read "George Clay, Private Investigator." Then I said, in as soft a voice as I could manage, "I'm sorry to tell you that Efrain Perez was murdered last night."

"Murdered!" There was horror in his voice, but anger, too. How well did he know Efrain, after all?

"I have been retained by the law office of Frank Coyne to investigate the matter on behalf of a client of his."

"Leonard Fitts."

"So you knew about Efrain's relationship with Mr. Fitts?"

"I knew. I didn't approve."

"Why not? You and I..."

"Efrain had a very promising future ahead of him. I didn't want it sullied by a youthful indiscretion."

There were so many questions I wanted to ask Alex, but I decided to start by giving him some information first, to soften him up toward me. I could tell he was angry because I'd invaded his turf, brought his sexual inclinations to his office door.

"Let me tell you what I know," I said. "First of all, I know that you didn't kill Efrain, because I was with you all night. I intend to respect your privacy."

"Thank you."

"Leonard Fitts hired me Wednesday to follow Efrain because he thought Efrain was cheating on him. I checked out Efrain's building and prepared to watch him yesterday, Thursday."

Alex nodded.

"I went to my other job Wednesday night. That's when you and I made eye contact. I want to make it clear to you that I had no idea you were connected to Efrain at that point."

Alex's body language softened. "Then how did you know where to find me?"

"Yesterday I followed Efrain from his apartment to the beach, where he suntanned for an hour or more with a friend. Then he came to this building and rode the elevator to this floor."

"You are very attentive."

"It's my job. He spent nearly four hours here, then walked out with you. What were you doing all that time?"

"I was tutoring him," Alex said. "And lest you think that is a euphemism for something else, let me explain."

He pointed to a photograph on his wall. "The man on the left is my father. This was taken at a meeting of sugar growers in La

Habana in April of 1957. The man in the middle is Fulgencio Batista."

"The dictator."

"There, you and I may have a difference of opinion. Despite his restrictive policies, he was the elected president of Cuba."

I had briefly dated a Cuban guy who was passionate about his anti-Castro politics, so I had learned a bit about the island nation. There was a lot more to discuss about Batista, but I wasn't going to get into it.

"So. Your dad and Batista were pals."

"More like business partners," Alex said. "Batista had his finger in many pies." He frowned. "And his dick in many women."

"Straight guys will do that."

"He had several bastard children, Batista. One of them with a woman who worked on our plantation in Cienfuegos."

"Efrain?"

He nodded. "My father thought it would secure his relationship with Batista by providing him with women when he visited. Then when he discovered Elena was pregnant, he persuaded Batista to acknowledge his parentage, on the condition that my father would raise Efrain as his son."

"So Efrain was your brother?"

"Not by blood, you understand. And when I left for boarding school in the US, he was still a child. I saw him on occasions when I went home, but we were more like acquaintances than brothers. My mother had died of cancer by then, and Elena ran the household."

He sighed. "I was working in international banking in New York when my father decided that this country bumpkin Castro might be a real threat. I helped him transfer the bulk of our family assets here and to Switzerland, leaving only the family home. After Castro killed my father and seized Campo Real, I had no further contact with anyone there. Then, two years ago, a man I knew notified me that Efrain was here, in Miami. That as soon as Castro opened the port of Camarioca, and boats could get out, people loyal to Batista and my father had smuggled Efrain here."

"How did you feel about that?"

"I honored my father's wishes. I met with Efrain, who was a country boy who hadn't had the opportunities I had. I gave him an allowance to live on, got him tutors to improve his brain and his manners." He took a breath. "And twice a week I met with him, to teach him about Cuban history and politics, world affairs and international finance."

"To what end? You weren't planning to marry him off, were you?"

"Perhaps. In the future. But my friends and I, we wanted him to be a valid candidate for president of Cuba, to follow in his father's footsteps."

It took a moment for that to sink in, as everything I knew about that cute dark-eyed boy shifted. "He wasn't killed because someone mistook him for a hustler," I said.

"No, I don't think so either."

"You realize, this gives a whole new direction to this case," I said. "Do you have a copy of Efrain's birth certificate? Or something that proves he's Batista's illegitimate son?"

"That paperwork is locked up in a safe deposit box. It has been appropriately authenticated."

"You'll have to turn that over to the police."

"And what do you think they will do about it?" He pounded his fist on the table. "Relations with Castro are already very fragile. They won't want to risk an international incident over the death of a single homosexual boy."

"You believe someone from Castro's government killed him?"

"Who else?"

I leaned forward. "Tell me, Alex. How many anti-Castro groups are there in Miami at present? Besides the remnants of Brigade 2506, that is?"

That group, under the auspices of the CIA, had organized a

raid on the Bay of Pigs in 1960, in a colossal failure. I was sure there were more such groups still existent. Did Alex belong to one of them? Were those the men I'd seen meeting at the Cockpit?

"There are many," he admitted.

"Including the group you belong to?"

"No one I know would have killed Efrain!"

"Are you so sure, Alex?" I leaned forward. "This young man was your brother in all but blood, and he is dead, because you and some other men decided to make him the figurehead of your operations, whatever they are. Suppose one of them had his own candidate? Another Batista bastard, or a Cuban with better pedigree or better qualifications."

Alex didn't say anything.

"Look, I feel like shit. If I had followed Leonard and Efrain back to Leonard's house instead of fucking around with you, I would have seen Efrain strike out on foot. I would have followed him, and I might have been able to save his life. My hands are already in this up to my elbows. I need your help to find out what happened."

"I don't know that I can do that," Alex said. "These are men I've trusted all my life. Some of them were friends of my father's. One of them has been my best friend my whole life. I can't turn on them."

I backed my chair away and stood up. "I understand. I wish I had someone in my life I felt that close to."

Then I walked out.

When I got back to my office, I called Frank Coyne's office. After a couple of minutes, he came on the line. "Good news. Leonard Fitts has been released from custody and from suspicion in Efrain's murder. The police found a knife in the canal with blood that matches Efrain's, and a fingerprint that doesn't match Leonard's. Apparently, a valuable gold coin Efrain wore around his neck is missing, too. The police are calling it a robbery murder."

"What does that mean for me?"

"It means you're off the hook," Coyne said. "You get to keep the retainer from Leonard and from my office for a couple of days' work."

I thanked him and asked him to keep me in mind for future jobs, then hung up.

I didn't think a random thug had killed Efrain Perez for his necklace, but there wasn't a damn thing I could do about it. I was off the case.

I went to work that night at the Cockpit, half-hoping Alex Reyes would show up to make amends, or at least offer his body, but no such luck.

The next two weeks continued the way my life was going at that time. I worked four nights a week at the Cockpit, usually with nothing more than the occasional minor disturbance or kid trying to get in with a false driver's license. I checked out the finances of a store clerk who seemed to be living larger than his boss anticipated, and found he was. I did some background checks for a clothing manufacturer looking for a controller who wouldn't steal from them. And I followed a woman who was cheating on her husband in a cheap motel on Biscayne Boulevard.

Then on a Monday night close to midnight, Alex staggered into the Cockpit. It was clear he'd already had a couple of drinks, either at home or at a bar. His tie was gone, his shirt collar was loose, and he wasn't wearing the hat I'd first seen him in.

I missed that hat.

The bartender didn't want to serve him, but I persuaded him to order a Cuba libre, heavy on the Coke, and promised the bartender I'd look out for him.

I put my arm around Alex's shoulder as I led him to a table. The physical closeness made me feel good—and not just in a hot and horny way.

I settled Alex in a chair and sat across from him. "Of all the gin joints in all the towns in all the world," I said, "what brings you here?"

I expected him to say that he missed me, that he was horny, that he wanted me inside him again. Something like that. Instead, he said, "I saw the coin."

That shunted my engine to a different track, and it took me a minute to figure it out. "The coin Efrain wore?"

He nodded. "It was from a Spanish treasure ship called *Nuestra Senora de la Regla* that sank off Cuba in 1715. Some divers found silver and gold coins from the wreck in the early fifties, and of course Batista got his share. He gave it to Efrain when he was a kid, and Efrain never took it off."

"You're sure it was the same one?"

"It had a tiny nick in the corner. I saw it around Efrain's neck enough times to recognize it."

"Where did you see it?"

Tears welled up in Alex's eyes and he started to cry. "Around my godson's neck."

I had to get up to check some IDs at the door, and I left Alex to drink his rum and Coke. It was after midnight by then and the bar was quiet, so I made my apologies and loaded a still-very-drunk Alex Reyes into my Chevy and drove him home.

I sat him down at his kitchen table, poured us both big glasses of water, and took the chair across from him. "Tell me about your godson."

"Rico Perdana and I met at Havana airport when we were twelve years old," he said. "Both of us bound for boarding school at St. Paul's. We bonded quickly, calling ourselves the only Cubans in New Hampshire."

At my urging he drank some water. "We became best friends. His father was one of Batista's generals, and both of us were being groomed for the next generation of Cuban leaders. We spent every day together for six years, even when we'd come back to Cuba for vacation. When we graduated, I went to Wharton and Rico chose the University of Miami. He said he'd had enough of cold weather."

"I can believe that," I said.

"Batista grew more and more unhinged as he tightened his grip on power. A year before he was deposed, he decided he didn't trust Rico's father anymore, and had him shot to death in the courtyard of the *Palacio de la Revolución.*"

"Jesus."

"Rico was safe in Miami, but Batista imprisoned his mother and his sister, and they died within months. My father paid the rest of Rico's tuition at UM and set him up in a real estate business in Miami. When I started transferring my father's assets out of Cuba, I invested in several of Rico's projects."

I nodded along.

"Then I moved to Miami, and Rico married Estrella, and he asked me to be the godfather to his son Humberto, named after his father. Of course, I agreed."

"As you would. He was your best friend." I motioned to the water, and Alex drank again.

"Tonight, I went to dinner at their house. Berto was so pleased to show me the coin his father had given him, to wear in memory of his late *abuelo*." Alex started to cry again. "How could he do it? Why?"

"Do you think Rico wants to be the president of Cuba?"

He looked at me.

"With one presumptive heir out of the way, Rico might consider himself the next best choice," I said. "His father was a trusted compadre of Batista."

Alex shook his head. "He wouldn't."

"What about the men you meet with. Is Rico one of them?"

He nodded.

"Would the others support him, with Efrain out of the way?"

Alex's whole body sunk into itself, tears streaking his face. I muscled him up from his chair and half walked, half dragged him to the bedroom. I sat him on the bed, got him some aspirin from the medicine cabinet, and then carefully undressed him, from his fine linen shirt to the white sleeveless undershirt, the polished brogans, fine silk socks, and sleek trousers. I left him his boxers, because I didn't want to tempt myself.

Then I stripped down to my boxers myself and crawled into bed beside him. I pulled him close to me, his back to my front, and wrapped an arm around his shoulders.

He was asleep quickly, but it took me a while longer, as I considered the options either of us had.

I woke at six, as usual, only this time Alex was awake beside me. "I can't confront him," he said, as if no time had elapsed between our conversation of the night before. "Can you?"

"I need to piss, and then I need coffee," I said. My morning wood pressed against my boxers and I hurried into the bathroom to relieve myself.

When I finished, I pulled on my trousers and walked out to the kitchen, where Alex stood in a silk bathrobe, making coffee.

Neither of us spoke while the java was brewing. "Suppose your best friend, the father of your godson, killed your adopted brother?" I asked, once I had some caffeine in my system. "What do you want to see happen?"

"I don't know," he said, looking down at his coffee, in a fine china cup.

"You can't go on this way," I said gently. "Suspecting, but not knowing. For all you know now, one of the other men in the group orchestrated Efrain's death, and gave Rico the coin as a memento to pass on to Berto."

"What kind of man does that?" he asked. "Takes another man's life?"

There were so many answers to that question, but I picked the one that I thought mattered most in this case. "A man who has undergone a loss so painful that he feels the only way to make that pain better is to make someone else suffer."

"I was in school in Philadelphia when Rico's father died. Studying for final exams. I talked to Rico every day, but I couldn't pick up and fly to Miami to be with him. Fortunately, there were other Cubans here he could talk to."

"Is that how he got involved with this group?"

Alex nodded.

"And then he brought you in when you moved here?"

He looked up at me. "He was the star, you know. Young and handsome and well-educated, fluent in English and Spanish. The perfect leader for our people."

I understood something then. "Then Efrain arrived from Cuba. And he had a better pedigree, even if he was a bastard."

"Rico fought against him for a while, but eventually he went along with the will of the group. Then about a month ago one of the other men saw Efrain out with Leonard Fitts and reported back. That we could not put forward a *maricon* as the leader of Cuba."

"It would be tough."

"Efrain swore to me he was seeing Leonard for fun, because he was generous with his money. That when the time came, he would buckle down, be straight. Marry a woman, even."

"Did you believe he could?"

"The idea of power was intoxicating to him." He sighed. "I couldn't, but I believe Efrain could have." He looked up at me. "Have you heard of this man, Alfred Kinsey?"

"The one who ranks men and women based on their attractions?"

He nodded. "Efrain said he was a three on Kinsey's scale. Equally attracted to men and women. Men were playthings, he said, while a woman was for settling down."

"I wish I could believe that," I said. "It would make my life a lot easier."

"Mine, too."

Neither of us spoke for a few minutes. We drained our coffee, and Alex poured more. Finally, I said, "There was a fingerprint on the knife the police found in the canal. The next time your group is ready to meet, bring them to the Cockpit."

I leaned forward. "I'll work something out with the waitress to get a glass Rico used, with his fingerprints on it. I'll take it to the police. If there's a match, we've put it in the police's hands.

If there's no match, then your conscience is clear."

"If his fingerprint matches the knife, I'll have destroyed my best friend's life."

I shook my head. "I'm sorry to tell you that if the print matches, your friend destroyed his own life, without any help from you."

Alex was still uncertain, so we agreed that if he wanted me to secure Rico's prints, he would catch my eye when his group was next at the Cockpit and tip his hat to me.

I was keeping a close eye on the group on Wednesday evening. I quickly figured out who Rico was; he was the only one young enough, besides Alex. After an hour or so, they erupted into an argument, and I was about to walk over and ask them to keep it down when Alex turned to face me. He tipped his hat to me, then walked out of the bar.

I'd cued the waitress as soon as I pegged Rico, and she had already put aside a martini glass he had used. I used a dish towel to carefully put it in a paper bag, then I stowed it in my car.

The next morning, in an effort to preserve my private eye's license, I called Frank Coyne's office. When he came on the line, I told him what I was holding, though I didn't go into detail about how I'd come across it. He agreed I was still under his contract and gave me the name of the police detective to whom I should deliver it on the beach.

He'd already called the guy when I got there. I dropped off the bag and walked out. There was always the chance that the print wouldn't match—but I didn't count on that.

It took a couple of days for the results, and the next thing I heard was when the headline on the Miami *Herald* blared "Prominent Real Estate Developer Tied to Beach Homicide."

None of the back story had made it into the papers. Just that Federico Perdana had been arrested in connection with the death of Efrain Perez.

I kept on going about my life, though I worried about Alex Reyes and the effect the whole situation was having on him. But I resisted going after him. In his mind, probably, I'd been the engine that led to his best friend's imprisonment, so I was tainted.

Then one Friday night, he came into the Cockpit around midnight, wearing that hat. He went up to the bar, ordered a Cuba libre, and smiled my way.

SONS OF SOUNDVIEW

Adam Meyer

They say you can't go home again, and maybe that's true, but deep down inside I'm not sure I ever really left Soundview. Chances are you've never even heard of the place. Soundview sits right at the tip of the Bronx just before you fall into the East River, and it's where I read my first comic book, kissed my first girl, and stole my first car. All that was a long time ago, of course. I haven't read anything but the newspaper in ages, I'm married with a kid, and the only vehicle I drive these days is my own Buick LeSabre, which is safely parked in the carport of my suburban split-level.

Back when I got the message from Max Goldfarb, I was still single and living in a long-term hotel in Manhattan and using my now-lapsed PI license to earn a few extra bills. Even then, I hadn't been back to Soundview in ages. Probably not since my mother's funeral. But Max said he had a job for me. I was more than a little curious, both about my old neighborhood and about why Max, my oldest friend, wanted to hire me.

I waited in his outer office, flipping through the *New York Times* sports section. Despite seven innings of no-hit ball by Tom Seaver, the Mets had lost again, on track for another last-place finish. In that fall of 1968, it was hard to imagine they'd ever compete with my beloved Yankees.

"Mr. Finnegan?" said a woman looking down at me. She

must've been a decade younger than I, in her early twenties, her dark-blond hair cut in a stylish bob. "Mr. Goldfarb will see you now."

I followed her through a set of ornately-carved wooden doors into a wide office. Everything had a high shine to it, the brass lamps on either side of the blocky cherrywood desk, the floor-to-ceiling windows, the maple floors. Even Max's hair was shining, slicked back with grease and starting to thin on either side of his high forehead.

"Max, great to see you," I said. "You look good."

I put out a hand to shake, but he pulled me in close for a hug. For a moment I felt like we were the same boys who'd played stoopball in front of his old brownstone on Taylor Avenue, and then he pulled away, studying me.

"You look good, too. Thanks for coming, Finn."

When Max and I were growing up, some kids just went by their last name or some variation. Finnegan had shortened to Finn easily enough.

The woman with the blond bob ducked out, closing the door behind her. I turned back to Max, but my eyes went past him to the tall windows all around. Below was a sprawling mix of brownstones, silvery high-rises, and straight-edged roads, with a band of blue water and the edge of a dense green island in the distance. It was a lot better than the view from my place, which was a rusted fire escape and a sliver of brick wall.

That made me wonder just where Max's path and mine had split. We'd lived nearly identical lives for years, "joined at the hip" as my mother liked to say. The only difference was that Max's family was Jewish and spent their holidays eating cold whitefish and trading barbs in Yiddish, while mine were Irish and fought loudly. By the time we turned fourteen, we'd started to go our own separate ways. I found myself running with the kids who passed stolen bottles of Wild Irish Rose back and forth and bopped to Elvis on their Regency transistor radios. Max was more likely to stay home, reading books by Dale Carnegie and

Shelby Foote.

"It's nice to get back to the old neighborhood," I said.

"So you live in Hell's Kitchen now. You like it there?"

"It suits me."

That was true. Some people hated the crowded sidewalks and the smell of fried plantains. But I loved the sense that I was in the beating heart of a vibrant city.

"You know they're calling it Clinton now?" Max said, smiling.

I smiled back. "Maybe in real estate circles. Not the folks I know."

Max's smile dimmed a little. "You must be wondering why I brought you in. You're a PI now, I hear."

After getting out of the Army, I'd done various odd jobs, including running errands for an old private investigator who'd cut his teeth working for J. Edgar Hoover during Prohibition. By the time I worked as his apprentice, he was busy chasing insurance fraudsters, not bootleggers, and when he died, he left the firm to me. In effect, he gave me a handful of longtime clients, most of whom were dead now.

"I usually handle small cases," I said, glancing out the windows at the sweeping view. "You would probably do better with one of the bigger agencies..."

"I'm sure they do good work. But this isn't that hard of a job."

I nodded, trying not to take that as an insult. Realizing what he'd said, Max waved his hand.

"I didn't mean that; it's just...you know the neighborhood, it'll be easy for you to find your way around. Besides, I want someone who can ask questions and do it quietly, someone I can trust." He leaned across the gleaming wooden desk, his eyes fixed on mine. "Back in June, there was a fire in one of my apartment buildings, over on Story Avenue. It burned the walls and caused some smoke damage, no one hurt. End of July, same thing happened in my rental unit on Leland. Earlier this week, there was a fire in one of my places on Underhill. It wasn't too bad, but that's only because the fire department caught it early."

"Sounds like you need the police."

"I've talked to the police. They had me file a report and that's it." Max shook his head, his gelled hair catching the sunlight. "Besides, you did some arson investigation in the Army, right?"

I had a flash of memory, me and some fellow soldiers using gasoline to torch a bridge on our way out of a rural village in North Korea. "Not exactly."

"Look, so far these fires have been small stuff. But if whoever's doing this keeps it up, things could get out of hand. I don't want to see anyone get hurt."

"And you don't want to get an insurance check that's less than what you could make selling the place on the open market."

I'd meant it as a friendly dig, the kind we used to take at each other while drinking egg creams on his front stoop, but the look in his eyes told me I'd hit closer to the mark than I meant.

"Neighborhood's not what it was when we were growing up, you know? The *schvartzes* are taking over, and families like ours are all moving out to the suburbs. That's where I'm going to start investing. Nassau County." Max peered out the window, looking past the slate rooftops and soot-covered chimneys to the clouds. "I know a guy putting some investors together to build something out at the old airstrip where Lindbergh used to fly from. It'll be lots of stores, inside not outside, and feel like a real town center. Like Soundview Avenue when we were kids."

I smiled, remembering how I could go from the butcher to the baker to the candy shop without breaking a sweat. But I had trouble imagining kids doing that out at some old airfield.

"Whoever's setting those fires, I want you to make them stop." Max studied me, his eyes as dark as the black glass marbles we used to play with as kids. "You think you can do that?"

I looked closely at Max and nodded. "I'll handle it."

After leaving Max's office, I headed out to see the buildings where the fires had been set. Max's secretary had given me three sets of keys, one for each location. There was nothing much to see at the first two, since any damage from the blazes had already been repaired.

At the third building, the one on Underhill Avenue, I headed down to the basement. According to Max, that was where the fire had started.

When I got down there, the air was so heavy with the smell of smoke I nearly choked on it. The super there had loaned me a flashlight, which I used to scan the area. A long row of wooden shelves had been reduced to ash. Most of the walls were exposed brick, and in the corner I found a spot where the red had been covered with black, the charred black streaks angling into a V shape. A faint dusting of ash had spread across the floor beneath it.

I sifted it through my fingers, feeling the lightness of it, like black confetti.

Some kind of paper or cardboard, probably. The kind of thing that would light with a splash of gas or kerosene. Just enough to get the fire going.

I looked around the basement some more, but I didn't learn anything more about who had set the fire. The door leading downstairs had a cheap lock and was just around the corner from the mailboxes. A high-traffic area. Maybe whoever had done it had been seen by someone who lived there.

I went around the building to talk to some of the residents. They were mostly Black, with a few Jewish and Italian and Irish folks in the mix, too, mostly older. I asked everyone I met if they had seen anyone with matches, anyone hanging around in the lobby near the basement door, anyone who had shown a special interest in the fire downstairs.

No one had.

If whoever had set the fire had avoided being seen, then maybe they had found some way to slip in and out of the building quietly. I returned the flashlight to the super and asked if there was a back door. He pointed me down the hall to a heavy steel door. A fire exit.

Slipping out into the alley behind the building, I heard voices.

A pair of young Black men leaned against the wall. They were maybe fourteen or fifteen, one wearing blue jeans and a green Army jacket like the one I had in North Korea, only it was so big his hands disappeared inside the sleeves. The other was half a head taller, dressed in corduroys and a white T-shirt, his arms bare despite the faint bite in the air. This second boy held a cigarette, its tip gleaming red as he took a puff.

"You boys live here?" I asked.

"Yes, sir," said the one in the Army jacket.

The taller one frowned, knocking some ash off his cigarette. He studied me closely, his gaze shifting from my soot-covered fingers to my cheap suit from Gimbels. "What do you want, man?"

"Just asking some questions for a friend of mine." I nodded at the door I'd just come out through. "You boys know anything about the fire that happened here the other day?"

"Yeah, sure, we saw smoke coming up from the basement. It was hairy."

I focused on the taller boy, the one with the cigarette. "You wouldn't know anything about how it got started, would you?"

He dropped the cigarette, looking at me closely. "You saying we done it, man?"

"I'm asking. There's a difference."

The boy ground out the cigarette with his sneaker. "Nah, we ain't done it."

"You hang out here sometimes, though. Maybe you saw who did."

He shrugged, pulling out another smoke but not lighting it. "I didn't see nothing. Life's a lot easier that way, you know?"

"You a shoe?" asked the boy in the Army jacket, studying me closely.

I held my hands up, palms out. "No, not a cop. Just asking questions for a friend of mine. Me and him grew up around here."

"Maybe things different when you lived here." The taller boy's deep brown eyes bore into mine. "Most folks don't like questions. 'Specially from strangers."

I nodded, thinking that maybe things in the old neighborhood hadn't changed that much after all. "If someone's setting fires around here, it could be dangerous for you, your neighbors. You wouldn't want to see that, would you?"

"Maybe. Be better than watching *Bonanza* or something."

The second boy laughed. The taller boy smiled to himself. An audience of one was still better than nothing.

"Besides, what we got to worry about?" The taller boy lit the new cigarette. "Got that white boy taking care of things for us, don't we?"

"What white boy?" I asked.

The two exchanged a look, and the one with the cigarette shrugged. "He's about our age, but fire's his stick, you know? He goes around like he's real badass, says he's on the lookout for fires, he can put them out, but you ask me he's all show and no go."

"Did you see him here the other day? The day of the fire?"

"Nah, man."

"Where can I find him?"

"Don't know."

I looked at the boy in the Army jacket. "How about you?"

He glanced at his friend and shook his head. "Me neither."

The boy with the cigarette laughed and pulled out his lighter. "I got an idea. You looking for smoke, better find some fire first. Don't you think, man?"

I headed back out to the street, tracing the sidewalks along Soundview Avenue where I'd once zoomed back and forth on my green-and-white Schwinn. I looked around for familiar faces, but the people I'd known growing up here were gone and most of the shops were, too. Many of the low-slung brick storefronts had been bulldozed to make way for high-rise apartments.

Max had said he hired me in part because I knew the neighborhood, but it was the opposite. I was a stranger here now, and that put me at a disadvantage. If he really wanted to know who had set the fires, he'd need someone who knew the current mix of residents, who still felt at home here. However, he'd paid me a week's wages to get him some answers, and I doubted he'd take the money back. He had too much as it was.

If I was going to pocket his cash, at least I needed to earn it.

I headed up Randall Avenue toward the Bronx River, where a row of old storefronts stretched before me. The names and sometimes even the businesses themselves had changed. The old luncheonette was now a White Castle, the butcher shop, a place called LRM Loans. Then finally a place I remembered, Fleishman's Variety Store. As a boy I'd often lingered at the window, studying the new Erector sets, wondering how many nickels I'd need to save to buy one.

I went inside, hearing the familiar jingle of the bell and smelling the familiar scent of old linens and fresh licorice. I made my way past a rack of Wise potato chips to the front counter. A woman leaned down behind it, and it was only when she rose that I realized I knew her.

Judy Fleischman.

Her hair was brown and long and rolled down her back in a long wave of silk. She wore a blue-and-green-striped turtleneck with an apron over it. Growing up she'd always been as tall and skinny as a boy, but now her hips were curvier and her lips more pink than I remembered.

"Can I help you?" she asked, blotting her hands on the front of her apron.

"I uh...Judy, it's Finn. Frances Finnegan. You probably don't remember me but—"

"I remember." Her smile looked the same as it had when we were fourteen, bringing out a dimple in her right cheek. "You kept asking to borrow pencils in algebra class."

"I always gave them back, right?"

"Usually." She frowned at me. "I heard you went into the Army, moved away. And your mom died...but that was years ago. Sorry, she seemed like a nice lady."

"Thanks." I looked around the store, fighting a wave of déjà vu. "What about your dad? He still run this place?"

"He likes to think so." A frown crossed her face but quickly passed. "He's off today, his back's been...anyway, I help him out a few days a week. I'm an actress so I've got the flexibility, as long as I haven't got any auditions. I hate to say it, but usually I don't."

An actress. I could remember her being in all the school plays, always with big parts but never the lead. I'd always thought she did it for fun, the way I played first base at pickup baseball games. I never realized she'd dreamed of being Lou Gehrig.

"Anything I might've seen you in? I go to the pictures once in a while."

"I've never been in a movie. Been on Broadway a few times, just as a spear carrier, and I was on a couple episodes of *Playhouse 90*. But that was years ago." She shook her head, her long hair swaying. "I suppose it's a dream I ought to give up on, but I haven't, not yet. And what about you? I heard you became a spy, like James Bond or something."

"A private investigator, not a spy. And it's not that glamorous, trust me."

I smiled at her and she smiled back. Our well of small talk had run dry.

"I'm doing a job for Max Goldfarb," I said. "He owns some buildings around here, you know."

"Yeah, I see Max around sometimes. But what's wrong?"

I explained to Judy about the fires and that I was looking for whomever had started them. She listened with great focus, her gray eyes lingering on mine. I wanted to keep talking, just to feel the pull of her gaze a little longer. "I'm looking for this kid, white kid, a teenager...he acts like he's a volunteer firefighter or something."

Something flickered in her eyes, a sign of recognition. "And what do you think he can tell you?"

"If he's got his eye out for fires, then maybe he's seen whoever did this."

My interest in him went deeper than that, but I didn't want Judy to know that. In case it caused her to shut down.

"There's a boy that comes in here..."

"What's he look like?"

"Like lots of boys, I suppose. Clean-cut, dark-haired. He seems lonely and I talk to him sometimes...he told me he's got his own firefighting company. Wants to do the real thing when he grows up. His father owns a hardware store, but not around here. It's over on Gun Hill Road, maybe."

"What's the store called?"

She shook her head. "No idea."

"The boy, what's his name?"

"Dale, I think, or Donny or...I don't know, like I said he just comes in sometimes."

I wrote that down, Donny or Dale, and looked back at Judy. I didn't have anything else to ask but I didn't want to stop talking, either.

"Thanks for the help."

"Maybe you'll come back and let me know if you find him," she said.

I told her that I would.

I headed up the street, away from the store that Judy's father owned. There was a series of tall new buildings where old brownstones had been, rising up into the sky and casting huge shadows across the sidewalk. There were benches out front and old men, some Black and some white, sat there reading the *Daily News* or feeding pigeons. I stopped a few of the men and asked about the boy, but no one seemed to know anything about a homegrown firefighter.

At the next building I came to, I saw a white woman in a housecoat, maybe mid-fifties though she might've been twenty years older. She had a small poodle on a leash and was letting him sniff some dandelions in the overgrown grass.

"Ma'am? You mind if I ask you a question?"

She looked at me as if I had just kicked her poodle. "Yeah, what?"

"I'm looking for a boy, wants to be a firefighter, his name might be Donny or Dale or—"

"Davey," she said, shaking her head. "Lives down the hall from me. Always causing trouble for me and Ira."

It took me a moment to realize that Ira was her dog.

"Always gives Ira these funny looks, says Ira barks too much, which is nonsense. As you can see Ira is as sweet as pie, and that Davey...." She leaned in close, whispering as if she had a secret to share. "He's no good."

"You said he lives down the hall from you." I nodded at the courtyard behind her. "In this building here?"

"That's right. Seventh floor."

Ira began to tug at the leash and the old woman followed, still shaking her head as I made my way past her.

The seventh floor smelled of boiled meat, and my shoes squeaked as I stopped at the door marked 7H. A man farther up the hall had confirmed that a teenage boy named Davey lived here. There was a mezuzah tucked up in the corner of the door, a small gold box that supposedly has a scrap of the bible in it. The old Jewish ladies on my street used to kiss it on their way in and out of their houses.

I knocked, studying the intricate pattern in the gold box. A moment later, a boy's face peered out.

"You looking for my dad? He won't be home for a little while."

"I'm looking for you, Davey. I've got some questions about a fire."

The boy frowned. "The one on Pugsley Avenue?"

I nodded, not bothering to correct him. "That's right."

"I helped put that out, you know. Before the real firefighters got there. It would've been a lot worse if I hadn't helped out." He stopped himself then and studied me, looking suddenly guarded. "You said you have questions. What kind?"

"Well, a friend of mine owns a bunch of buildings around here, like that one on Pugsley Avenue. He heard about you putting out that fire, and he wanted to give you a reward, but he had no idea where you lived." This wasn't true, of course, but I'd learned over the years that lies opened more doors than the truth, sometimes literally.

"A reward? He doesn't need to do that..."

"Still, I'm sure he'd like to know something about you." I nodded at the front door to his apartment. "You mind if I come in? It'll make it easier for us to talk."

As he stepped back and let me inside, I studied the boy more closely. He had thick black hair over a high forehead and ears that stuck out a little from his head. He was skinny and almost good-looking, and surely would be when he finally grew into those ears.

The walls were covered with modern paintings covered in red and yellow squares, but the furniture was old-fashioned. A golden couch with wooden arms, a big Zenith in a wooden cabinet, a pair of silver candlesticks sitting beside a pile of textbooks on the ornate dining table. A brass coatrack stood near the door, holding a man's trench coat and a woman's teal-colored jacket. Looking around, I was surprised at how much it reminded me of the house I'd grown up in, although we had no TV back then, no abstract art, either.

"My name's Francis Finnegan, but people call me Finn. I used to live a few blocks away from here."

He almost smiled. "I'm David. People call me Davey."

"So you like fighting fires, Davey?"

"Yeah, I want to be a firefighter someday. Or maybe a cop." He mimed making a gun with his right hand, and I noticed a small red mark on the side of his middle finger. "My dad thinks I should go to college, but I don't like studying."

"Never liked it much, myself." I noticed a Yankees cap on the table, beside the textbooks, and a small spiral notebook nearly hidden behind it. "How come you want to be a firefighter and not, I dunno, a ballplayer?"

"I'm pretty good at baseball but I just like the idea of putting out fires, I guess." He stuck his hands in the front pockets of his jeans and shrugged. "It's dangerous work but I'm not scared."

"Of fire?" I studied him more closely. "Seems like you ought to be."

"I used to be, I guess. But my mom died last year...cancer. Now nothing scares me anymore. Sometimes I just think, whatever happens, it'll be okay—either I'll live, or I'll get to be with her, in heaven."

I looked at the teal-colored coat, frowned. Following my gaze, Davey said, "That's my stepmother's. She doesn't like me very much."

"I'm sure that's not true."

His eyes challenged me. "It is."

I nodded, thinking of the year my father died. I was fourteen, about the same age Davey must've been. That was when Max and I really started to drift apart. With my dad gone, I found myself spending more and more time with "the juvies," as my mom used to call the kids who hung out on Rosedale Avenue after dark. I got into trouble with them over the next few years, some smalltime, like getting drunk or having fistfights, and some more serious, like shoplifting or stealing cars for joyrides.

"You want a drink, water or soda or something?" he asked.

"Sure, water would be great," I said, but not because I was thirsty. I looked around as he went into the kitchen, picking up the Yankees cap on the table and reached for the small notebook beside it. I looked at the first page I came to. Big block letters filled the lines. Phrases jumped out at me: *watch the world go by, honor thy father, different wavelength.*

"You a writer?" I asked, flipping pages. It looked like poetry or maybe a stream-of-consciousness journal.

He whirled, turning off the faucet. "Hey, what're you doing?"

"Sorry, didn't mean to pry. But I was curious."

He started for me and reached for the notebook. I held it just out of his grasp.

"I like to get my thoughts down sometimes, that's all. Now please give that back."

"You got a lot of big thoughts, Davey?"

He shook his head, noncommittal. Suddenly he didn't know what the right answer was and that seemed to make him nervous.

"Here."

I held the notebook out, waited for him to grab it. As he did, I closed my other hand around his wrist, pulled his right hand toward me. There it was, what I'd noticed earlier. A small fresh red lump on the inside of his middle finger.

"How'd you get that?" I asked.

"It's a blister. From playing baseball."

"I played ball for years, never got a blister like that. Probably that's from a match or a lighter." I let his hand go, studied him closely. "You started that fire, didn't you? The one on Pugsley Avenue, the same one you put out."

"No way."

I moved in close enough so that he could tell I was serious. "You lie to me and I can't help you. You tell the truth and maybe I can."

He looked at me with fear in his eyes, tried to turn away. But I brought a finger to his chin, made him meet my gaze. Finally, he blinked, looking like he was about to cry.

"I started that fire on Pugsley, okay? It was an accident, though. I was practicing being a firefighter...trying to put it out real quick. But it got out of control, faster than I thought...I didn't mean for it to get so big...." He brought his knuckles to his eyes, wiping away tears. "That's the truth, I swear."

"You do that a lot? Start practice fires?"

He looked away, saying nothing. But I knew.

"You started a bunch of other fires the last couple months, too—on Story and Leland and Underhill, and maybe even some others I don't even know about."

He studied the worn parquet floor and said nothing for a moment. "You going to tell my dad? He'll kill me."

I took a step closer, anger flooding my arms, heating my fists. "You listen to me, Davey, and you listen good—no more fires. You want to be a cop or a firefighter, the last thing you need is a goddamn record. You don't want to go to college, then fine, but then you better at least do something where you can learn what it takes to be a man, like go into the Army. I did it myself and I can tell you, it'll be good for you, teach you some discipline."

He nodded quickly, listening. His eyes still glimmered with tears.

I thought about the last time I hung out with those kids on Rosedale Avenue. I was seventeen, and me and a bunch of guys had taken an old Chevy for a joyride. After a couple spins around the neighborhood, a police officer spotted us. Everyone piled out of the car and started to run, but I tripped getting out and twisted my ankle. My friends left me behind, and the cop—his name was Officer Toye, a good Irish lad like me—caught up quickly. He grabbed me by the arm and shoved me against a wall and asked me what the hell I thought I was doing.

I hemmed and hawed and tried to explain that it was my friend's fault, not mine, and he put a hand against my chin and turned my face to the wall. "Just shut up, all right, you dumb kid."

"You going to arrest me?" I asked.

He said he wasn't sure yet, and then he told me he wanted to tell me something important, something I'd do well not to forget. After all those years, I couldn't remember it word for word, but I knew it well enough. I repeated it for Davey as best I could.

"All of us, we're better than the worst thing we've ever done, and we're not as good as the best thing we've ever done. We're just somewhere in the middle, trying to get the balance right. You understand?"

Davey nodded weakly. "Yes, sir."

Of course, he probably didn't understand any more than I had at his age. But Davey seemed a lot like I'd been, neither good nor bad but somewhere in between. He'd veered too far to the edge, sure, but all he had to do was correct course and steer back to the middle and he'd be all right.

"Listen, I'm not going to tell your father. Matter of fact, I'm not going to tell anyone about this. But you gotta promise me that was the last fire you're going to set, that you'll do what your father and stepmother tell you to until you're old enough to make up your own mind about what's right and what's wrong. You hear me?"

"Y-yes."

"All right then."

I slipped a business card out of my wallet, tucked it into the brim of the Yankees cap, clapped it down on his head. Looking out beneath the dark brim, his eyes bright beneath thick brows, he looked no older than eight or nine.

"If you ever need anything, call me," I said. "And I'll check up on you in a few months, see how you're doing. I still know some people here in the neighborhood, and if anyone tells me you started any more fires, I'll be back with the cops, next time. You hear me?"

"Yes, sir. I won't do anything like this again."

I took one last look at the apartment and went back out into the hall. The woman I'd seen earlier was walking toward me with her dog, Ira, straining at the leash. Davey watched from his doorway, his dark brows furrowed, his face shadowed beneath the Yankees cap.

"Good boy," she said, tugging Ira toward her apartment with a hint of anxiety. I looked up at Davey's door, but he was gone.

The next day, I went back to Max's office and I told him I had found the person who had set the fires.

"Did you let him know he needs to quit it or else?" Max asked.

"Trust me, he got the message."

Something in my tone made Max hesitate. "Who is he? One of those *schvartze* troublemakers?"

"He's just some dumb kid like you or me. Didn't mean any harm."

"Yeah, well, he did plenty of it." Max leaned in across his oak desk, eyes blazing. "You know how much it's cost me to fix things up after those fires?"

I nodded. "No, but I can guess. Just like I can guess how much it would've cost to fix Mr. Edelstein's shop window."

Twenty years ago, we'd sent a baseball sailing through the plate glass front of Edelstein's bakery while playing a game of catch. We'd never told our parents or Mr. Edelstein, either, racing off as fast as our long legs would carry us.

Max turned back to his window and his expansive view, his gaze softening as he looked at the sprawl of buildings all around. "A broken window's different from a fire. Besides, we were twelve. How old's this kid?"

"Young enough not to know better."

Max nodded. "If you're sure he won't do it again, I trust you."

"I'm sure. He seems like a good kid. He's working through some things, but he'll be all right."

Max put a hand to the glass, tracing a line with his finger. "All right then. But like I said, I'm done here in the city. Things are starting to get bad, and they're only going to get worse. You might think about getting out yourself."

"Someday," I said. I thought about telling him how I'd seen Judy at her father's old shop, and how I thought I might swing by on my way to the subway back to Manhattan, just to say hello.

Before I had a chance, Max nodded at me. "Good to see you again, Finn. Let's do it again soon, all right?"

Almost a year to the day after my return trip to the Bronx, Judy and I got married at the VFW hall just a few blocks from her father's store. Max stopped by the party for a little while, although I hadn't seen him since that day in his office. It was nobody's fault. He and I traveled in different circles, and he was a busy man. He gave us a gift—a check for a hundred dollars, enough to cover the cost of our honeymoon—and hugged us both. He said his shopping mall had opened and taken off, and there were so many customers they practically lined up outside. He told us we ought to leave Soundview behind and think about coming out to the suburbs.

With everything going on that day, I can't say I thought of that kid Davey much, but he did cross my mind. I mentioned his name to a few people at the wedding party, locals who might've known him, and someone—I can't remember who—told me his family had moved into the new Co-Op City.

After that I pretty well forgot about him, even though I'd sometimes wake in the night, dreaming of fire, and see a face looking at me through flickering orange flames like the ones I'd seen on that bridge in Korea, blackened lips curling in a smile. "You want to burn together?" he said, and I turned away, or thought I did. When I woke up it was hard to remember the details.

In the end Judy and I took Max's advice, and we moved out of New York City like a lot of couples hoping to start families. There was too much crime, too much danger. The fires that had started in the Bronx had become an epidemic, with whole blocks burning to the ground. Muggings were up and murders were, too, so Judy and I bought a house out in East Meadow, Long Island, in one of the developments Max built. He'd helped finance more than a dozen by then, and he might've set his sights on even more, except that he died in a helicopter crash over Long Island Sound in the spring of 1974.

As for Davey, I assumed I'd never hear from him again, but he did call me once, about six years after we met. It was a couple months after Max died.

In those days, I commuted an hour each way on the Long Island Railroad to my job at Farmers Insurance, where one of my old contacts from my private-eye days had gotten me a job as a claims adjuster. It wasn't glamorous work, but it paid the mortgage, and I was usually home in time to see the baby before he went to sleep each night.

That night I was rocking my four-month-old son against me, trying to get him to stop wailing, when the phone rang. Like his old man, he wasn't much of a sleeper.

"Judy!" I called, waiting for her to pick up the extension. When she didn't answer, I grabbed the phone myself. "Hello?"

"Finn?"

"Yeah?" I said, impatiently. It had been a few years, like I said, and I didn't recognize the voice on the line. Davey had still been a boy when we'd met and this was a grown man. "Who's calling?"

"It's David. 'Course I was Davey then. You remember me? From Soundview?"

"Davey, I mean David, sure, I remember you. But...how'd you find me?"

My old number had been disconnected years ago.

"The white pages, man. I knew your name—I still got that

old business card, believe it or not—so I just looked you up. Of course, I was hoping it was you and not someone else."

I laughed, feeling the baby settle against me. "How are you, David?"

"Good. I'm good. I went into the Army, just like you said...I'm out now. But it was great, I learned so much. Back in New York now, living in Yonkers. Just applied for a job at the post office."

"That's good, nice and steady."

I remembered how Davey—David, that is—had once dreamed of being a firefighter, and I almost asked him if he still did. But the baby was wriggling in my arms and the smell of meatloaf burning rose in my nostrils and I let it go.

"Glad things turned out okay for you," I said.

"Yeah, they sure did."

The baby was wailing again now, his cries an icepick in my ear.

"Look, I gotta run but...if you ever get out to Long Island, look me up."

"Sure, I'd like that. By the way...you were right."

I frowned. "Right about what?"

I listened for his reply, but there was a dial tone in my ear. He'd already hung up.

I thought about him that night, that kid from Soundview, and then not much for the next couple of years until one day when I walked out to the driveway to pick up the paper. I wore the slippers Judy had gotten me for Father's Day and an old robe that had hung on a hook on my bathroom door back in my Hell's Kitchen apartment, and unrolled the slightly-thick copy of *Newsday*. There on the front page was the headline, NOTORIOUS SON OF SAM CAUGHT, and below it a photo of a slightly scruffy man with dark curly hair and ears that stuck out a little. His name was David Berkowitz.

I knew he seemed familiar to me, but it wasn't until I turned to page three and started reading more about the man who had terrorized New York City for the previous thirteen months that I realized why.

Things hadn't turned out okay for Davey—*David, I usually go by David now*—after all.

Did I deserve any blame for what he'd become, for what he'd done? If I had reported him to the police back in '68, maybe he wouldn't have had a chance to kill half a dozen people with his infamous .44 caliber handgun. If I'd checked up on him more regularly, the way I had promised both him and myself, maybe I could've helped steer him back to the middle of the road and away from those dangerous edges. If I hadn't urged him to join the Army, maybe he wouldn't have learned how to use a gun. If I had—

Enough.

I put the rubber band back on the paper and took it out to the round tin trashcan in the driveway. It made a *plonk!*, sounding as if it had landed at the bottom of a deep well. I looked out, around the big old Plymouths and Oldsmobiles gleaming in my neighbors' driveways, the medium-sized oaks rising from their lush lawns, then went back inside.

Soundview was still my home, but I had come a long way since then, and maybe that's all anyone could do really. *And maybe that's enough*, I thought, as my son ran toward me on strong skinny legs.

"Daddy!"

Turning away for just a moment, I reached back and shut the door behind me.

PEACE TRAIN

Hugh Lessig

Anyone else calling about a job wouldn't interest me. Not now. Not with the world turned upside down. But it's Peg, and straight off I ask if she's getting a divorce. She sputters a laugh and says this is about Rodney. He's run off. I don't do missing kid cases and tell her so. She says it isn't like that, and will I please stop running my mouth and come see her because the clock is ticking. I hardly get out of bed these days, but yeah, it's Peg. I slap on some Aqua Velva to hide the bourbon oozing from my pores and head over there.

We were high school sweethearts in 1944. I lied about my age to enlist in the Marines at sixteen and didn't return to Powell's Junction until a few years after the Japanese surrendered. By then, she'd given up on me writing so much as a post card and married Floyd fucking Gates. I get to the Gates residence around noon and don't see Floyd's van in the driveway. He's got his own TV repair business and makes house calls between stops at KJ's Tavern and the gentlemen's club, parking the company van where anyone can see it.

She's standing in the doorway as I come up the sidewalk. She says, "Come inside and close the door."

I get that a lot. Powell's Junction is a one-horse town, a pass-through on the way to the Pocono Mountains. I'm the only private investigator unless you drive to Allentown. So if you're seen talking to me, half the town knows hubby is either cheating or got mangled at the stone-crushing plant and is doing homework for a lawsuit.

We take opposite ends of the couch. She's wearing a polka-dot blouse, blue jeans with rolled-up cuffs and dainty slippers. Her blond hair frames green eyes that lost their homecoming-queen sparkle sometime between V-J Day and the grassy knoll. She clears the coffee table of morning and afternoon newspapers, the headlines all about the incoming Nixon administration.

"I missed you in the Labor Day parade," she says.

The town always throws a big shindig to end the summer. In previous years, the parade featured a float with veterans of past wars. I refused to participate this year and they canceled the float. "Military uniforms aren't quite the inspiration they used to be, times being what they are," I say.

Peg wrings her hands, eyes rimmed red from crying. "It started when Walter Cronkite said we've already lost."

I resist the urge to correct her. Uncle Walter actually said of Vietnam that "we are mired in a stalemate that could only be ended by negotiation, not victory," and he was being generous. I saved a magazine article that quoted him. It sits in a pile with the photo of that guy shot in the street, wincing as the bullet struck, and pictures of Marines at the US Embassy, firing blind over the fence during the Tet Offensive. I can't look away. I smell fear in newsprint. I turn on the news and taste blood in the air. I haven't taken a case in two months, unless you count my detailed investigation of Jim Beam.

"So about your son," I say.

She throws a letter on the table from the Selective Service System. Rodney Gates is to report for induction into the Army on December 18, one month from now. I last saw him in the grocery store over the summer. He wore a green tank top and cut-off jeans with wire-rimmed sunglasses that were tinted orange. When I coached him in Little League, his hair had always been parted neatly to one side.

Peg sinks back in the couch. "He's turned into a flower child. When he was little, he played with his GI Joe. He has a footlocker with all the accessories. A medic kit, a Jeep, a tent, a poncho, a rolled-up map. He even has this little scuba outfit with a mini-submarine that runs in the bathtub."

"He's eighteen now, Peg."

"What's that supposed to mean?"

"Just what I said. If this isn't a missing persons case, you must know where he is."

"He always threatens to hop the train near Powell's Dam. Maybe he thinks it will take him to Canada."

"Always threatens? So he's wanted to leave before."

"There might have been other times."

"Tell me about them."

She shakes her head as if to shoo away a fly. "You know Floyd, Mr. Husband of the Year. When he gets plastered, he'll hit Rodney for no reason—although Rodney eggs him on with his music and his backtalk." She pushes a blond lock to hide a sickly green bruise high on her forehead. Damn Floyd hits more than his kid.

"You said the clock was ticking."

"Floyd is out looking," Peg says. "I was hoping you could find my son first."

Before I go, she wants me to see Rodney's room. His old GI Joe figures are piled in a corner, a nasty tangle of arms and legs and torsos. The trench graves on Okinawa looked something like it. A buddy of mine, a Black guy named Hodge, got the job of digging graves because they didn't allow Blacks to fight. I looked him up a few years ago and he was in a VA hospital under psychiatric care. Having never seen combat, he came home full of scars.

"Brock?"

"Sorry. The mind wanders. You wanted to show me something."

She points to his record player. My taste in music stops with Bill Haley and the Comets with some Chubby Checker thrown in for good measure. That's what I've always liked about Powell's Junction. Change comes slowly here. The turntable spins and I brace myself for a screeching guitar with reverb. But it's just some guy talking.

This record is a message to young people, to people under the age of twenty-five, and certainly to people under the age of forty. If you're over the age of forty, I'm not sure you should listen to this record. What I'm going to say might make you mad.

I turned forty earlier this year, so I guess I'm in the mad category. According to the label, the record was made by one Timothy Leary, whose name sounds vaguely familiar. It is titled "Turn On, Tune In, and Drop Out." The words roll around in my head. I don't know about the first two phrases but dropping out sounds like my idea of a plan. I can't stop seeing hollow-eyed Marines and burned children, the hard stares of villagers. I saw those faces on Okinawa. Now they stare at me from the television every damn night. Turning off the TV doesn't help. I need to find that circuit breaker in my brain and flip it on.

"This Leary fellow is on dope," Peg says. "He did some experiments with students at Harvard and talks about the psycho-chemical revolution. He says he's taken LSD three-hundred-and-eleven times."

"That sounds like a lot. I'd better get Rodney."

Her hand rests on my arm before I pull away.

Hopping the train near Powell's Dam is a local runaway tradition. A trestle bridge spans the water, and the track approaches in a sweeping arc. It requires the engineer to slow down, and it's easy for someone who's hiding behind a white birch or a stand of Mountain Laurel to run out and grab a car. The train once carried black diamonds from anthracite coal country to New

Jersey. Now it's logs and textiles and wandering souls. The track runs roughly parallel to the Old Pocono Pike, the main highway north out of town. I park the Corvair along the shoulder and hump it through the woods until I see the tracks through the trees.

The smell of wood smoke leads to a clearing where a sagging orange pup tent sits next to a fire ring of smoldering embers. A faint humming in the distance seems like a stray noise at first, then settles into a pattern. I follow it to the trestle bridge and find Rodney sitting cross-legged near the ledge, eyes closed, mumbling away. I clear my throat to announce my presence.

"Yes, I hear you," he says.

"It's Coach Haven. What are you doing out here?"

He sighs. "Expanding my consciousness. The merging of dark and light, electron and proton. Looking for inner meaning."

"I guess playing shortstop wasn't fulfilling enough."

Rodney waves a hand as if to banish the thought. "All human games end in a tie, coach. The chances of succeeding in any human game are always statistically dubious."

That sounds like this Leary fellow. I sit in the dirt a few feet away, the ground dry and crumbling like week-old coffee cake. Rodney sits too close to the ledge for my taste but doesn't seem to care. He wears striped bell bottoms and a T-shirt that once was white. A backpack is within arm's reach. His sandals appear to be fashioned from rope and tire squares. A blond ponytail rests on the nape of his neck.

"I suppose mom sent you," he says.

"She's worried."

"Mom and you used to be a thing. I saw a picture in her yearbook of you two dancing in the gym. You both belonged to the debate club and sat next to each other for the group picture. She was giving you the side eye." He chuckles. "I guess you didn't like her well enough."

"There was a war going on, Rodney. A different one, but a war all the same. I had to leave."

He smiles dreamily, eyes still closed. "Here comes the lecture. How I need to serve my country and come back a war hero like Brock Haven. He rides in the Labor Day parade and speaks at the American Legion on Memorial Day. He coaches Little League. He shows off his medals. Not my bag."

"I don't show off my medals."

"It seems like you do."

"Well, I fucking don't."

Silence settles between us. I try to think of something profound to say and come up with a question. "So, who's this Leary? It seems I've heard of him."

"Hell, man, he's been in the news for a couple of years. Harvard professor. He's into LSD, which I can't find in Powell's Junction. But you can get grass two blocks from the high school. Leary is about exploring your sensual equipment. How we're addicted to symbols, and when someone tries to break away from that addiction, society responds with screaming neurological pain."

The train isn't due for another thirty minutes. I want to keep him talking until then, which shouldn't be a problem. "Does this guy sing? Play guitar? It must get boring listening to him yap on a record. Although he seems to have a relaxing voice."

"You have the album?"

"Your mom let me listen to yours. I stopped at the part where you're supposed to get lost if you're over forty."

"Sorry, coach. You're from a different time."

"I was once a teenager when the world was spinning out of control. Don't forget that."

Behind us, a rustling in the bushes gives way to a guttural cry of triumph. Floyd Gates stumbles into the open, eyes blinking in the sun, pointing like a lucky gold digger. "God damn, Brock, but you're easy to follow."

When I was discharged from the Marines and came home in 1951, Floyd was five years out of high school and still a greaser. He wore tight-fitting T-shirts with a cigarette pack rolled up in one sleeve. Hair jelly was his catnip. Biker's boots and a six-inch switchblade completed his ensemble. Now he wears a light-blue work shirt with his name scripted in an oval at the breast pocket. He's cut back on the hair jelly and traded his biker's boots for steel toes.

But he still carries the switchblade. He flicks it open with a flip of his hairy wrist.

"Easy with that, Floyd."

"Stay out of this, Brock. I came to get my boy."

I place myself between the two men, facing Floyd. I can hear Rodney's feet shuffling on stones. Floyd circles to my right. That smirk on his face takes me back. He was in the gym that night in 1944 when I told Peg I planned to enlist. I remember the satisfaction on his face as Peg begged me to reconsider.

"You got no call to stand between a father and his son," Floyd says, "even if that piece of shit isn't worthy to be called anyone's son, not fit to be called a human being. Stays in his room and listens to faggots."

I want Floyd to make a move. He's the type to do something stupid, and that switchblade doesn't scare me. But I hadn't planned on Rodney stepping out behind me. With a high-pitched wail, the kid shoves me aside and runs straight at his father, arms flailing. I dive for him and miss.

Father and son roll in the dirt toward the ledge. Floyd ends up on top, his knees pinning Rodney's shoulders. He slaps his son in the face again and again. I wonder if Floyd hits Peg like this and the boy begs for it to stop, and if later they sit down with TV dinners and pretend everything is fine. Rodney pushes at his father's face, but Floyd's movements are practiced and calculating. He's got beating down to a science. With all the suffering in the world, there is no room for this.

I grab Floyd by the collar and toss him away from the boy, maybe with too much gusto.

Rodney's face is a red mess. Blood trickles from both nostrils and the skin is broken under one eye. He blinks and looks past me. "Where'd he go?"

I look over the ledge and see Floyd draped on a rocky outcropping. He's fallen a good thirty feet and isn't moving. As Rodney stands beside me, the body slips off and falls the rest of the way, smacking against a jutted rock before cartwheeling into the water. A swarm of blackbirds, startled by the noise, launches from the woods behind us and flies overhead in a beautiful swirling pattern.

Then things get very quiet.

"Coach...."

The boy collapses, his T-shirt dark with blood. Floyd's switchblade has plowed a furrow along his inner arm, and a red pool spreads like water. The boy's cheeks were beaten red just seconds ago. Now they're turning white before my eyes.

Rodney's backpack is within reach. I shake out the contents and find a pair of tie-dyed T-shirts covered in Chex Mix. I apply pressure to the wound with the first shirt as Rodney keeps trying to sit up, insisting he's fine.

"Lay down," I say. "You'll just make it worse."

He giggles through his fear. "I had a medic kit with my GI Joe, you know? Little things of morphine, bandages, iodine swabs, even a plasma bottle. I always wanted to get this surgical kit to go with it, but Sears was always out. Guess we could use a medic kit now."

"Calm down, shortstop. I've seen machine-gun holes, grenade holes. Yeah, a switchblade hole can be trouble, but your dad was never good with that thing. He always held it like an ornament. You'll be listening to Timothy Looney Tunes again in no time."

"I know. Dad just wanted to hurt me, Coach. The blood'll stop soon."

The way he tosses off those lines throws me for a loop. No wonder he wants nothing of Vietnam. He's already living in a war zone. Handing him an M-16 will only make things worse.

He'll either kill himself or take out his fury on someone as innocent as himself. I try to summon this truth and put it into words. Instead, my own truth spills out. "Can I tell you how I got my medals?"

He tries to roll away from me. "War stories are so out, man."

I press harder on his arm. "Just listen. I've never told this story. We had taken control of Okinawa, but pockets of resistance cropped up here and there. I was at an airfield, walking out farther than I should have. I came across this cave. We had found souvenirs in other caves: an officer's sword, a few hats and buttons. A buddy of mine came away with a luger. So I went inside and saw this kid trying to hide in the shadows. At first, I thought he was a villager, but then he threw himself at me. A real live Japanese soldier. He was half my size, nothing but skin and bones. I stabbed him in the neck with a Phillips head screwdriver because that's all I had. I could have stopped myself, but I lashed out and he bled to death before my eyes. I tried to stop the bleeding, but it was too late. Before his body went slack, he looked up as if to say, 'You didn't have to do that.' That's how I became a hero."

"I don't...I don't get it."

"That cave had a cache of explosives. It could have killed dozens of Marines. The kid was guarding it, maybe waiting for the right moment to touch it off, or maybe too scared to move. It doesn't matter. He stayed at his post while we took over the island. I ended up the hero and he got buried in a mass grave."

Blood congeals around the shirt. The kid was right. Ol' dad just wanted to hurt him.

"You're not that frightened soldier, Rodney. You will make it. You will move on with life and make your own mistakes and fall in love and affect those around you. When it comes time, people will mourn your death, but that's not today. You will leave marks in the sands of time."

"I don't want to leave marks."

"I get it, Rodney. I do. Turn on, tune in, and drop out, right?

I've been dropping out all year. I get drunk and look at the TV and think of that kid who died. Of all the kids who died before me. Of the kids dying now, on both sides. I wish I could drop out with you. I wish I could disconnect."

"Sounds like you have a lot to disconnect from, Coach."

"Yeah. I do."

"I wish I could help."

With my free hand, I pull out my wallet and shake out the black-and-white photo in the billfold. It shows a Japanese woman in traditional dress staring into the camera with a Mona Lisa smile. "The boy in the cave had this photo. I've carried it with me every day. I've wanted to find this woman so she knew her son died a hero. I see images from Vietnam and think of the mothers on both sides. I put this photo on the nightstand next to the bourbon and stare at it before going to sleep. I became a private investigator to remind myself that other people have problems, too. But no missing kid cases. Can't do them."

"Coach, stop talking. I get it."

"Excuse me?"

"Give me the photo."

"It's not yours to take. I didn't mean it that way."

"You took away my burden. Let me do this for you."

I fashion a tight bandage using the shirt sleeves. We say nothing for a few minutes. Rodney takes the photo and puts it in his backpack. When he sits up, we both study the railroad track. Then he looks at me and asks a question with perfectly clear eyes.

"You want to know about the train," I say. "See there, the apex of the curve? That's where you want to jump on. Take a running start and target the last car. The engineer will be focused on the trestle. Careful of the shot rock piled next to the track. If you trip, it's all over. The boxcar will have a ladder and the rungs can get wet. Grab as hard as you can with your good hand."

"Will the train go to Canada?"

"It will barely go to Jersey. The next town will be Truxton. It sits in a valley. You'll see it as the train approaches. Before it hits the station, step off and start walking. Then you have three alternatives: Get a job waiting tables and scrounge up money for a bus ticket. Maybe that gets you to Canada. Or keep riding the rails and end up in Jersey City. Or come back and get drafted."

"How do you know so much about the train?"

"Because I hopped it once. I caught a deadbeat husband trying to do it, and for a while it seemed like a good idea for me. But I can't run from what's inside my head."

Rodney checks the bandage on his arm. Then he reaches for his backpack and starts rummaging around. "I want you to have something, too," he says.

Peg must have heard the Corvair pull up. She opens the door before I can knock, her arms encased in thick yellow gloves. She wears one of Floyd's work shirts instead of that polka-dot blouse. Her lower lip trembles.

"I defrosted the fridge and now I'm cleaning the oven," she says. "I clean when I get nervous. And now I'm looking at the blood on your hands. Please, Brock. Don't say it's my boy."

"Your son is okay, but he's left. They'll find Floyd in the dam."

She collapses in my arms. I carry her inside to the couch. Floyd was a good dancer in his day, and I imagine he went the extra mile to make her happy while I was in the Marines not bothering to write, not seeming to care. Maybe she's remembering that version of Floyd now. Or maybe she only recalls the Floyd who beat her and Rodney. It's hard to tell if she's experiencing relief or sadness. She finally looks up, expectant.

"Your husband had a knife," I say. "He stabbed Rodney and was beating him to kingdom come. I tossed him off and he fell in the dam. I let Rodney hop the train. He'll make it to Truxton and decide what to do from there. I have no regrets about Floyd. He hit you, and don't tell me otherwise. He was an angry drunk and didn't deserve either of you."

Peg sits up on the couch. "I need to go to Truxton."

"Let the boy find his own way."

"You go then. I'll hire you. I'm fixed for life insurance and Floyd has savings."

I hold up my hand to stop her. "It's not about the money. Rodney doesn't know how he fits into this crazy world. I dig the feeling, as they say. He's doing it a different way than I did. This turn on, tune in, and drop out business—yeah, it's drugs. But Rodney isn't the drug type. He's a hard thinker, always was. When he played shortstop, he was consumed with finding the perfect angle. He's got some thinking to do. And given where Uncle Sam wants him to go, he might be doing the right thing. I know he's breaking the law, and it sounds odd coming from a buzz-cut, float-riding old fogey like me."

"So you're on his side now," she says.

"I'm saying he may be ahead of his time. I don't have a good feeling about this war, and between all the gobbledygook, this Leary says one thing that halfway makes sense. It always takes one generation for a new idea to become accepted."

"Don't tell me you have that record, too."

"I have Rodney's notes on it. He gave them to me, thinking I might get something out it. I was reading them before I came here. Your son's got a good heart, Peg. For now, just let him be."

The radiator hisses steam as she peels off her rubber gloves. When it falls silent, the air seems perfectly still. Her voice comes out as a whisper: "I should put away his toys. There was a time when he liked simple things."

"Keep the GI Joe stuff handy. He might want them someday."

She scoots across the couch and kisses me softly. Suddenly I'm back under the bleachers and it's 1944 and the world is turned upside down again. A heartbeat passes as I gently push her away.

SUNDOWN TOWN

Mark Troy

Horatio slid the exposed photographic paper into the developer solution and gently rocked the tray back and forth while he sang "Reach Out, I'll Be There" to time the process. The darkest areas emerged first—a helmet-like afro and a pubic triangle. Then came eyes and nipples, followed by the other lines and shadows that finally coalesced into a portrait of a nude woman at the end of the third verse. Horatio drained the developer and moved the paper into the stop bath and then the fixer. He hung the photo on the drying line with the others and repeated the process with the next image. When finished, he turned off the red light and flipped on the overhead, which changed his darkroom back into a kitchen. He ducked under the string of photographs and took a Falstaff from the Sears Coldspot. Then he surveyed his work.

The woman, mid-twenties, appeared in three photos, but in only one was she fully nude. Horatio had had to move close to the window for it. He'd had only seconds to set it up and snap it before retreating to the concealed spot from which he'd shot the others.

Two men showed in others. One wore a clergy collar.

Horatio returned to the refrigerator for another Falstaff and a half-eaten paper carton of Chinese noodles. He parted the heavy blackout curtain separating the kitchen from the living room of the small apartment where a Goodwill sofa faced a portable black-and-white television on an upended orange crate. Before sitting, he cleared away some books on photography from the St. Louis County Library and a months-old issue of *Jet* magazine, with boxer-turned-actor Floyd Patterson on the cover. A folded letter marked a place in one book. Horatio removed it and reread it. It was dated three days earlier and embossed with the great seal of the state of Missouri. Horatio's gaze settled on the two words he'd read many times since its arrival the previous day—"application denied." He crumpled the paper into a ball and threw it across the room.

"Fuck that," Horatio said. "Denied, denied, denied. Always denied."

Horatio stroked the crook of his elbow where a few tiny bumps itched as they always did when he felt stress. *Denials, just fallin' like shit bricks from the sky,* he thought.

Horatio threw the box of noodles across the room. It hit the wall with a wet plop and joined the crumpled letter on the floor.

Horatio parked his '61 Karmann Ghia in the public garage near the St. Louis County government buildings. He slung the camera bag containing his Canon SLR and Vivitar 150mm lens over his shoulder before locking the little car. Clayton, especially this part of the town, was suit city. The sidewalks teemed with white faces in suits who moved to the side for the man in the Army field jacket, striped jeans, and jump boots.

Greenwald Investigations occupied a suite on the third floor of the Pierson Building a block from the courthouse. The other four floors held law offices and title companies. Horatio pushed through the revolving door into a lobby filled with more suits. A blazer-clad security guard came out from behind a reception desk in the center and approached him tentatively. Horatio figured him for a county deputy supplementing his retirement.

"Can I help you?" the man asked, looking up at the larger man.

"Yeah," Horatio said. "You can stay outta my way."

"Are you sure you're in the right building? The government assistance office is located in the government annex. That's two streets over."

"Ha-ha. Next words outta your mouth better not include 'parole office' or you be the one needing government assistance."

The guard retreated behind his desk. "No need to be huffy, sir. Is someone expecting you?"

"Oh, they expecting me all right."

The guard picked up a telephone receiver. "Can I call up and say you're on your way?"

Horatio grinned at him. "Be obliged. Greenwald Investigations."

The guard pushed some buttons on the phone. "Who should I say?"

"Just tell them the soul brother is here."

The guard blanched. He said into the receiver, "Yes, this is the lobby. I have a—"

"Soul brother," Horatio said. When the guard hesitated, Horatio gestured with his hand for him to continue.

"Um a soul brother, who...Yes, of course." The guard replaced the receiver in the cradle. "They're expecting you, Mr. Cutter."

"Now that weren't so hard, were it?" The man eyed Horatio's hand nervously as Horatio reached into his jacket pocket. "You validate parking?" Horatio asked. He produced a ticket.

"Yes, yes, yes," the man breathed. He stamped the stub, eagerly, it seemed to Horatio, and returned it.

"Now if you'll be kind enough to escort me to the elevator."

The guard scurried out from behind the desk. "Follow me, Mr. Cutter."

The elevators were no more than thirty feet away, clearly visible. The man pushed forward, head down, not looking at Horatio. People in front of the elevators cleared a path. The doors slid open on the nearest elevator. Men in suits and women in dresses paused in mid-conversation, hesitated, and then sidled quickly past Horatio. Horatio stepped into the empty car. The guard reached in and pushed button three.

"Going up?" Horatio said to the handful of people outside. The doors slid shut. "Guess not."

Mack Greenwald had taken over Greenwald Investigations after his father had built it up to the largest PI firm in Missouri with offices in St. Louis and Kansas City.

"So you couldn't just come up without mau-mauing the guard?" Greenwald said when Horatio had been shown in. He was hanging a photo on a wall celebrating his influence with the city's elite.

"'Mau-mauin', I never heard it used as a verb. You make it up? Anyway, I was just havin' fun with him. Mau-mauin', I guess, 'cause he wasn't gonna let me up. Wanted to make him say 'soul brother' and sweat some."

"Did he? Sweat, I mean?"

Horatio grinned. "Oh, hell yeah, he be sweatin'. How come it's so hard for whitey to say 'soul brother' but 'spade' just rolls off their tongue?"

Greenwald shrugged. "Could be they think there's another meaning that'll trip 'em up. A spade, though, that's a shovel, right?"

"Good one, Boss."

Greenwald stepped back and admired the picture he'd hung. He beckoned Horatio over. "Take a look at this."

The photo showed Greenwald and two other men posing with Bob Gibson in his Cardinals uniform. "Game one," Greenwald said, referring to the ongoing World Series with Cardinals versus the Detroit Tigers. "Gibson pitched lights out. You proud of your boy?"

"What you mean 'my boy'?" Horatio asked.

"Well, he's Black, right? And you're Black. He's one of you."

"I got it, man. Being Black is like being in a club, is what you're sayin'? We all be rooting for each other. One for all and all for one."

"Look," Greenwald said, "I didn't mean to offend you."

"No offense, man. I get you. So, how'd you meet my man, Gibson?"

"Roger's got a box at Busch behind the plate." Greenwald indicated one of the men in the photo. Horatio noticed the same man appeared in another one, handing Greenwald a plaque beneath a Chamber of Commerce banner.

"Must be nice to know bigshots," Horatio said.

"Gets you into high places." Greenwald took a seat in an armchair and gestured to a chair facing him. "Were you able to get anything?"

Horatio extracted some photos from a side compartment of the camera bag and spread them on a coffee table between them. "This here's the church. Guess you never seen it, it being in Kinloch and all."

"Can't say I have," Greenwald said.

"Not too many white faces get down Kinloch way. The church, it got a building attached to it, probably built later, where they hold meetings. Open room in front, some offices in back for the minister and secretary. I scoped it out ahead of time. The minister, he's a white man. You know that?"

"That's what I was told," Greenwald said. "Did you find any evidence of a radical agenda when you scoped out the meeting area? Pamphlets? Leaflets? Posters promoting violence or fomenting revolution?"

"Leaflets? You mean like Huey P. Newton's Ten Point Program leaflets?"

Greenwald's eyes lit with excitement. "You saw some of those?"

Horatio laughed. "Just mau-mauin' you, man. Was some cards on a table with the Beatitudes. 'Blessed are the poor' and stuff. Painting of JC and the twelve at The Last Supper and some posters of Martin and Bobby. Couple banners sayin' 'Peace' and

'Love.' Might be radical shit to some people."

Greenwald moved the photos of the church to the side and picked up two more. In one, a youngish Black man, wearing a sporty blazer over a white turtleneck and plaid slacks was exiting a three- or four-year-old Buick Skylark.

"He doesn't dress like any radical I've ever seen," Greenwald said. "Do radicals drive Buicks?"

"He ain't no radical," Horatio said. "Check it out." He took a magnifying glass from the camera bag and gave it to Greenwald. "See here?" He pointed to a rectangular decal on the car's windshield.

Greenwald examined it. "Laclede something," he read.

"Junior High. In Wellston. Drove by this morning and spotted that Skylark in the assistant principal's spot."

"Does he have a name?"

"Randolf Burton."

Another photo showed the man at the door of the annex building being greeted by a white man wearing a clerical collar. "Reverend Jonathan Krueger," Horatio said. "I got more shots, but you get the idea. Burton and Krueger went inside. Burton came out a half hour later and left."

Greenwald sat back in his chair. "So far it's all pretty normal."

"You mind I ask what this is all about?" Horatio asked.

"The North County Chamber of Commerce is worried about the racial violence in DC, Detroit, Chicago, and LA spilling down here. Somebody picked up a rumor of planning meetings being held at the church. The police are blowing it off, so the Chamber engaged our services to investigate."

"But you couldn't send no white face down to Kinloch to peep through windows."

"Right," Greenwald said. "It appears to have been all for naught."

"Well hold on, Boss. Got a couple more pictures to show you." Horatio laid out another set. The first one showed an attractive young woman approaching the church annex.

"Brown sugar," Greenwald said. "Did I say that right?"

The woman wore a curve-hugging, striped mini-dress above textured hose and high-heeled ankle boots. Her most striking feature, though, was the voluminous 'fro surrounding her head.

"She working that whole Black-is-beautiful thing," Horatio said.

"Her hairdo, definitely a militant look." Greenwald studied another photo showing the woman going through the door. "Where was Krueger at this time? Was this before or after Burton?"

"During. Krueger and Burton was meeting in a back room. I went around and heard them talking."

"What was the woman doing?"

"My guess is she was undressing."

"Undressing?" Greenwald seemed surprised.

"Why you surprised? Cheatin' makes the world go round. It's what you hire me for."

"You shoot any pictures of her nude?" Greenwald seemed excited at the thought.

Horatio hesitated. "Nope," he lied. "Taking photos through windows ain't exactly ethical."

"Ethics," Greenwald said. "Ethics don't mean anything until you have a license to lose. Which you don't."

"Too dark, even if I wanted to."

"Pity about the light." Greenwald appeared genuinely disappointed. "Thought we could get something good on the reverend."

"Hold on, Boss." Horatio brought out another photo. "So I went back out front and waited. Burton leaves. About twenty minutes later, the girl comes out. Notice anything?"

Greenwald peered at the photo. "Top buttons of her dress are undone."

"Check her legs. Smooth, right? Where's the pantyhose? You ask me, the girl and Krueger wasn't making revolution. They was doing the old horizontal hoochie coo. Burn, baby, burn."

"I don't know what to make of this."

"So the girl showed up in a cab that waited down the street for her to come out. Seems to me she had this planned and got money from somebody."

"We need to find out more about this girl," Greenwald said.

"Way ahead of you, Boss. I followed the cab. Little place in North St. Louis. Here's the address." Horatio wrote it out on paper.

Greenwald took the paper and stacked the photos together. "Great work."

Horatio closed his camera bag. "I was wonderin' about you puttin' me on permanent. You said you was gonna think about it."

"I did," Greenwald said. "Have you heard from Jeff City?"

Horatio's spirits fell. He sighed. "Yeah."

"What did they say?"

"Denied."

Greenwald grimaced. "Sorry. Did they give a reason?"

"Nope. I can't figure it. Got a clean criminal record. A distinguished service record."

"High marks on the test, too. So what grounds could they have?"

Horatio thought about it. "Had to guess, it's my picture. Part of the application process."

Greenwald grimaced again. "I'm truly sorry, Horatio. What century are we living in? You'd think this was still the nineteen-hundreds the way my people treat your people. I'm not condoning the militants, and especially the Panthers, but sometimes I think we created the conditions for them to form. You take my meaning?"

"Yeah, right on, Man."

"I can't hire you as an agent without a license. Wish I could. You know that. I can throw some more freelance assignments your way if something comes up."

"'Preciate it."

Greenwald stood, signaling the end of the meeting. "See

Clara on your way out. She has an envelope for you."

Horatio parked the Ghia on Mable Avenue, which bordered Kinloch Park. He shouldered his camera bag and wound past honey maple trees abloom in fall-red colors to a picnic table flanked by golden-leafed sumacs. A young woman occupied the table, watching a group of children romping on monkey bars and swings on the other side of a spray pad and wading pool, both of which were closed until summer. He put the camera bag down beside a small transistor tuned to WESL, soul radio from East St. Louis. Gladys Knight sang "I Wish it Would Rain."

"Okay if I sit?" Horatio asked.

The woman looked up at him. She wore owlish eyeglasses with tinted lenses, giving her a modish, yet scholarly look. Her clothes were anything but modish—a faded sweater jacket with patched elbows worn over a shapeless jumper—but clean. They exuded a faint, baby powder smell of Ivory soap. Only her 'fro remained from her appearance the previous evening.

"Do I know you?" she asked.

"Not yet," Horatio said. He removed a photograph from his camera bag. He laid it between them. The nude in the window. "You, right?"

The woman pushed it away. Her face hardened. "They told me there would be a peeper. So it be you, huh? Peeper? They said put on a show 'cause the man wants to see. I thought they was meaning a white man, but peeping is peeping. You got your show. What you want from me? Money? I ain't got none."

"Don't want money. Want some answers is all."

"Ain't got none of those neither. So why don't you just git?"

"Who were you working for?"

"What makes you think I was working for anybody, Peeper?" She took a pack of Kools from her purse, shook out a cigarette, and lit it. She blew a cloud of menthol into the air.

"You said they told you there would be a peeper," Horatio

said. "I want to know who 'they' is."

"Why you askin' me, if you're in with them?"

"I ain't in with them. I never met them."

"But now you want to meet them so you can sell them more pictures?"

"I want to know what's going on. What were you doing in the church?"

"I told you. I was givin' a show. Got paid for it."

"Sleeping with the minister? Was that part of the show?"

The woman's eyes flashed in anger behind the glasses. "No. You sayin' I'm a whore?"

"No, but somebody wanted me to see something and I need to know who."

"So they use you, just like they use me." She sucked hard on the cigarette, causing the ember to glow angrily.

"Who are they?"

"Shit. You naive? Whitey's who." The woman ground the cigarette into the tabletop and brushed it into the grass. "Don't matter their names. They use you. They use me. You get what I'm saying? They usin' all us Black people."

Her eyes welled up. She put her face in her hands and sobbed. Horatio laid his hand gently on her shoulder. "What's your name?" he asked.

"Bernadette," she said between sobs.

"I'm Horatio, Bernadette, and I'm gonna put an end to them usin' us, but I need your help."

"Put an end to it. You are really, truly one naive brother." She raised her head. "You see that little man over there? The one wearin' the red jacket an' the blue sock cap?"

Horatio saw the boy she described playing a running game with some other children about his age. Two adult women watched them. Horatio thought they might be a preschool class or a daycare.

"My little man, he's turnin' five this month."

"He lives with you?" Horatio asked.

Bernadette shook her head. "With my mama. Only way I can see him is this way. Child protective people, they let me visit him at Christmas and birthdays."

"Why?" Horatio asked, though he thought he knew.

"This," she hissed. She pulled up her sleeve and showed him her arm. Needle scars. They hadn't been visible in the photograph because of the lighting and position of her hand.

"Those ain't new. You been clean awhile," Horatio said.

"What do you know about it?"

Horatio pushed up his own sleeve and displayed the crook of his elbow.

"Another junkie," she sneered. "How long from your last fix?"

"Eleven months. Since I got back from Nam."

"Don't feel so proud of yourself. Three years for me and I still feel the urge. Once a junkie always a junkie. You ain't never shake the shit. An' you think you ever gonna get your child back? Hunh-uh."

"Bernadette, tell me. How are they using you?"

Bernadette dabbed at her eyes with her sleeve. "My mama takin' care of my little man. She clean them white folks' houses over there." Bernadette pointed across Mable Avenue where a wooded area separated the city of Kinloch from the city of Ferguson. "She do it so he can go to daycare and have clothes and toys. Food on the table. Bed to sleep in. She gone from mornin' till dark. You can't be in Ferguson after dark if you're Black. You know, right? Even if you're comin' home all tired an' all from workin', you gotta scoot when the sun goes down."

Horatio nodded. A sundown town. Ferguson was long known to be one. "That's against the law," he said.

"Ain't a law on the books, 'cause of civil rights, but everybody knows how it is."

On the playground, the adult women were herding the children together. Bernadette stood and walked over to the edge of the spray pad. One of the women stopped her son and pointed at Bernadette. Mother and son waved before the woman turned the boy back into the group. Horatio got off some shots while The Isley Brothers sang "Behind a Painted Smile."

Bernadette came back to Horatio. "They're going for a nap now." She picked up the nude photo.

"Yours," Horatio said.

Bernadette put it in her purse. She sighed deeply. "Wish I had a photo of little man. You live around here?"

"North St. Louis."

"Me, too. But I grew up here in Kinloch." She seized his sleeve. "Wanna see the sights? We might see Dick Gregory's house," she said. When they reached Horatio's Ghia, she said, "You weren't foolin' nobody followin' us last night. The cabby, he picked up this little red, white-boy car right away. He wanted to know should he lose you. I told him no. I figured I'd already showed you everything. What more could you see?"

"It's the only ride I can afford. Might have to find another way to tail people."

Bernadette directed him to drive down Mable Avenue. She had him take the first cross street toward Ferguson, but they were able to go only a few hundred yards before they reached a barrier of construction material and debris. Wooden timbers, culvert sections, and piles of concrete were piled haphazardly from one side of the road to the other without gaps.

Bernadette said, "The good folks of Ferguson, they blocked off all the roads in and out of Kinloch. They even had a city councilman wanted to build a kind of Berlin wall between the cities. It never passed, but they never move these barriers. Only one road to go in and out—Suburban Avenue where the bus runs."

Bernadette had him try two other streets so Horatio could see all the barriers for himself.

"One day a white lady my mama works for asks Mama to stay and do a few extra chores. My mama says okay, but when she's done, it's dark and she get worried about getting home.

The man, he says he gonna drive her. Only he gets her to the other side of one of these barriers and he says, 'Oops, look like you got a problem.' And then he tells her she better be careful if she want to keep workin' in these houses in Ferguson."

"Then did he take her home?" Horatio asked.

"He watched her climb over and around the barrier on her own. See, it was a message they own her, and she better do as they say."

"So how does that involve you?"

Bernadette directed Horatio to Suburban Avenue. "You know what happens to my little man if Mama loses her jobs?"

"I can imagine," Horatio said. "No more daycare, for starters."

"Not just daycare. She got no money for food, for prescriptions. Little man has asthma. He needs his medication. Maybe Mama gets evicted. If she can't provide, child protective takes him. He goes into foster care an' I never see him again." Bernadette wiped her eyes.

"A man came to you," Horatio said.

"All I had to do was go in the church and put on the show for the peeper."

Horatio winced. "Can we quit with the peeper?"

Bernadette touched his hand. "You feelin' bad? Ain't nothin' how I'm feelin'. If I do the show, Mama keeps her shitty jobs scrubbin' white people shit outta white people toilets an' I still get to see my little man from way across the park. Tell me all I gotta do is flash my baby maker? Yeah, I'm doin' it." She fished another Kool from her purse.

"You know the homes your mama works? Show me."

Horatio saw the Skylark, two cars ahead, turn off Florissant Road onto Frost Street in Ferguson. He followed. Sycamores, oaks, sugar maples, and an occasional cottonwood filled the manicured yards on both sides of the narrow street. Bicycles lay on lawns. Hoops hung over garage doors. Marvin Gaye sang "I Heard It Through the Grapevine" on the Ghia's radio.

The Skylark turned at the third intersection onto a street virtually identical to the one they'd just left. Nineteen-fifties era homes—single story, brick with stone accents, single car garage, nine-pane picture window perfect for displaying a Christmas tree. The Skylark slowed in front of a home in the middle of the block and stopped. Four houses back, Horatio stopped. There was nothing to distinguish the object of Burton's interest from the other homes in the neighborhood except the "For Sale" sign in the front yard. "Want a deal? Roger that!" the sign said above a phone number. The Skylark moved on. Horatio moved. He paused for a minute to snap a picture and make a note of the sign.

After a few more turns, the Skylark came to a stop near a barrier on the Ferguson side. Randolf Burton got out and waited. Horatio pulled over and climbed out of the Ghia.

"That little red car is hard to miss," Burton said. "You been following me from the school. Why?"

"You seem interested in a house for sale back there," Horatio said.

"So? You wanting to buy it?"

"Not my style," Horatio said.

Burton crossed his arms. "Uh-huh. So why you following me?"

"Reverend Jonathan Krueger."

"The reverend? What about him?"

"You visited him last night. What about?"

"Why should I tell you?"

"Some people think the reverend is doing some radical organizing. Fo-MEN-ting revolution, they say. You know anything about that?"

Burton broke into a grin. "Fomenting revolution. Yeah, you got us. We be fomenting. We're fomenters."

Horatio grimaced at the sarcasm. Burton, in his garish plaid slacks and burgundy turtleneck, looked more country club than revolutionary.

"What?" Burton said. "You think 'cause I don't wear no ratty Army jacket and don't have no Black Panther 'do I can't foment?"

"Okay," Horatio said. "Explain it to me."

"That house back there, I plan on buying it," Burton said.

"I don't understand," Horatio said.

Burton spread his arms. "See where we are. Ferguson. How many Black people live here? None. Fact is, we ain't wanted here. They erected these barriers to keep us out."

"And so you want to go to war over the barriers?"

"Shit, I don't want no war. I just want that house. It's a cute house. Got a kitchen with Formica counters and a wall of cabinets my wife will love. One bedroom for my two little girls and another bedroom for my boy. Safe street to ride their bikes. A garage to keep my fishing gear."

"But there's a problem," Horatio said.

"Damn right there's a problem. I call the real estate office to tour the house and they say they get back to me, but they never do. Can't disguise my Black voice."

Horatio understood. *Denied, denied, denied. Denials fallin' like shit bricks.*

"It's called redlining," Burton said. "The white bankers and the white real estate agents, they get together and they mark an area off limits. The agents won't show no house and the bankers won't give no mortgage. Civil rights be damned. Equality be damned. Yeah, no more drinking fountains for colored only, but that don't matter if there ain't any colored to use them."

Horatio thought he knew the answer to his next question, but he asked anyway. "What's the reverend's involvement?"

"He's the middleman. He talks to the agents and the banks, gets the deal, and I get the house. The redline is the battle line. We bust the redline, we win the revolution. You wanna raise your fist, go ahead. I wanna raise my kids in a nice home. Ferguson's gonna change. Other people, colored people, will follow. No burning like other cities."

***

Mack Greenwald looked at the two men seated with him at the table in the small conference room of the North County Chamber of Commerce office. To his left was real estate agent Roger "Roger that!" Schultze. To his right sat Charles M. Miller, president of Union Bank.

Greenwald said, "Tough game last night. I thought Gibson looked pretty good, but Lolich was just a little better."

Schultze shook his head, "We'd a won if Flood hadn't misplayed that ball in center. You ask me, there's too much darkness on the team."

"Too much darkness in baseball, period," Miller agreed. "Baseball is going too far with this anti-discrimination. Too many spades taking spots from good white players."

"Roger that!" Schultze said.

Greenwald opened a folder and removed the photos Horatio had given him. He fanned them out on the table between the men. "This is the guy who's been calling you, Roger." He stabbed a finger on the photo of Randolf Burton. "Assistant principal in Wellston."

"He should stay in Wellston," Miller said. "The colored are moving too far this way. We need to hold the line."

"How do we do that?" Schultze asked.

Greenwald pointed to the photo of Krueger. "The minister. He's aiding Burton. We'll have a chat with him and make him back off."

"What makes you think he'll listen?" Miller asked.

"Because if he doesn't, his ministry will be rocked with scandal. Consorting with a prostitute." Greenwald displayed the photos of Bernadette entering and leaving the church.

"You got them in bed together?" Miller asked.

"No, but this is enough. Unbuttoned dress, no pantyhose. He won't want to have to explain that to the press or to his synod. If he still won't play, we have this." He brought out another photo, a mugshot. "Same girl a few years back when she was arrested for turning tricks for smack."

"How did you get that?" Schultze asked.

The conference room door flew open and Horatio burst in, followed by the Chamber's secretary.

"I'm sorry," she said. "Mr. Cutter was listening outside. I couldn't get him to leave."

Greenwald rose to his feet. "Did you threaten her, Horatio?"

"Call me Mr. Cutter," Horatio said. "Like in the movie where the guy says 'call me Mr. Tibbs'. An' no, I didn't threaten her." He turned to the woman. "I threaten you, ma'am?"

She shook her head. "No, no. You're just—"

"Intimidatin'?"

She nodded.

"Gotta work on that. Thank you, ma'am. You can go."

Greenwald said, "What do you want, Hor—"

Horatio waggled a finger.

"What do you want, *Mister* Cutter?"

"Let's all get acquainted," Horatio said. "You, sir, must be 'Roger that!' Schultze. I recognize you from your pictures. Pleased to meet you." He held out his hand, but Schultze refused it. "Right on." He turned to the other man. "You must be Mr. Miller, the banker man, who's gonna give Mr. Burton a mortgage."

"That won't happen," Miller said.

"Oh, it will once word gets out what you fine citizens been cooking up."

Greenwald resumed his seat. "You don't know what you're talking about, Ho—Mister Cutter."

"Yeah, I'm just a uppity shovel. Ain't that what you mean? Why don't you finish telling how you acquired that mug shot of Miss Jordan? That's her name, by the way, Bernadette Jordan. Call her Miss Jordan."

"I arrested *Miss* Jordan," Greenwald said.

"When you was with the St. Louis Police Department,

wasn't it?"

Greenwald nodded. "You seem to know the answers."

"You kept in touch with Miss Jordan after you arrested her, didn't you?"

"To make sure she straightened out."

"Righteous of you. You even helped her mother find work, ain't that right?" Horatio looked from Schultze to Miller and back. "Her mother cleans each of your houses. Wipes up your messes. Takes out your garbage. Scrubs the shit out of your toilets."

Greenwald said, "I felt sorry for her. I made sure she had work."

"And made sure you had a hold on her daughter." Horatio took a cassette tape from his pocket and held it up. "She told me about the hold you had on her and her mama. She told me how you used her and used me, too. I got it here."

Greenwald said, "She can say anything she wants. It doesn't prove anything. Now, you've said your part. It's time you left."

Horatio sat down at the end of the table. "Oh, I ain't done. Lemme ask you, why exactly did you leave the police department?"

Greenwald glared at him.

"Was it because you got passed over for promotion?" Horatio turned to Miller. "You'll appreciate this. A Black brother got the job he wanted. You wouldn't think a soul brother'd have police friends, would you?"

Greenwald said, "The city was taking this affirmative action shit too far. That job was mine."

Schultze said, "Do we need to call the police?"

Horatio shook his head. "You don't want the heat. You're all in violation of federal law." From his camera bag, he removed a thick book. "Visited the County Library this morning. You know they got a section on government docs? I didn't either, but a sweet little librarian pointed me the way. Know what this is? It's a law President Johnson himself signed just this year. It's called the Civil Rights Act of 1968. You men read it? No? Well, me neither. But the librarian tells me Title Eight is where it's at. Title Eight got a name called the Fair Housing Act. You know what it prohibits? Exactly what you're engaged in. *Dee*-scrimination in sale and financing of housing based on race."

Miller slapped his palms down and leaned forward. "It's your word against ours. Nobody's going to believe you."

Horatio stood. "It ain't just my word. It's your words." He looked at Greenwald. "Not only did you get 'Roger that!' to hire Miss Jordan's mama, you urged him to hire her here at the Chamber's office. In fact, don't she come here in the mornings to sweep and empty the trash before going on to her houses?"

Greenwald didn't answer. Horatio took three steps to a corner of the room where a wastebasket sat. "Well, look here," he said. He withdrew a mini-cassette recorder and a microphone. "You're all recording stars."

"You son of a bitch," Greenwald said. "After all I did for you."

"About that," Horatio said. "There's another thing the cute librarian helped me find. The people on the board. So much knowledge in the library. You know which board I'm talking about? The board that approves and denies PI applications. Were you gonna tell me you're on it? It came to me when you said I passed high on the test, something only me and the board would know. All that, 'I'm sorry, what century are we living in?' was bullshit. You vetoed my application for a license."

Greenwald didn't answer.

"Thought so," Horatio said. He opened the door and called out, "Reverend, I believe these men are ready to deal on a house."

Greenwald said, "You're going to regret this day, Cutter. You'll never be licensed while I'm on the board."

"I can wait. The future is sooner than you think."

Reverend Krueger entered, followed by another man, whom Krueger identified as an ACLU lawyer. Horatio found Randolf Burton waiting outside.

"A new future for Ferguson," Horatio said.

"How did you do it?" Burton asked.

"I introduced them to their worst nightmare," Horatio said. "A spade with a library card."

Horatio sang "Bernadette" for timing as he rocked the developer tray gently back and forth. An image of a young boy, all smiles and missing front teeth slowly emerged. Bernadette's little man.

Bernadette's flat was dark when Horatio arrived. He'd framed little man's portrait and wrapped it as a gift. The front door gave when he knocked. He pushed it open and called Bernadette's name. No answer. The only sound was the static from an off-tuned black-and-white TV on a cart. He turned it off and called her name again. He switched on a floor lamp.

The flat was tiny and austere, like his own. A swaybacked sofa and a scarred end table completed the furnishings. The nude photo lay ripped into pieces on the bare floor.

Horatio went down a narrow hall, a feeling of dread filling his chest and pushing into his throat. He found her on the kitchen floor wearing only a bra and panties. A rubber tube was tied around her upper arm and a needle was embedded at the crook of her elbow. A spoon and a lighter lay near her outstretched fingers.

Horatio called her name again and knelt beside her. He felt for a pulse. She had none. He cradled her in his arms. That was when he found the picture, which had been under her body. It was her mug shot from Greenwald with words written on the back. "The future is now."

THE UGLY

Stephen D. Rogers

When we look back on the sixties, as we are doomed to do, as if living through it once isn't bad enough, I imagine people will be tripping over themselves making excuses for this cultural wasteland: it was the war, it was the drugs, it was the television brought to you in living color.

It's the decade, Man.

I killed men so that we didn't end up speaking German, and now you can't even speak English.

Or maybe time has passed me by. I'm not saying it's not a possibility that the sixties will bleed into the seventies and then the eighties. I just hope not. I still go into the office every day because that's my job. I still wear a suit and tie. More often than not, I wear a hat when I'm outside.

Call me a square, a drag, a downer. Call me whatever made-up word you want. When you need help, do you head to the nearest pad to find another hippie who can read your aura?

No. You knock on my door, because you know I can get the job done.

You got a problem with the fact that I have a problem with you? Go fuck yourself.

This time, it was a young couple sitting on the far side of my desk, their eyes red, and not because they'd been crying. I say couple, but I didn't see any rings, just a little too much familiarity.

"Free love" they call it because they don't realize the price they're paying.

"So when was the last time your mother saw your father?" I addressed Rainbow because it was his father who was missing. I resisted asking if Rainbow was short for John, Robert, or Charles.

"Two months ago now, and nothing since."

"Maybe it's good riddance."

Rainbow shook his head. "The old man wasn't like that. If he's not home for supper, something's wrong. My mother called the police, the hospital, even the morgue. He's just gone."

"Where's he work?"

"The factory on Riverside. He's a slave to the system."

Remember the roof over your head for your first eighteen years? The food and clothing you took for granted? Your father was a slave all right. Guess who benefited?

"I'll talk to the people down there, see where it leads me. You know any of his friends?"

"Not really."

Of course you wouldn't bother learning their names, paying them at least that much respect. They're the older generation. They're out of touch.

"He probably worked with most of them at the factory. Any chance he was seeing anyone on the side?"

"My father?" Rainbow laughed. "Nah, man, he welcomed the ball and chain."

I could smack this kid across the face, or I could take the money he'd placed on my desk as soon as he sat down.

Pragmatism won, and I slid the bills across the surface into my open middle drawer. I could always beat some sense into him later, assuming that was even possible.

I'd never been inside the factory where the father worked, and after stepping onto the floor, I still didn't know what they made except that the process involved men standing at unwieldy machines, flying sparks, and the sound of metal grinders.

Tapping on the shoulder of the nearest worker led me to the foreman, who led me to a breakroom so we could talk.

The room contained three wooden picnic tables, a folding table with two coffee urns, and a wall of lockers, labeled, but not actually locked.

After introducing himself as Bud Reilly, the foreman and I sat. I handed him a business card. "As I said out there, I'm looking for Frank Wilson."

"Did he do something wrong?" Bud kept his hair cut short, and I didn't imagine his eyes missed much on the periphery.

"Not as far as I know, unless you count not returning home one day."

"And not coming to work, which isn't like Frank. Listen, I don't know what I can tell you. He comes in every day, he does his job, he leaves. At least until he stopped coming in."

"Who does he pal around with?"

"Breaks are short. Maybe you talk to the other guys at your table, but mostly you focus on eating or finishing your cigarette. Out on the floor, they're one-man machines."

"Is there a place the guys go after work?"

"Probably. I drink on the other side of town, so they don't have to run into me."

"Trouble?"

Bud shook his head. "I just don't want them thinking they can't let off steam. I'm not the owner, but I'm not one of them, either."

"If I said I know for certain that Frank told someone who works here what he was planning to do, who do you see on the other side of that conversation?"

"Jimmy. I don't know that for sure, but that's who I see."

"Good." I placed a five on the picnic table. "I'd appreciate if you let Jimmy know I'll be standing outside at quitting time, and I wouldn't mind buying him a drink."

"I can do that."

"I appreciate your help." I dismounted the bench. "Is there anybody who didn't ask you about Frank when he quit coming in? Somebody you would have expected to ask?"

"They mind their own business."

I snorted. "That's not my experience with human nature."

"The work's steady, and the money's good."

"And they're all replaceable."

Bud shrugged. "That's up to the owner."

"Thanks for your help, and for passing my message to Jimmy."

"I hope you find Frank and can persuade him to come back. Not everybody is equally replaceable."

"I'll do my best."

Walking through the floor on my way out, I came across a pallet of finished product, piles of the small pieces collected in boxes, and I still didn't know what they made. I had the sense, however, looking at the men around me, that even if they couldn't point at a completed building or bridge, they could take pride in a job well done.

I left them to it.

Time to talk to the wife. I had wanted to get a sense of the missing man from his coworkers first, because spouses tend to see each other through the prism of their own self-interest. As a general rule, spouses react to my reports with shock.

"I had absolutely no idea."

Everybody but the milkman knew the truth, and the person who actually lived with the subject of my investigation didn't have a clue.

The couple lived in a triple-decker not far from the factory, dead center in a nine-block square of similar arrangements. Their neighbors would be assembly-line workers and firefighters, truck drivers and bakers, storeowners and stiffs. Half the women worked at least part-time jobs to make ends meet.

I parked on the street next to a kid jumping rope, donned my hat, and went to introduce myself to the woman of the house.

She opened the door wearing a bandanna on her head and with a cigarette between her lips. "Yah?"

"I'm looking into the disappearance of your husband."

"Why?"

It was a good thing I hadn't started here. I might have returned my client's deposit. "Rainbow hired me."

She rolled her eyes. "You must mean Robert. You might as well come on in if you're not going to leave." She walked into the house.

I took off my hat, stepped inside, and closed the door. Opened the coat closet and took a quick inventory. Followed her deeper into the house until I found her in the living room, sitting on the couch, tamping the cigarette in a beanbag ashtray.

"You're Marge, right?"

"Frank had so many wives?"

"I like to confirm what I'm told." I looked around. "You have a nice place here."

"Now that Frank's gone, maybe you can buy it from the bank." Marge motioned at a chair. "You're making me nervous, looming over me."

I sat, my hat in my hand. "Robert said your husband has been gone a while now."

"Listen. I'm no angel, and Frank is no prince. I get it. He disappears in the middle of the night? I'm supposed to be broken up. Honestly, it could have been either of us."

"I thought Frank didn't come home from work."

Marge lit another cigarette. "Robert told you that, right?"

I nodded.

"Robert asked where's his old man. I created options."

"Did he tell you he was leaving?"

She shook her head. "I woke when I felt the bed move. Thought he was going to the bathroom. A couple minutes later,

I heard the front door."

"What time was this?"

She shrugged. "The middle of dark. Anyway, he hasn't been home since."

"What do you tell yourself?"

"Maybe he got tired of punching a clock. Maybe he got tired of punching me."

"Any old girlfriends I should look up?"

"We were high school sweethearts." She smirked. "Can I make a suggestion?"

"Of course."

"Go down to Price's. Play some pool. Have some beers. Tell Robert you followed up every lead you could find, and his father is gone."

"Where do you think Frank is?"

Marge inhaled the world through her cigarette, spat the smoke out the side of her mouth. "I think if I cared to find him, I couldn't. I don't see how you can expect to do any better."

"What about your other children?"

"Robert was our first, and he tore up something inside me. When Frank had one too many beers, he blamed me."

"Frank's parents alive?"

She chuckled. "You don't give up, do you?"

"I've been paid to do a job."

She tapped her cigarette against the ashtray. "His father's dead, killed on a fishing boat, and his mother's insane."

"Insane as in—"

"She's in an institution. The last time we visited, Robert was a baby. She didn't recognize her own son. Didn't even remember having a son."

"Why now?"

"Why now what?"

"Frank wakes up in the middle of the night. Walks out the door never to return. Why now? What changed?"

"You're the detective."

"You said either of you could have left, but only one of you did. He didn't leave a month before that night. He didn't leave a week before that night. He left that night."

"I don't know what to tell you."

"Where would Frank go?"

Marge huffed. "He could have found a job anywhere."

"What did he take with him?"

"The clothes on his back."

"Nothing else?"

Marge shrugged. "Why would he? He's got nothing here he couldn't get anywhere else."

"Everything here is paid for. Why spend what cash he took with him replacing things he could take for nothing?"

"Maybe he thought I'd hear him. Maybe he thought I'd care."

"I don't know, Marge. Either you're not telling me something you know, or there's something you don't know."

"What did Robert tell you about us?"

"Not much. What does a kid understand about what goes on in a marriage? Especially after the kid moves out and turns his back on everything that world represents?"

"Is he still with that girl?"

"He's with some girl. I don't know if she's the same one."

Marge drew on her cigarette. "Did it look like he's been eating?"

"If you want to hire me, just say the word."

She laughed out chunks of smoke. "You can't blame me for trying."

"How about this? Tell me something I don't know."

"Sounds like that covers a lot of territory."

"Impress me."

Marge paused. "Not that I imagine it's related, but an old buddy of Frank's stopped in a couple months back. Dick something. He was on leave."

"How did Dick know where to find Frank?"

"He didn't. They just happened to run into each other. One

going into the bar. One coming out. Dick was in town to visit his sister."

If true, maybe his running into Frank held no significance beyond proving that, yes, it was a small world. "What did Dick have to say?"

"He liked my roast chicken."

There comes a point in every interview after which to continue would be a waste of time. The key to being an efficient investigator is to recognize that point and bring the interview to a swift close. In this interview, I felt like "roast chicken" was that point.

I asked to see Frank's belongings and chatted with Marge while I looked through them, hoping she might say more while I was otherwise engaged. No dice. Meanwhile, Frank didn't appear to have taken anything with him, or to have left anything behind for me to find.

After handing Marge a card and thanking her for her time, I headed back to the factory to wait for Jimmy to get off.

Adults go missing every day. It's a free country, after all, a country founded on the twin desires to begin again and to roam. What most people don't realize, don't want to realize, is that all paths lead to the same place.

Run as fast as you want. You'll always end up back where you started, viewing your new world with eyesight dimmed by the growing cataracts of your personal history.

Then again, missing adults also sometimes paid my bills. Case in point.

I placed my mind elsewhere until it was time to stand outside the factory so that Jimmy could spot me, standing against a lamppost.

If nobody approached, what next?

Bud had taken my money. That gave him a vested interest in talking with me again. Maybe he could point to another of Frank's coworkers, even though that approach, like interviews, could soon lead to diminishing returns.

Marge might remember something she'd seen or heard. She might remember the name of Dick's sister. She might remember why she married Frank in the first place. High school sweethearts didn't always.

Letting the lamppost take my weight, I tried to remember my own high school years. The girls I must have liked and tried to more than like. Cataracts.

The factory doors opened, and men emerged: singly, in pairs, in small groups. Men trudged home. Men headed for neighborhood bars.

One man paused on the sidewalk and looked around.

I touched the brim of my hat.

After a moment, he crossed the street.

"You the guy looking for Frank?"

I nodded. "Let me buy you a drink. Somewhere around here you like to unwind?"

We walked there in silence. Jimmy, maybe considering how much he wanted to tell me. Me, wanting him to come to the conclusion it was his choice.

One of the things I find most fascinating about interviews is how much people think they can conceal as if what they say, what their body says, doesn't fill in the gaps.

Jimmy led me into a tavern just slightly wider than the bar.

He forced his way past the men already seated to reach two empty stools near the back.

I bought us two drafts and waited until they arrived. "So you're a friend of Frank."

"You could say that." Jimmy lowered the contents of his mug.

"His son's worried."

"His wife not so much." He glanced sideways at me. "Right?"

"She's not as distressed as some I've seen. Do you know why that might be?"

Jimmy shrugged. "What does anybody know?"

"Frank knew something."

"The problem with Frank is he didn't respect the line between knowing something and doing something about it."

"He had his reasons."

"What, the kids he never had? Nothing we made was going to hurt them because they didn't exist. I don't care if he made up birthdays for them. Even Frank knew they weren't real."

I drank from my mug, pretending to swallow more than I did, buying Jimmy time to follow his thoughts to wherever they led him. Only then could he wave me over.

Jimmy shook his head. "We wouldn't even be having this discussion if that Army buddy of his hadn't shown up, talking about things he had no business sharing. If Frank hadn't then felt he needed to make a difference."

"Some people are just like that."

"You seen that Clint Eastwood movie, *The Good, the Bad and the Ugly*? That was Frank."

"How so?"

"Just like those three guys, Frank couldn't not go to the cemetery."

"He was trying to do the right thing."

"By talking to a reporter? How was that going to help?"

"Maybe Frank wanted people to know the truth."

"The truth." Jimmy snorted. "The truth is that the factory pays a living wage. It puts food on my table. It allows me to take my sick kid to the doctor."

"Who did you tell?"

"I told Bud, of course. He runs things. He needs to know what's up. Maybe Bud told the owner." Jimmy waved his hands. "Maybe the reporter told Frank to blow town. Maybe Frank just got tired of Marge."

With each "maybe," Jimmy had less to do with Frank's disappearance. I didn't blame him. Everybody needed to be able to sleep.

"Even if Frank did talk to the reporter, what's the worst that could have happened?"

"The mood of his country right now? We would have had protesters outside the building holding picket signs, pictures of people missing limbs. You want to explain to my kid why he can't go to the doctor and get any more medicine?"

"I can't argue with you there." I raised my mug.

"See? Even you understand. But Frank? He put the concerns of some kid that didn't even exist over my flesh-and-blood."

"You had no choice. You had to tell Bud."

"Of course, I did."

And Bud told the owners because that was part of his job, a job that put food on his table.

And the owners did whatever they had to do to protect what was theirs, because that's how they feed their families.

And so it goes, the circle-jerk of justification.

Just like now, I had to figure out how I was going to sell this lack of closure to my client, because that's how I managed to eat.

This case was on hold until the body turned up.

Probably until the sixties were dead and gone.

ABOUT THE EDITOR

MICHAEL BRACKEN is the author of several books, including the private eye novel *All White Girls*, and more than twelve hundred short stories in several genres. His short crime fiction has appeared in *Alfred Hitchcock's Mystery Magazine, Ellery Queen's Mystery Magazine, Espionage Magazine, Mike Shayne Mystery Magazine, The Best American Mystery Stories 2018, The Mysterious Bookshop Presents The Best Mystery Stories of the Year 2021*, and in many other anthologies and periodicals. A recipient of the Edward D. Hoch Memorial Golden Derringer Award for lifetime achievement in short mystery fiction, Bracken has received two Derringer Awards and been shortlisted for two others. Additionally, Bracken is editor of *Black Cat Mystery Magazine* and has edited several anthologies, including the Anthony Award-nominated *The Eyes of Texas: Private Eyes from the Panhandle to the Piney Woods* and the *Mickey Finn* series. Born in 1957, he experienced the sixties through the eyes of a child and still remembers stringing his own love beads.

ABOUT THE CONTRIBUTORS

JACK BATES remembers the sixties as a time of tormenting his older teenage sisters by crashing their dance parties, pulling the heads off their Beatles dolls, and drawing mustaches on the covers of their magazines. He's a three-time finalist for a Derringer Award for short crime fiction. He's also received awards for screenplays and television scripts.

C.W. BLACKWELL was born and raised in Santa Cruz, California, where he grew up hearing local stories about the Merry Pranksters and the first acid tests. He has been a gas station attendant, a rock musician, and a crime analyst. His crime fiction stories have appeared with Down and Out Books, Gutter Books, Fahrenheit Press, and *Rock and a Hard Place Magazine*. He is a 2021 Derringer award winner.

N.M. CEDEÑO is a former president of Sisters in Crime: Heart of Texas Chapter. Her short story, "A Reasonable Expectation of Privacy," tied for third place for Best Short Story in the 2013 Analog Readers Poll. On her first day as a student at the University of Texas, Ms. Cedeño's father showed her bullet holes from the Tower Shooting, which occurred on her father's last day of class at UT, August 1, 1966.

HUGH LESSIG's short stories have appeared in *Thuglit, Shotgun*

Honey, Crime Factory, Needle, and *Mickey Finn: 21st Century Noir, Vol. 1 and Vol. 2,* and *Guns + Tacos*. He turned ten years old in 1968 and spent most of it glued to the TV, wondering if his parents had always been scared of what they saw. He lives in Hampton, Virginia, and works in public communications.

STEVE LISKOW (SteveLiskow.com) has been a finalist for both the Edgar Award and the Shamus Award, and he has won the Black Orchid Novella Award twice. He was attending summer classes at Oakland University when the Detroit riot erupted less than thirty miles south of the campus. He and his dorm mates watched the events on television, and two residents of his dormitory lost their homes in the fires.

ADAM MEYER is a Shamus award nominee whose short fiction has appeared in *The Beat of Black Wings*, *Malice Domestic: Murder Most Theatrical,* and *Crime Travel*. His TV credits include several Lifetime movies and true-crime series. He's also the author of the thriller *Missing Rachel*, and the YA novel *The Last Domino*. Although he wasn't born until the seventies, he grew up hearing all about life in New York in the sixties. He lives online at AdamMeyerWriter.com.

TOM MILANI spent his career as a technical editor for a federally funded research and development center. "A Hard Night in Hamburg" is the first story he sold. His best friend in elementary school introduced him to the Beatles, and it was love at first listen. Some fifty years later he still marvels at their musical alchemy and wonders what it would have been like to be there at the beginning of the transformation.

NEIL PLAKCY's experience of the sixties was bracketed by two events. He came home from elementary school one day in 1963 to find his mother and their housekeeper crying on the front porch after the assassination of JFK. And then four years later, the vibrant inner core of his birth city, Trenton, New Jersey, was decimated by riots. Learn about his fifty-plus mystery and romance novels at www.mahubooks.com.

STEPHEN D. ROGERS is the author of *Shot to Death* and more than eight hundred shorter works, earning among other honors two Derringers (with seven additional finalists), a Shamus Award nomination, and mention in *The Best American Mystery Stories*. His website, StephenDRogers.com, includes a list of new and upcoming titles as well as other timely information. He mostly experienced the sixties through television, some brought to him in living color, and all of it too complicated for him to comprehend.

MARK THIELMAN (MarkThielman.com) is a criminal magistrate working in Fort Worth, Texas. A two-time Black Orchid Award-winning novella author, Mark's short fiction has been published in *Alfred Hitchcock's Mystery Magazine* and various anthologies. He lives in Fort Worth with his wife, two sons, and an oversized dog. Seven-year-old Mark was forced to watch parts of the '68 Democratic national convention when his dad hogged the only television in the house and the networks pre-empted all the good shows.

GRANT TRACEY was born in Toronto. Recently he received the 2020-2021 Distinguished Scholar Award from the University of Northern Iowa. He has published more than fifty literary stories, and in 2015 turned to writing crime. He is the author of the Hayden Fuller Mysteries Series, and a third novel, *Neon Kiss*, is at press. Favorite authors: Chandler, Thompson, and Spillane. In 1964, Grant attended his first hockey game with his father at Maple Leaf Gardens.

MARK TROY grew up in St. Louis, Missouri. He entered high school in 1961, a year in which "Pony Time" reached number one for Chubby Checker. Mark cut his teeth on Cardinals baseball and remains an avid fan to this day, even while living in Texas. Mark is the author of "Shaft on Wheels," which appeared in *The Eyes of Texas*, and *Dos Tacos Quatemaltecos y Una Pistola Casera,* episode twelve, season two of the *Guns + Tacos* series.

ANDREW WELSH-HUGGINS began the sixties in diapers and ended the decade riding up and down the streets of Lima, New York, on a bike with the absolutely coolest banana seat. When not dreaming of those halcyon days, he's an Associated Press reporter, the editor of the 2020 anthology *Columbus Noir,* and the author of seven mystery novels featuring Andy Hayes, a former Ohio State and Cleveland Browns quarterback turned private investigator.

ROBB WHITE was an undergraduate at Kent State during the sixties. The long hair, beard, and ideals are long gone, but nostalgia for "Crystal Blue Persuasion" and "Suite: Judy Blue Eyes" remains. He is the author of two private-eye series. "Inside Man" was chosen for *Best American Mystery Stories 2019. Murder, Mayhem & More* cited two of his hardboiled novels for its Top Ten Crime Books of 2018 and 2019.

On the following pages are a few
more great titles from the
Down & Out Books publishing family.

For a complete list of books and to
sign up for our newsletter,
go to DownAndOutBooks.com.

Moonlight Kills
A Dick Moonlight PI Thriller
Vincent Zandri

Down & Out Books
January 2022
978-1-64396-244-3

When Dick Moonlight PI and his professional impersonator sidekick, Fat Elvis, uncover the head of a decapitated, long blond-haired woman under the floorboards of an under-construction luxury home, they come into contact with a husband-and-wife construction team who also fancy themselves Hollywood filmmakers. Only, it turns out that the filmmakers aren't interested in making romcoms, but instead, snuff films.

With Fat Elvis the perfect candidate for a starring role in their new film, Moonlight is hired by the police to go undercover and expose the operation.

Razing Stakes
The De La Cruz Case Files
TG Wolff

Down & Out Books
February 2022
978-1-64396-245-0

Colin McHenry is out for his regular run when an SUV crosses into his path, crushing him. Within hours of the hit-skip, Cleveland Homicide Detective Jesus De La Cruz finds the vehicle in the owner's garage, who's on vacation three time zones away. The suspects read like a list out of a textbook: the jilted fiancée, the jealous coworker, the overlooked subordinate, the dirty client.

Motives, opportunities, and alibis don't point in a single direction. In these mysteries, Cruz has to think laterally, yanking down the curtain to expose the master minding the strings.

Sheehan's Dog
Les Roberts

Down & Out Books
February 2022
978-1-64396-247-4

Former Irish mafia hitman Brock Sheehan lives quietly on a boat fifty miles from Cleveland. When his long-lost nephew, Linus Callahan, tracks him down and asks him for assistance, he agrees to help. A few days earlier, the nephew got into a bar argument with a multimillion-dollar basketball player just released from prison for running a high-level dog-fighting ring. Then the athlete is murdered, and Linus becomes the Cleveland police department's "person of interest."

Investigating the athlete's former dogfight ring, Brock winds up with a pit bull of his own, which he names Conor. And eventually, with Conor's instincts, he discovers and turns over to the police the real killer of the dog-killer turned sports legend.

Hell to Pay
A Diggy and Stick Crime Novel
Andy Rausch

Down & Out Books
March 2022
978-1-64396-248-1

Dirty ex-cops Robert “Diggy” Diggs and Dwayne “Stick” Figgers have found themselves in a terrible situation. After Kansas city drug lord Benny Cordella discovers that they have wronged him, he devises an insane plan: he's going to force them to commit suicide. This, he believes, will send them to hell, where they will track down Dread Corbin, the man who killed his daughter. Of course, Diggy and Stick don't believe this is possible, but they will soon discover that hell is real.

Hell to Pay: Diggy and Stick Book One is unlike any crime novel you've ever read before. It's dark, dangerous, edgy, and laugh-out-loud hilarious. Buckle up for one hell of a ride!